SYNDICATE

SYNDICATE

A DICK FRANCIS NOVEL

FELIX FRANCIS

CROOKED
LANE

NEW YORK

Published in the United States by Crooked Lane Books, an imprint of The Quick Brown Fox & Company LLC.

Crooked Lane Books and its logo are trademarks of The Quick Brown Fox & Company LLC.

Library of Congress Catalog-in-Publication data available upon request.

ISBN (hardcover): 978-1-63910-859-6
ISBN (ebook): 978-1-63910-860-2

Cover design by TK

Printed in the United States.

www.crookedlanebooks.com

Crooked Lane Books
34 West 27th St., 10th Floor
New York, NY 10001

First Edition: September 2024

10 9 8 7 6 5 4 3 2 1

For grandson,
Alfie Lowe,
born 9 November 2023

With my thanks to
Harry Herbert,
chairman and managing director of
Highclere Thoroughbred Racing,
one of the world's leading racehorse
syndication companies

and also to my wife
Debbie
for her love, help, and support

1

I WAS HARDLY DARING to breathe, not wanting to move even an inch, but my heart was beating so fast I feared it would burst clean out of my chest.

Come on. Come on.

I didn't so much say it as think it.

Come on. Hang on. You can do it.

The pounding in my chest increased both in rate and in intensity.

Epsom Downs. The first Saturday in June. The Derby.

* * *

"Whatever happens, don't be late. Our first guests will be arriving at seven, and you have to be here, dressed and ready. And please try to remain sober."

My wife of twenty-five years, Georgina, was leaning over the banister at the top of the stairs.

I looked up at her. "Yes, dear."

Whose crazy idea had it been for us to hold a party on Derby Day?

Mine probably, but nearly a year ago, when we'd booked the marquee and the caterers, I hadn't been expecting to own the favourite for the race. And today was our actual silver wedding anniversary, so it had been an obvious choice.

I say "own" the favourite for the Derby but that wouldn't be entirely true. I possessed just one twelfth of the horse in my own name, but I managed the whole animal as the syndicate organiser.

"I need the place cards," Georgina said. "Have you done them?"

"They're on my desk," I said.

"Can you get them for me?"

"But I have to go. The traffic is always horrendous around Epsom for the Derby."

"A couple of minutes won't make any difference."

I glanced at the grandfather clock in the hallway—twenty past nine.

Did she not realize how important this race was for me? I had hardly slept a wink all night because of my nervousness, and I'd been up since five. All I wanted to do was to get going, to ensure I was at the racecourse in good time.

Calm down, I told myself. *It's just another race.*

Except it wasn't just *another* race. This was the Epsom Derby, the pre-eminent flat race in the U.K., if not in the whole of Europe.

I walked into the kitchen, on the way to my office at the back of the house. Our daughter, Amanda, was sitting at the kitchen table in a dressing gown, eating toast and typing into her mobile.

"So are you looking forward to this evening?" I asked jovially.

"No," she replied blandly, without looking up. "Darren says it's stupid to have a combined party. I should be having my own birthday party, and not having to share it with James and all your dreary old friends."

The party was to be a celebration not only for Georgina and me, but also to mark our son, James's, twenty-first, and Amanda's nineteenth birthdays. James's birthday had been two days previously, and Amanda's was next Friday.

"But you were really keen on the plan to hold a joint party. Indeed, if I remember correctly, it was your idea in the first place."

"Well, I'm not keen anymore," Amanda said, still not looking up from the screen. "Darren says we would have much more fun, like, down at the pub, wearing jeans and T-shirts than having to dress up here in fancy suits and bow ties."

Darren was an unemployed twenty-six-year-old college dropout who had been Amanda's boyfriend for the past eight months, and as far as Georgina and I were concerned, he was not a suitable match for our daughter. In fact, he was totally unsuitable.

Not only was he eight years older than Amanda, but he had also been convicted for joyriding in a stolen car the previous summer in the nearby town of Didcot. And we were also extremely worried about the way he tried to control our daughter's life. He demanded that she tell him where she was at any given time, and he became angry if she didn't or if she went out anywhere without him. He even stipulated what she could wear. And he had done his best to cut her off from all her other friends, especially the male ones.

She had planned to go travelling during her gap year between school and university, but Darren had put paid to that too, telling her she would be better off getting a job and staying here. So, instead of backpacking around Australia with a girlfriend for three months at the beginning of the year, she'd spent the time working as a checkout girl in the local Tesco supermarket, something she still did.

"Darren says I should have had a party last year for my eighteenth birthday, not this year for my nineteenth."

I didn't actually care one iota what Darren said, but decided not to say so. I wasn't in the mood for another argument with her—not here, not today.

"If you remember," I said calmly, keeping a tight hold on my temper, "we all decided that it wasn't sensible to have an eighteenth birthday party right in the middle of your A levels, and that we would do it this year instead as a joint celebration."

"Darren says it's just because you want to do it on the cheap."

"Darren doesn't know what he's talking about. Now, please be helpful to your mother today. She has lots to do to get ready for this evening."

Amanda finally looked up from her phone.

"Where are you going all dressed up?"

I was wearing morning dress and carrying a top hat.

"To the Derby. Potassium is running."

"Will he win?"

"I hope so."

God, I hoped so.

I went through into my office and picked up the place cards from my desk—one hundred and forty of them in four stacks, one for each of the four long tables set up in the marquee. Amanda and James had a table each for their friends, while Georgina and I had one apiece for ours. I carried the cards back through the kitchen, where Amanda was still sitting at the table.

"Remember what I said about helping your mother," I said to her.

She looked up at me and didn't answer.

"Please," I said imploringly. "Mum's not very happy about me being out all day at the races, and you know how stressed she can get."

"Okay," Amanda said reluctantly.

"Right. I must get going or I'll be late."

I went back into the hallway and put the place cards on the hall table.

"The cards are all in the right order," I called up to Georgina. "I'll see you later."

"What time is the race?" she asked, coming back onto the landing from our bedroom.

"Twenty past three."

She drew her breath in through clenched teeth. "That's cutting it a bit fine."

"We're actually lucky," I said. "It's usually run at four thirty, but it's been brought forward so as not to clash with the football at Wembley."

"Well, don't be late. Leave as soon as the Derby is over."

"I can't just leave if Potassium wins."

Georgina waved a dismissive hand, which I took to mean she rather hoped he wouldn't win.

"It would pay for the party," I said.

And some, I thought.

The Epsom Derby might not be the most valuable horse race in Europe, but the purse was still £1.5 million, with £850,650 of that going to the winning connections. To say nothing of the future value of the horse as the Derby winner. Potential stud fees could easily run into the tens of millions.

The way things had been going in recent months, with increased inflation, higher wage costs, and people being more careful about buying racehorses, my personal finances, and those of the syndicate company, could really do with the boost. A year ago, when we'd planned the party and booked the marquee plus the caterers, my business had been buoyant. No expense had been spared. Now I was worried that we couldn't afford it.

Too late to think of that now, I told myself. *We're committed.*

* * *

As expected, the traffic between the M25 and Epsom Racecourse, through Ashtead, was bumper to bumper and mostly stationary with it, but I eventually drove into the car park reserved for owners and trainers just before midday.

I parked my Jaguar as close to the exit as I could, ready for a quick getaway, and climbed out, collecting my coat and hat from the car boot.

My hands were shaking.

"Morning, Chester. Lovely day for it."

I turned to find Owen Reynolds, a racehorse trainer in his mid-fifties. He was walking towards the car-park exit.

"Ah, good morning, Owen," I said. "And how is Potassium today?"

"Never better. He seems to have slept well and ate up his breakfast at six o'clock before departing my yard at seven. He's already safely here in the racecourse stables and raring to go."

"All good then?" I asked.

"I think so," Owen replied. "We could have done without that band of rain that came through in the night, but I don't think it will have made much difference to the going. And this sunshine should help dry it out."

Potassium had shown that he preferred racing on firm ground, having suffered his only defeat at Newmarket in early May, when the turf had been very soft, almost a bog.

Owen and I walked across the road towards the racecourse entrance together.

"Have you backed him?" I asked.

Owen was renowned for being a betting man.

"I put a grand on him to win this race the day he broke his maiden at Newbury, well over a year ago."

"What price did you get?"

"Twenty-five-to-one."

Some bookmakers were now quoting Potassium as short as two-to-one.

"You did well."

"Only as long as he wins. How many of the syndicate are coming?"

I laughed. "What do you think? No one wants to miss out on this one."

"Have they all got badges?"

"Some have had to buy them, as Epsom are so miserly with their allocation, and not all of them will be able to get into the parade ring, but they're all here, some with their extended families too. Many have booked restaurant hospitality."

"Let's hope Potassium doesn't let them down."

"Or us," I agreed.

Being the favourite in the betting certainly didn't guarantee success. Far from it.

In the past thirty years, only eight horses that were favourite or joint-favourite have gone on to win the Derby, and since its first running in 1780, there have been three winners returned at odds as high as a hundred to one.

Owen Reynolds and I walked towards the entrance into the Queen Elizabeth II enclosure.

"Excuse me, Mr Newton," said a man on my left, just outside the gate. "Could I have a word?"

I looked across and recognised one of the BBC radio reporters, complete with microphone and headphones.

"I'll see you later, Owen. In the saddling boxes."

Owen walked on, waving a hand while I turned to the reporter.

"Just a quick interview for our listeners," he said. "Ready?"

I nodded.

"I have here with me Chester Newton, syndicate manager for Victrix Racing, the owners of Potassium, which is the favourite for today's big race. Well, Chester, do you expect Potassium to win?"

"I wouldn't exactly say that I expect him to win, but I hope he does."

"And will he make all the running as he has in the past?"

"Race tactics are for the trainer and jockey to decide, not the owner. But the Derby is a mile and a half, and that's a lot farther than the horse has ever raced over before, and all his six previous races have been on straight, mostly flat courses, while here he will have to negotiate the stiff rise to the top of the hill and then the sharp downhill bend at Tattenham Corner."

"Are you making your excuses early?" asked the reporter, with good humour in his voice.

"Not at all. I'm just saying that to win a Derby requires a special horse, but we feel that Potassium is that special horse."

"You heard it first here folks, straight from the horse owner's mouth. Thank you, Chester Newton, and now back to the studio."

The racecourse gateman scanned the Privilege Racecourse Access app on my mobile phone, and I walked into the enclosure.

In spite of what I had told the reporter, did I, in fact, expect Potassium to win?

He was certainly in the best shape of his life. Even though he had failed to triumph in the 2000 Guineas at Newmarket on his last outing, he had been training really well since. Sixteen days ago, Owen and I had opted for the horse to miss the ten-furlong Dante Stakes at York, instead running him over the full Derby distance at home on the gallops on the same day, upsides with two older horses from Owen's yard, and Potassium had still been pulling at the end.

But if I'd learned just one thing during my more than thirty years working with horses, it was that nothing in racing is ever certain. It had a habit of producing the totally unexpected—Devon Loch's collapse in the 1956 Grand National was testament to that. So, while I wouldn't say that I exactly *expected* Potassium to win, I'd be sorely disappointed if he didn't.

Hence my nervousness.

I looked again at my watch, desperate for the time to pass quickly, but the hands stubbornly refused to move round the dial any faster. I had been itching to get here early, and now that I was, I didn't know how to fill my time.

Potassium was the only Victrix runner today.

In all there were forty horses owned by the Victrix Racing syndicates that I managed, all but six of them running on the flat. Owen Reynolds had four of them, including Potassium, while the others were spread amongst nine other trainers all around the U.K., and one in Ireland.

Some of the syndicates had twelve members, as with Potassium, but most had twenty or even twenty-five, depending on the original cost of the horse and my expected take-up of the shares.

I would buy the horses at the bloodstock sales in the autumn, in either the U.K. or Ireland, and then hold a "yearling parade," where prospective syndicate members were invited to view the horses, sign the ownership papers, and enjoy a good lunch.

I had now been doing this job for the past twenty-four years, having initially set up Victrix Racing when I was thirty with just a single syndicate made up of willing friends and family prepared to invest their hard-earned cash in my new venture.

Over time, I had acquired a pretty good idea of which horses to buy and how many shares in each to make available, as well as establishing a comprehensive list of people willing and able to participate in shared ownership.

I didn't purchase the most expensive horses, those that went for in excess of half a million pounds. Indeed my top limit would be less than half of that, and most were around the hundred thousand mark.

Sometimes they turned out to be really good buys, and sometimes they didn't. Potassium was definitely in the former category, having cost exactly a hundred thousand guineas at the Newmarket October yearling sale, a remarkably low price for a horse that turned out to be the champion European two-year-old of last year.

Now aged three, Potassium had stepped up to compete in the Classic races for three-year-olds, including the Two Thousand Guineas and The Derby, where success would put him into the "greats" list.

I didn't normally keep any of the horse shares for myself but there was something about this particular animal that had made me think we were onto a winner. So, by December, eighteen months ago, when the last of the twelve shares had still not been taken by anyone else, I decided to buy myself an early Christmas present and registered the final share in my own personal name.

And how glad I was now that I had.

My share of Potassium's prize money, won in his six previous races, had already repaid my initial investment of nineteen thousand pounds. Anything won today would be a bonus.

All my fingers and toes were crossed.

CHAPTER

2

I HAD SPENT THE time since my arrival at the racecourse wandering around and chatting to other members of the Potassium syndicate and other friends, but I'm not sure that I could recall any of the conversations—my mind had been elsewhere.

Why was I so nervous? I asked myself.

If Potassium didn't win today, it didn't make him a bad horse. There would be more races to come, and as a former European two-year-old champion, he should already have a career assured as a stallion at stud.

So why the nerves?

Partly, I suppose, because this race really was the *big* one, but I was mostly nervous because of what it would mean for my business.

After more than twenty years of ever-increasing success, there was no denying that there had been a significant drop in our form during the past two. A combination of bad luck, and quite likely bad judgement on my part, had caused some of our horses not to fulfil their expectations, and I knew there were continuing murmurings on the racing grapevine that Chester Newton had lost his golden touch.

When I had started out in the syndicate business, after spending ten years as an assistant trainer in one of the foremost training yards in the country, there had been very little competition, but that had all changed. Prospective members now had a whole plethora of syndicate companies to choose from, and the only real difference between them was who was buying the horses and who was doing the managing. If my members lost confidence in me as that person, my business would wither and die faster than a rose bud starved of water.

I hoped that winning The Derby would banish the tittle-tattle and re-establish Victrix Racing as the blue-ribbon company for syndicate owner-ship. But losing it with the race favourite could also sound the company's death knell.

Potassium looked wonderful in the parade ring, relaxed and assured, while many of those around him were sweating up badly in the hot after-noon sunshine, including me in my top hat and tails.

Owen Reynolds welcomed those members of the owning syndicate lucky enough to have the parade-ring badges, and he seemed to be the calm-est of us all, joking about the high levels of security, even though it wasn't a laughing matter. But I knew Owen fairly well, and I reckoned that this was his way of dealing with his own nerves, which I was certain were jangling beneath his serene exterior, just like the rest of ours.

Finally, our jockey Jimmy Ketch joined us, wearing Victrix's distinctive racing silks of royal blue and white vertical striped body, black sleeves and white cap, and everything suddenly became very serious.

"Now remember what we discussed," Owen said to Jimmy earnestly. "Sit tight behind one or two others uphill for the first five furlongs to settle him. Then, at the top of the rise, pull him out into free air and push him on fast down the hill, hopefully getting a jump on the others as they take a breather. Go steady around Tattenham Corner, then kick hard again. Don't worry about going well clear. He loves to be in front and he hates to be caught."

It all sounded so simple.

A bell was rung by an official—the signal for the jockeys to get mounted.

Jimmy walked over to where Potassium was still being led around, and Owen gave him a leg up, tossing the jockey's petite frame effortlessly up onto the tiny saddle.

"Good luck," called out one of our syndicate members as the horse and jockey walked past us before going out onto the track.

The start for the Derby is at the lowest point of the course and is impos-sible to see from the lawns of the enclosures, not least because of the hospital-ity marquees placed close to the far rail, and all of the sponsor's tall advertising hoardings erected on each side of the winning post. And it was such a scrum to get to the viewing steps on the grandstand reserved for owners and train-ers. So I decided to remain in the parade ring and watch the race on the big television screen set up at one end.

Quite a few of my fellow syndicate members clearly had the same idea, and we stood there in a group, staring at the screen in silence, too preoccu-pied by our own hopes and dreams to enter into conversation.

We watched as the fifteen horses made their way to the start, had their girths tightened by the starter's assistant, and then were expertly loaded into the starting stalls.

Potassium had been drawn to start from stall nine, considered a reasonably good draw because the Derby course, although mostly a left-handed, elongated horseshoe shape, initially curves to the right, giving the higher drawn horses the early advantage.

"They're off!" shouted the racecourse commentator through the public address system as the stall gates opened, accompanied by a huge roar from those in the enclosures and also from the masses on "the hill," where the fun fairs and alcoholic liquid refreshment were both in full flow.

All fifteen runners appeared to make an even break, and I frantically searched the image on the screen for Jimmy Ketch's white cap as they sorted themselves out. After a brief moment, I found him, tucked in behind some of the early leaders, just as he'd been instructed. Potassium was always eager to be at the head of the pack, but we didn't want him to run too free too early—not with a full mile and a half to cover.

The field was well bunched as they first swung right-handed and then crossed the course to the left-hand running rail, all the time climbing steeply.

Even though the Derby is a "flat race" because there are no jumps, Epsom racecourse is far from flat. In the first half mile of the Derby, the horses have to climb one hundred and sixty vertical feet, almost the height of Nelson's Column in Trafalgar Square. This can sap a horse's energy, especially if it gets racing too early. Hence our aim was to keep Potassium well covered up behind the other runners at this stage. However, as they reached the crown of the hill, I watched as Jimmy Ketch eased him a little wider, thereby finally giving him a clear view of the track ahead.

Potassium took this as an invitation to go to the front, and, as we had hoped, he stole a march on others, who were taking a breather, by suddenly opening a four-length lead going down the hill towards Tattenham Corner. And still he didn't slow down. Far from taking the sharp left-hand bend steadily, as he'd been instructed, Jimmy kicked hard into Potassium's ribs beforehand, and the horse fairly hurtled around the corner and into the home straight.

By the time he passed the three-furlong pole, Potassium had established a lead of almost eight lengths, and I began to believe he really could win. But the others were in hot pursuit, and now they began to close the gap.

One of the major factors that had attracted Potassium to me when I'd first seen him as an unnamed yearling at the sales was his front end—his huge chest. In deciding which horses to buy, I always took careful note of what was known as the depth of a horse—the greater the depth, the larger the lungs and hence the greater the amount of oxygen available to be delivered to the muscles, which in turn indicated that the horse might be able to sustain its gallop for longer.

Almost all horses slow down in the latter stages of a race as they begin to run out of puff. Those that appear to be increasing their speed towards the finish are actually the ones that are sustaining their gallop for longer, and therefore slowing down the least.

Now I was banking on the fact that Potassium's large lungs would be able to sustain his gallop long enough for him to reach the winning post while still in front.

At the two-furlong marker, his lead had been cut from eight lengths to six, and that was halved by the time he reached the one pole.

At Epsom, the ground rises again in the final half furlong, further depleting a horse's stamina, but as Owen Reynolds had said in the parade ring, Potassium loved to race in front, and he hated to be caught.

As two of the other runners closed in on him rapidly, he stuck his neck out and found more. But would it be enough?

Come on. Come on. Hang on. You can do it.

The three horses flashed past the winning post side by side, with Potassium closest to the far rail.

"Did we win? Did we win?" shouted one of the other syndicate members, grabbing me from behind and sending my top hat spinning off my head.

"I don't know," I replied.

"Photograph. Photograph," announced the judge over the public address.

Had Potassium held on? Or had he been caught?

I stared at the screen as it showed the slow-motion replay of the finish.

It looked worryingly that Potassium might have been headed right at the death, but the TV camera position was some ten yards short of the finish, which meant it wasn't looking straight along the line, as the photo-finish camera would be.

The replay was run over and over on the screen and, the more it was shown, the more convinced I became that Potassium had lost. But the length of time the judge was taking to declare the result meant it must be very close.

The noise level of the crowd swelled again as everyone was discussing the possible outcomes, and some bookmakers were even shouting their odds for bets on which horse's head had reached the line first.

"Here is the result of the photograph," announced the judge through the loudspeakers, causing the crowd to fall silent in expectation. "First number nine. Second number two. Third number ten. The distances are a nose, and the same."

I leaned down and calmly picked up my top hat from the grass.

Potassium was horse number nine.

We had just won the Derby.

*   *   *

My moment of isolated calm quickly evaporated as I was swamped by other syndicate members, all of them cheering loudly and slapping me on the back.

"We won! We won!" shouted the man who had previously grabbed me.

His name was Nick Spencer, a millionaire London property lawyer who owned many shares of Victrix horses. He was usually a quiet and measured man, but now he was literally jumping up and down with excitement.

"Indeed we did," I replied quietly, still hardly daring to believe it.

All my racing life, my burning ambition had been to win an Epsom Derby, and now it had finally happened. Yet strangely, at this moment of triumph, I was totally relaxed, subdued even. I realised that my overriding emotion was one of relief rather than elation. Maybe that would come later.

"Come on, Chester," said Nick, seizing my left arm and dragging him with me. "Winner's circle, here we come!"

Unlike at many British racecourses, such as Ascot, York, Cheltenham, and Aintree, where the unsaddling enclosures for the first to fourth placed horses are positioned within the parade rings, Epsom had a space reserved exclusively for the race winner—a railed circle situated right in front of the Queen Elizabeth II grandstand.

As Nick and I moved through the throng, I was accosted by the same BBC radio journalist as had met me at the racecourse entrance earlier, again with his live microphone at the ready.

"So, Chester Newton, owner of Potassium, do you think he was a lucky winner?" he asked, thrusting his microphone in my direction.

"In what way?" I replied.

"The TV images clearly show that in just another stride Potassium would have only been third. So don't you think he was lucky to win?"

I stopped walking and looked straight at him.

"But the race distance wasn't another stride long," I said in a strong but measured tone, resisting the urge to get angry about such a ridiculous question. "The winner of the Derby, as in every other race, is the horse that gets from the starting stalls to the finish line in the shortest time, and today, here, that horse was Potassium. So he's a worthy winner. There was no luck involved. The race was run exactly as we had planned it, right down to that last winning stride. It is a famous victory for Potassium, and also for Victrix Racing."

The reporter seemed quite taken aback by the forcefulness of my reply, and I was a bit surprised by it too, but I was determined not to allow Potassium to be labelled as a "lucky winner" when he'd won the race fair and square. But I suppose it was better than being labelled as an "unlucky loser."

By the time I'd elbowed my way through the crowd to the winner's circle, Nick Spencer and all the other Potassium syndicate members were already in there, many with their partners, such that there was hardly room for the horse.

Owen Reynolds had a grin on his face as big as that of the Cheshire Cat as he led the winner in. Why wouldn't he? Never mind anything else, he'd just won twenty-five thousand pounds from his bet.

The jockey, Jimmy Ketch, raised his arms above his head in a victory salute that sent the other syndicate members into greater raptures.

I, meanwhile, leaned quietly on the white rail, taking in the ebullient scene. Inside me was forming a warm glow of satisfaction, and I could feel that a smile was slowly spreading across my face.

Surely my business would be safe after this?

If only.

CHAPTER

3

"WHERE ARE YOU?" Georgina asked when I called her from the car as I drove it out of the car park at a quarter to five.

"I'm just leaving the racecourse," I replied.

"I thought you'd be nearly home by now."

"I've been busy doing post-race media interviews and getting the Derby trophy packed up and into the car."

"So Potassium won, then?"

"Didn't you watch it?" I asked in disbelief.

"No," she said. "I forgot. I was busy changing the seating plan. My mother has decided not to come after all as Dad's not feeling very well today, and she doesn't want to leave him overnight."

Georgina's parents were now in their mid-eighties, and her father suffered from angina and a failing heart, meaning he was effectively housebound by his need for additional oxygen provided to a mask through a long plastic tube from an oxygen-generating machine.

"But at least that means I won't have to pick her up from the station," Georgina went on. "Bloody Richard and Sarah Bassett have also let us down again. Sarah rang to say they think they may have caught a cold and aren't coming, but I think it's just an excuse not to bother to come down from London. Who does that on the day of a party, especially when we've already had to pay for them?"

I wasn't really listening to her.

How could she have forgotten to watch the Derby when I had a runner, let alone the favourite?

"Did either James or Amanda see the race?" I asked.

"I've no idea," Georgina said. "They've both been absolutely useless. That wretched Darren turned up at midday in a taxi. Then, about an hour later, Amanda announced that they were going down to the pub for some lunch. And James went with them. None of them are back yet."

I could tell from her voice that Georgina was getting very stressed.

"Keep calm, my love," I said. "It will all be fine. There shouldn't be much more for you to do except to change clothes and beautify yourself."

"You must be joking," she said. "The caterers clearly have absolutely no idea about how to dress a table properly. They've put the wineglasses all over the place rather than in nice straight lines. I'll have to go and sort it out."

"Does it matter?" I asked.

"It matters to me."

Yes, I thought, and the Derby had mattered to me, but obviously not to her. Not anymore.

I sighed.

Once upon a time, when we were first married and I was still trying to establish Victrix Racing, we had always gone to the races together, and Georgina had used her considerable charms on the then meagre number of my syndicate members, encouraging them to buy more shares in my horses. And she'd been good at it too, often flirting with the older men who had plenty of spare cash to invest in my bloodstock.

But that had all changed over time.

As Victrix had become more and more successful, she had become bored with the continuous need to kowtow to potential owners. She told me one day that we should start believing that it was us doing them the favour, not the other way around. And in a way, she was right.

Syndicate membership allows people to own a share of a horse that they would never be able to afford to own in its entirety.

Most of the flat-race horses I bought as yearlings were kept by Victrix for two years, running in races as two- and three-year-olds. After that, they were usually consigned to the "horses-in-training" sales and sold on to new owners to become stallions or brood mares, or to stay in training as older horses, sometimes as jumpers. Occasionally, we kept a horse ourselves to run as a four-year-old and, rarely, at five.

I charged a fixed annual amount that included all the training fees, vet, farrier, transport, race-entrance charges, and other costs, with the first-year amount including the price of the horse. For example, if a yearling had cost £100,000 at auction, I would likely syndicate it with twenty shares, each costing £10,750 in the first year and £5,750 in the second.

Only if the prize money won by a horse exceeded a quarter of a million pounds, or if it was subsequently sold for at least twice what it had originally cost, did Victrix take a ten per cent share. Otherwise, all prize money became the property of the shareholders, and the proceeds of any sale were also divided equally amongst them.

I insured all the Victrix horses against mortality during our ownership, and for all other eventualities prior to me selling the shares, but otherwise the company carried the risk over large veterinary or equine hospital bills.

But not every syndicate company worked to the same model. Indeed, there were a number of small-share syndicating companies that made it possible to buy a share in a racehorse for as little as a couple of hundred pounds.

Some did not even buy the horses in the first place, simply leasing them. Almost all of those were female horses, owned by breeders, who effectively rent out their horse to a syndicate while they raced, so having others pay the training fees. At the end of two or three years running on the track, the fillies returned to the breeders to become brood mares—to create the next generation.

Other companies invoiced shareholders only for the initial cost of the horse and then sent variable monthly statements to cover the training fees and other expenses, but I found that my members welcomed an all-inclusive fixed price, as it gave them certainty over their total outlay, with no unwelcome and unexpected extra charges. Indeed, I wasn't able to ask them for more, whatever the reason—it was clearly printed in the share agreement that there would be no additional payments asked for.

Horseracing is always a gamble.

"So when will you be back?" Georgina asked.

"In about an hour and a half, depending on the traffic on the M25."

"That won't give you much time to change."

"I can't help that. As it is, I've left before I really wanted to. I would have liked to stay and celebrate with the other owners. They're having quite a party in one of the restaurants."

"But you'd have had to drive home anyway," Georgina said.

I'd have arranged a taxi, I thought. *And would have left my car overnight in the racecourse car park. Or maybe even slept in it.*

Because it's not every day you win the Derby.

As it was, I'd probably had one glass too much of champagne, but what was a man to do when offered another by the reigning monarch in the royal box, as had been the case after the prize giving?

"I'll be there as soon as I can," I said with resignation. "Bye for now."

I disconnected.

At least I *would* be having a party tonight, even if I might have preferred to be at the one in the racecourse rather than the one at home.

I tried to call James and Amanda, but there was no reply. The phone signal in our village was pretty poor at the best of times, and particularly so within the thick walls of our eighteenth-century local.

I called the pub's landline, a number I knew by heart.

"The Red Lion," said the man who answered.

"Jack," I said. "It's Chester Newton."

"Ah. Our Derby winner. Well done."

"Thanks."

"It was on the TV here in the bar. We've been celebrating ever since. Are you coming round to join us?"

"I'd love to, but I can't because we're having a party at our place tonight. But are James and Amanda still there?"

"Sure are. They've been leading the singing."

I could hear it in the background.

"Could you please tell them to go home before they get too drunk?"

"Might be a bit late for that."

Oh God. That wouldn't go down well with their mother.

"Tell them anyway and don't serve them any more. They're meant to be co-hosting tonight."

"Okay. Will do."

He hung up, and I smiled.

At least some of my family had watched the race.

* * *

The traffic on the M25 wasn't too bad, but still I didn't get home until gone half past six, and Georgina wasn't happy as she met me in the hallway, already dressed and ready.

"Don't worry," I assured her. "I'll be all set by seven." I ran up the stairs. "Are the kids back yet?"

"Yes, but they're all the worse for wear, especially that bloody Darren. He can hardly stand up." She wasn't amused.

"Has he got a suit?" I called, removing my shirt and tie on the landing.

"Charity-shop purchase by the look of it. But whether he can dress himself in it is anyone's guess."

I was laughing as I dived into the shower.

Did I care?

Not really. Because I'd just won the Derby.

* * *

Our first guests arrived at seven o'clock sharp, and I was down in the hallway wearing my black tie and ready for their all too prompt appearance.

"Chester, my boy. Well done. Well done, indeed. Saw it on the telly. I told Mary, here, that you'd probably still be at Epsom celebrating."

But nevertheless, they'd arrived here bang on the dot of seven.

Duncan Matthews always called me "my boy" even though, to my sure knowledge, he was six months younger than I.

"I got home about half an hour ago," I said.

I gave Mary a welcome kiss on the cheek, and one of the catering staff offered them each a glass of champagne from a tray.

Duncan looked around him at the empty house. "Are we the first?"

"Indeed, you are," I said.

"Ah, well, someone has to be." He took a glass from the tray and downed half of its contents in one go. "We have a taxi coming for us later."

As well as being a good friend, Duncan was also our GP at a doctors' surgery in Didcot, and while he was always quick to recommend to his patients that they should consume fewer units of alcohol per week, he never seemed to follow his own advice.

"Go on through to the terrace," I said, pointing the way. "It's a beautiful evening, so we're having drinks outside."

More guests arrived, and I also ushered them onto the terrace.

"Where are the damn kids?" Georgina asked, coming into the hallway.

"They're still upstairs. James was coming out of the bathroom in his underpants when I came down. He told me that no decent party should start until at least nine o'clock, preferably ten, or even eleven."

His mother looked appalled. "But we're meant to be eating at eight thirty."

"So let's hope they're down by then."

"They'd bloody well better be."

Maybe Darren had been right, and it had been stupid to mix the generations at the same party, but I wasn't going to get stressed over it. Not now. Not today.

Yet more guests arrived, but there was still no sign of anyone young.

"Congratulations, Chester, with Potassium," said a large man coming through the front door—his white dinner jacket a good two sizes too small for his expanding waistline.

"Thank you, Malcolm," I replied.

Malcolm Galbraith was a local racehorse trainer. He claimed that he was originally from the rough end of Glasgow, but he had married a London girl called Barbara, and they now lived in a village over the hill from us. He trained jumpers almost exclusively, and had one of the Victrix steeplechase horses in his yard.

"He just hung on nicely. Owen must be pleased." He said it without any great warmth.

The relationship between racehorse trainers was a strange mixture of camaraderie, rivalry, and envy. In some ways they were a tight knit group, bound together by their unique position between the owners on one side and their horses on the other, much like football managers sandwiched between the club's directors and the players. But they were always in bitter competition with each other, and not just on the racetracks during the races. They also competed ferociously in the endless struggle to find owners prepared to send them enough horses to fill their stable yards.

"Owen was very happy when I left him at Epsom," I said.

"Isn't he here tonight?" Malcolm asked, looking around in surprise.

"No. He decided that, win or lose, his job was to look after the horse this evening."

"Good for him," Malcolm said.

In the lives of the best racehorse trainers, the horses came first, second, and third. Any human considerations came way down the pecking order.

By about quarter to eight, most of Georgina's and my guests had arrived and were drinking champagne out in the garden, but there was little sign of anyone under the age of thirty.

I was still in the hallway when James came down the stairs, now appropriately dressed.

"You did tell your friends that the party started at seven?" I said.

"Sure," he replied. "But they're always late. Gary texted me that our uni group were all meeting at the Red Lion first for a beer."

Gary was James's best friend, Gary Shipman, a local lad who'd been at school with him in Didcot. They had then travelled the world together during their gap year and were now fellow students at Bristol University.

"I'm sure they'll be here soon," James said.

They'd better be, I thought. *Or Georgina will explode.*

"How about Amanda and Darren? What are they doing?"

"Bonking again, I expect," James said. "I heard them at it in her room before lunch."

It was too much information. Especially in my own home.

I took my glass of champagne through to join everyone else outside. If the young weren't here by half past eight, their food would just get cold. I wasn't going to worry about it. Instead, I just smiled at my friends and sipped my drink, deciding that I would not worry about anything at all tonight.

Sadly, it didn't quite turn out like that.

CHAPTER

4

WE SAT DOWN to eat at twenty-five minutes to nine, by which time the young had finally arrived from the pub, and Amanda and Darren had also appeared from whatever they had been doing together upstairs.

Amanda was in a new white dress that, in my opinion, was much too short. She was also wearing a pair of sharply pointed white shoes with five-inch-high stiletto heels, on which she was having difficulty standing up straight. To top off her ensemble, she had a white silk scarf tied tightly around her neck.

Darren, meanwhile, was slightly less flamboyant in an ill-fitting dinner suit plus a bright scarlet bow tie.

But at least they were here and almost respectable.

The marquee looked wonderful. The four long tables were candlelit, and all the wineglasses were arranged in straight lines, at least to start with. And at the far end there was a black-and-white-checked dance floor under a starlight canopy attached to the tent roof.

I was placed at the end of my table, facing inwards towards the dance floor.

"It all looks lovely," said the woman on my left. "You've done it so well."

"Thank you, Victoria. But that's down to Georgina. I've been at the races all day."

"Of course you have," she said, laughing and laying a hand on my arm. "Well done with that too. Brian and I watched the race. And it was so exciting to see you interviewed on the television afterwards."

Victoria and Brian Perry were our immediate neighbours on one side. He was a long-retired naval commander who now mostly busied himself with his garden while she arranged the flowers in the church every Sunday, and not much went on in the village without both of them knowing about it—and telling everyone else. It was that sort of place. Even the monthly village magazine was called *The Gossip*.

But they had both been very kind to Georgina and me when we had first arrived with two tiny children, ages one and three.

My mother and father had both died in a Thames boating accident when I'd still been a teenager, and Georgina's folks lived north of Leeds, so Brian and Victoria had stepped in to be like an extra set of grandparents to our little ones and would often babysit at a moment's notice, even overnight.

How angelic our kids were back then, I thought.

Clearly much had changed in the meantime.

The catering staff expertly served the first course—warm smoked trout with a dill sauce—and there was the reassuring sound of clinking cutlery and quiet murmurings as people ate. Even the young seemed to be behaving themselves—at least so far.

I reached forward for my glass of wine but opted to take the water instead. I didn't want to get drunk. Not yet, anyway. I had a speech to make. After that—well—we'd see.

"So what will Potassium do now?" Victoria asked me. "Will he race again?"

"Oh yes, I hope so," I said. "A few more times this year, provided he stays fit and well. The owning syndicate members would expect it. But we're still to decide exactly where. Today showed that a mile and a half is his absolute limit in distance, so that will rule out the St Leger or the Melbourne Cup."

The Derby course had been remeasured in 2017 and found to be six yards longer than a mile and a half—and those extra six yards had almost been Potassium's undoing. The St Leger is run over two furlongs more, making it the longest of the five annual three-year-old "Classic" races, while the Melbourne Cup—*The Race That Stops the Nation*—is the world's richest two-mile handicap. I'd always wanted to have a runner in the Melbourne Cup, but it wouldn't be Potassium.

Between the starter and main courses, I took the opportunity to walk up and down the tables, speaking to our guests. All of them, bar none, congratulated me on the Derby win, and the youngsters' tables set up a chant of "Potassium, Potassium" that everyone joined in with.

I stood tall and took in the accolade, waving my thanks.

It had been a truly fairy-tale day. And this evening, my family and our best friends were gathered together for the celebrations—Georgina's and my wedding anniversary, our children's birthdays, and of course the Derby win. I'd even managed to have the magnificent solid-silver round Derby trophy placed on a display table on the edge of the dance floor.

What could be better?

"Enjoying yourself, Dad?" James said, coming up to me with a can of lager in his hand.

"What do you think?" I replied with a grin. "But don't get too drunk. You've got a speech to make later, remember."

We had agreed that all four of us would say a few words after dinner before the dancing started. We had decided against having a live band, opting instead for a DJ who could play dance music suitable for all ages, and I now strode over to where he had set up his lights and sound equipment, at the far end.

"Did you bring the wireless microphone we discussed?" I asked him. "For the speeches."

"Sure. I have two of them, just in case. And both have new batteries." He pointed to where they lay on the table to one side. "Just push the 'on' button on the bottom of either, and you'll be connected directly through all my speakers."

"Great. Thanks."

I wandered over to where Georgina was sitting at the end of her table, deep in conversation with those on either side.

"Well, my darling wife," I said to her, stroking her bare shoulders in a seductive manner, "can you remember what we were doing at this precise moment on our wedding night twenty-five years ago today?"

She was silent for a few seconds, thinking.

"We were sitting on the hard shoulder of the M6, waiting for the recovery truck to arrive after your bloody car broke down."

I laughed. "Exactly! What happy days, eh?"

"If you say so," Georgina said without much humour in her voice.

Did I say so?

Yes, I did.

The first ten to fifteen years of our marriage had certainly been extremely happy, blissful even, as we had started our family and moved into this house, and as my syndicate company had grown and grown, and with it the reputation of Victrix Racing as a serious player in the bloodstock industry.

After a couple of years here, the struggle to meet the monthly mortgage interest payments had begun to ease as the business had flourished, and family life in the Newton household had been really good.

One of the reasons we had bought this house was because it came with a small paddock behind it, together with a wooden building comprising three stables and a tack room, so we quickly acquired a couple of ponies for the children to learn to ride.

Both Georgina and I came from horsey families, and we had met at Haydock Park races, where I had been representing my unwell boss, the trainer of a horse that was owned by Georgina's parents. We had been introduced in the parade ring, stood side by side on the grandstand as the horse won the race, and had gone out to dinner afterwards to celebrate. We had then spent the night together in passionate ecstasy and had hardly slept apart ever since, even for one night.

However, over time, I suspect that all marriages evolve and change, and it would certainly be fair to say that ours was no longer as close and loving as it had once been. In fact, I couldn't remember when we had last had sex. Probably not since when we'd snuck away to Portugal for a weekend last August, some ten months ago. And it was safe to say that our sex then hadn't been an unqualified success. More of a frustrating disaster.

It was because Georgina seemed to have lost all interest in that department.

Not that either of us seemed determined to move on separately. I think we had become very used to our lives together, and it suited us both, although we no longer did those little things that were once so much a part of our romance, like one of us waving as the other drove away, even for a short trip to the post office or the local shop.

I went back to my seat at the far end of my table.

"All good?" Victoria asked as I sat down.

"All perfect," I replied with a smile. Well—almost.

I hadn't actually seen Amanda to tell her to keep moderately sober for her speech, but what trouble could she get into surrounded by her best friends?

Lots of trouble, I thought. Especially when drinking was involved!

The main course was fillet of beef, served sliced on wooden boards placed on the tables so people could help themselves, along with roasted new potatoes, cauliflower cheese, snow peas, and individual bowls of green salad with a balsamic dressing.

If we had known that this would turn out to be the hottest day of the year so far, we might have gone for something a bit more summery—and maybe a bit cheaper—but the beginning of June in southern England had a habit of being rather cool, especially in the evenings.

And the beef was excellent—tender and tasty.

Victoria on my left had plumped for the vegetarian option, a sliced roasted loaf of lentils, chestnut mushrooms, and cheese.

"Good?" I asked.

"Delicious," she replied.

A dessert of Eton mess followed, and everyone seemed happy and full.

I leaned back in my chair, contented. All that painstaking preparation of the seating plan had come to fruition, with animated conversations taking place all along each of the tables. Even the young were chatting away, with smiles and laughter to the fore.

I pulled the notes for my speech out of my jacket pocket, to have one last quick look through before I started. Mostly the notes were about how wonderful my wife and children were, even if they weren't always. But it's what people want to hear on such an occasion. I would, of course, also mention my other great love—Potassium. How could I not, on today of all days?

"All set?" I asked Georgina, going over to her. "You're up first, then James, followed by Amanda, with me at the end."

"Are the others ready?" she asked.

"I'll check."

James was ready, but I couldn't see Amanda anywhere. I walked over to her table.

"Where's Amanda?" I asked her friends.

All I received were shrugs and shaken heads.

I looked around for Darren, but there was also no sign of him.

"Maybe she's in the loo," one of her girlfriends said. "I'll go and check."

Dammit, I thought. Stupid girl. She knew perfectly well when the speeches were going to start.

I went back to Georgina.

"I can't find Amanda. One of her friends has gone to check in the loo. But Darren's not here either."

"Are they in the house?"

"They'd better not be."

We had decided that, after everyone had arrived and moved through into the garden, we would lock the house to keep people in the marquee. Consequently, we had hired a toilet trailer, with very smart ladies' and gents' loos, which was positioned outside, close to the far end, behind the DJ.

I walked over to the house, but the door in from the terrace was still locked. There were lights on inside, but I could see no one in there, so I went around to the toilet trailer and met Amanda's girlfriend coming the other way.

"No sign of her in there," she said.

"Okay. Thanks for looking."

"But I found this on the ground outside."

She was holding the white silk scarf Amanda had been wearing around her neck. I took it from the friend with increasing concern, and went back into the marquee to Amanda's table.

"Does anyone know where Amanda is?" I asked loudly of those sitting at the table. "We have found her scarf." I held it up. "And where is Darren?"

I'd bloody murder the two of them if they'd gone back to the pub.

"Darren's there," one of the girls said, pointing.

He was coming back into the Marquee from the garden. I went over to him. "Where's Amanda?" I demanded.

"I've no idea," he replied. "I've been outside looking for her."

We went back to her table.

"Who else is not here?" I asked.

They all looked to their left and right.

"No one else missing," said the girl who'd been to look for Amanda in the loo. "I'll call her." She lifted her phone.

Amanda's phone wouldn't ring if she were in the Red Lion, because of the lack of signal. But would she really have gone there on her own when all her friends were here?

However, her phone did ring. We all heard it, and as one, our eyes swivelled towards it lying under a napkin at her place at the table.

For the first time, I was becoming more than slightly worried. Amanda's mobile phone was like an extension of her left hand. She never normally went anywhere without it, not even to the toilet. Was she ill? Or maybe blind drunk?

By now, everyone else was beginning to sense that something was amiss.

Georgina came up to me. "What's wrong?"

"We can't find Amanda," I replied.

"Is she in the toilet?"

"We've tried there, and we found her scarf on the ground outside. Darren says he doesn't know where she is—that's if he's telling us the truth."

"What are you implying?" Georgina asked with concern.

"Nothing. But I don't trust that boy. I never believe a single word he says."

Georgina looked at me. "Perhaps she's gone into the house."

"The terrace door is still locked. I have the key with me."

"But she has her own front-door key. She could have just walked round and gone in there."

I thought it unlikely Amanda would have had her front-door key with her at the party, but nevertheless, I took the terrace-door key from my jacket pocket and gave it to Georgina. "You go and check the house. If she's not there, I'll organise a search of the garden. She's probably just had a skinful and fallen over somewhere, but she might have hurt herself."

Or be unconscious from drink, I thought.

Georgina now looked worried, and she hurried off towards the house.

I went over and picked up one of the DJ's microphones and pushed the 'on' button.

"Turn it up," I said to him. "Ladies and gentlemen." My voice boomed out of the speaker system at maximum volume. "Sorry about the delay in getting the speeches underway. We seem to have mislaid our daughter." I paused. "Amanda, if you can hear this, please come back to the marquee as quickly as you can."

Everyone fell silent and began staring at the two entrances, one towards the house and the toilet trailer, the other towards the garden, but Amanda did not materialise through either.

Georgina reappeared from the house, shaking her head.

"Could we please organise a search of the garden?" I said through the speakers. "I am sure she's fine, but she may have fallen and injured herself or become ill. If you feel able, could you please fan out and look for her?"

James took control of his friends and was barking orders about where each of them should go.

I looked at my watch. It was five to ten. The sun had been down for more than half an hour but there should still be enough light left in the late-evening western sky for people to see. In addition, we had some candle lanterns positioned at various strategic points, such as on either side of the steps down from the terrace and on the route to the loos.

All but a few went out into the garden while I stayed inside.

I used my mobile phone to call the village pub.

"The Red Lion."

"Jack, it's Chester again. Is Amanda in the pub?"

"I haven't seen her since earlier this afternoon. Not since you called before. Is everything okay?"

"Yeah, fine, I think. But we can't find her. If she turns up, could you call me on this number?"

"Will do."

He disconnected.

Where the hell was she?

People slowly started returning to the marquee from their searches, and there were no jubilant shouts of discovery from anywhere.

Darren wandered in, and I went over to him.

"Look here, Darren," I said, "if you know where Amanda is, tell me right now."

"I don't," he replied, spreading his palms out wide. "We had a bit of a row, and she went off in tears, but that was ages ago."

"What did you row about?"

I could tell that he didn't want to tell me.

"Come on," I insisted. "What did you and Amanda row about?"

"She was paying more attention to the boy on the other side of her than she was to me."

"You stupid bastard." I said it with feeling.

Georgina came across to stand by me. She was now in tears.

"I'm going to call the police," I said.

CHAPTER

5

I NEVER DID GET to make my speech.

At first, when I called them, the police weren't particularly interested.

"How old is your daughter," asked the person who answered.

"She'll be nineteen next Friday," I replied.

"And how long has she been missing?"

"About an hour."

How the balance of one's life could change so rapidly in just a single hour—from happiness and joy to foreboding and terror.

"Adults are not officially listed as missing until they have not been seen for at least twenty-four hours, sometimes even longer."

"But we're in the middle of her birthday party," I said. "She is due to be making a speech, but she can't be found. We have thoroughly searched the house and garden, and she's not here. All we have found is the scarf she was wearing."

"Even so, she's not really been missing long enough," said the policeman. "She might have just gone for a quiet walk on her own."

"In the dark? From her own birthday party? Without her mobile phone? And what about her scarf we found?"

"People sometimes do the strangest things," he replied drolly.

I felt I was getting nowhere.

"I believe my daughter must have been abducted. I just hope it has nothing to do with me winning the Derby this afternoon."

"In what way could that be relevant?" the policeman asked.

"Because my horse is now a very valuable commodity," I said slowly, not wanting to believe what I was saying, "and that might make my daughter a target for kidnappers."

"I'll get someone there right away," he said, changing his tune. "Stay where you are, and don't let anyone else leave the party. They might need to give a statement."

I disconnected.

I had gone into the house to use the landline and, in spite of what I had said to the policeman, I didn't really believe that Amanda had been kidnapped. I tried to convince myself that there must be a less dramatic reason, and she would soon turn up, and eventually we'd all be able to laugh about it.

I went upstairs and into every single room to look for her. I searched under the beds, in the wardrobes, and even behind the shower curtain in the bathroom. Nothing.

"Amanda," I shouted loudly from the landing, "if you are here, show yourself. This is no longer a joke. I have called the police."

There was no sudden appearance, and no sound.

I went back outside and into the marquee, where people were standing in various groups discussing what to do.

"Ladies and gentlemen," I said again into the microphone, "we are still unable to locate Amanda, and I have now called the police to report her missing. They are sending a car. I have been asked to keep everyone here as you might be needed to make a statement. So I suggest we all sit down again in our designated places so that we can check that everyone is here and no one else is missing."

Everyone slowly moved back to their seats while I went over to Amanda's table and stood at the end to address her friends.

"If anyone knows more about this than they are saying, now is the time to come clean, before the police get here."

I stared at each one of them in turn, but no one responded.

"Darren, here," I said, pointing at him, "tells me that he and Amanda had an argument, and she went off in tears. Did anyone else see that? Did she tell any of you about it? Did anyone see her crying?"

I tried to establish exactly when she had last been seen, but they had all been drinking heavily, and most of them couldn't really remember anything.

"She came to the loo with me," said one of the girls, "just before the main course was served. I was feeling sick, and she showed me where to go."

"Did she stay with you?" I asked.

"No. She said she would wait outside, but when I came out, she'd gone."

I looked around at her friends. One of them was even using a phone to take a photo of me. But it gave me an idea.

"Look at the photos you have taken this evening," I said. "Check to see if Amanda appears in them. The police might want to see those to have a description of what she's wearing."

Every single one of them picked up their phone and began scanning through the photos.

"Also look at the time record on each picture, and sort out when the most recent was taken of her."

Georgina came over to me. "What are you doing?"

"Checking if anyone has taken any pictures of Amanda during the evening, and when. Go and ask James and his friends to do the same. There may be one of her in the background. Maybe even one of her leaving the marquee. That would give us the time she went missing."

I didn't hold out much hope, but it gave them, and me, something to do. Anything to take my mind off what might be happening to my daughter. I had visions of her lying out there somewhere, cold and afraid, maybe in the fields at the back of the house.

"Did anyone search the paddock and the stables?" I asked no one in particular.

"James did," Georgina said. "He took a torch while you were calling the police."

Brian Perry came over, looking deeply concerned. "Shall I go and check that she hasn't gone through the gate into our place?" he asked.

Brian and I had installed a gate between our respective gardens to make it easier for the children to go over there when they'd been small, to save them having to go out onto the road. As far as I was aware, it hadn't been used for years, but it had never been removed.

"Thank you, Brian, but I think we should all stay here until the police arrive."

"But we recently had a pond created in the garden."

He didn't need to elaborate on what he meant. I had a vision of Amanda, Ophelia-like, lying face up, beautiful and drowned in Brian's pond.

I quickly turned around to find James.

"James, go with Brian. Take your torch."

They hurried away, and I wondered if I should have gone with Brian rather than sending my son.

However, I more than half expected Amanda to waft back in, totally unperturbed, wondering what all the fuss was about. But she didn't.

The noise level rose somewhat as everyone was discussing the situation.

What should we do? Putting on any music seemed inappropriate. So did offering any more drinks, especially to the two young people's tables, as they had clearly had enough already.

We had been saving cheese and biscuits for a late-night snack at midnight, but I went over and told the catering manager to serve them to the tables now.

James and Brian returned, both shaking their heads.

"I also went into our house," Brian said, "but it was all dark, and there was no sign of her."

"Thanks," I said.

We waited. And then we waited some more.

I felt powerless. I thought I should be doing something more. Like driving around the village looking for her. But maybe not after the number of glasses of wine I had already consumed. I felt fine but I might be close to the limit, or just over. Perhaps I should walk or arrange a search party made up of other guests.

Staying here seemed all wrong, but the policeman on the phone had been adamant that everyone was to remain.

*　*　*

The first police car didn't arrive until thirty minutes after my phone call, by which time I was almost climbing the walls, or I would have been if the marquee had had walls.

James had gone out to the driveway to meet it, and in due course he brought two uniformed officers in high-visibility yellow jackets around the house to the marquee. I went to greet them on the dance floor.

"My name is Chester Newton," I said. "I was the person who called the police. It's my daughter who has gone missing."

The two officers looked at everyone still sitting at the tables in their smart attire.

"This is her birthday party," I said. "Along with a silver wedding anniversary celebration for my wife and me."

One of the two took a notebook out of his jacket pocket and made some notes.

"Your daughter's full name?" he asked.

"Amanda Rose Newton."

He wrote it down.

"Date of birth?"

I gave it to him, and he wrote that down too.

"Is this house her home address?"

"Yes."

"When did you notice that she was missing?"

"At about ten to ten, when she couldn't be found for the speeches. But the last photograph we have found of her this evening was taken at three minutes past nine. No one has seen her since."

"At 21.03?"

"Yes."

He wrote it down and also looked at his own watch.

"Did she leave with anyone?"

"No one from the party," I said. "Everyone else is accounted for."

"Can you give me a description of what she was wearing?"

I showed him a photo that one of her friends had taken of Amanda in her white dress and silk scarf. The dress was short and strapless, which I thought was obviously not appropriate attire to run away in, not that the policeman made any such comment.

"Did she have access to any vehicles?"

"She has her own car, a battered old blue Ford Fiesta, but it's still in the driveway. I checked. And no other cars are missing."

"And you have searched the house?"

"Yes. Thoroughly. And the garden. There's no sign of her. But we did find her scarf. It was on the ground outside the ladies' loo."

I held it out to him, but he didn't take it. Instead, he made some more notes, and I was becoming frustrated by his lack of urgency or action.

"Shouldn't you be organising a search of the local area," I said. "Or maybe getting a helicopter up to look for her?"

He glanced up at me from his notebook.

"Your daughter has been missing for less than two hours. Do you have any idea how many people are reported to the police as missing?"

I shook my head.

"In this country alone, a person is reported missing every ninety seconds. That's a hundred and seventy thousand missing persons every year."

I stared at him in disbelief.

"We can hardly send a helicopter up for all of them, now can we?" he said. "Now, does your daughter have any medical issues?"

"In what way?"

"Does she suffer from any form of mental illness? Or any other condition for which she takes regular medication?"

"No."

"What is the name of her doctor?"

"Dr Duncan Matthews," I said. "He's here tonight as one of my guests."

I turned around and searched for him. I knew that he was sitting at Georgina's table, and I found him quickly. "Duncan," I called, "could you please come over here for a moment?"

He came and joined the policemen and me.

"Good evening, sir," said one policeman. "I understand that you are Miss Amanda Newton's doctor. Can you tell me if she takes any regular medication, for example, for any adverse psychiatric condition?"

"She does not have an adverse psychiatric condition," Duncan said slowly and clearly. "The only regular medication she takes is the contraceptive pill, which I have been prescribing to her for about three years. At her own request."

That was news to me, but I suppose I shouldn't be surprised. Maybe I ought to be pleased that she was sensible enough to take precautions against becoming pregnant. But—for three years?

"Is there any other medical reason you might be aware of that could explain her sudden disappearance?" the policeman asked.

"Absolutely not," Duncan replied. "I have been Amanda Newton's doctor since she was two years old, and I consider this to be totally out of character."

"In your professional capacity as her doctor, would you describe Miss Newton as being vulnerable or particularly at risk?"

"There is no medical reason for believing so, but I judge that any young woman of nineteen who has disappeared without explanation, especially at night, should be considered to be at risk."

The policeman made another note. "Thank you, Doctor."

Duncan went back to his seat, and the policeman turned back to me.

"My dispatcher said something about you believing that your daughter might have been abducted. Why is that?"

"Why else would she not be here at her own birthday party? And what about the scarf? She wouldn't just take it off and drop it."

He didn't seem convinced.

"I also wonder if she might have been a target for kidnappers," I said. "I have a very valuable horse. It won the Derby this afternoon."

That seemed like a very long time ago now.

"Have you received any ransom demands?"

"No," I replied.

I took from his body language that he didn't believe for one second that Amanda had been kidnapped. But if not, where was she? Would she really go missing for a couple of hours during her birthday party if she hadn't been forced away by someone?

The policeman snapped shut his notebook.

"I will make a report and circulate your daughter's details on the National Police Computer. Checks will also be made to ensure she is not in police custody or a patient in a local hospital."

The two officers turned as if to leave.

"Is that *all*?" I said, grabbing one of their yellow jackets. "You haven't even looked for her!"

The policeman turned back to face me.

"It is my assessment that this is a low-risk missing person situation and that your daughter has most likely gone away from here at her own volition. She is an adult, and choosing to leave, even in the middle of her own birthday party, is not a crime, nor is it a police matter."

"But there is one other thing," I said, lowering my voice. "It seems Amanda had an argument tonight with her boyfriend. The boy in question has shown controlling behaviour towards her in the past, and I am really worried that he might have something to do with her disappearance."

"What's her boyfriend's name?"

"Darren Williamson," I said. "I believe he's already known to you."

"Why is that?"

"He was convicted of joy riding in a stolen car in Didcot last year."

"Is he here?"

"He's over there." I gestured towards where he was sitting.

Darren saw me pointing at him. His eyes widened, and he suddenly stood up and bolted for the marquee exit.

6

"Cocaine."

"What?"

"He was in possession of a quantity of cocaine."

One of the policemen had moved remarkably swiftly and had intercepted Darren just as he reached the exit, bringing him down with a masterly executed rugby tackle.

"So is that why he ran?" I asked.

"He claims so. He said he was trying to get outside so he could dump it before it was found on him. He vehemently maintains that he has nothing to do with your daughter going missing. But he also told us that both he and your daughter shared a line of coke before they came downstairs earlier. That might have affected her reasoning and could explain her subsequent behaviour."

I'd always known that boy was a bad influence on her.

By now it was almost midnight, and the two policemen were in the house with Georgina, James, and myself, all of us sitting around the kitchen table. Our guests had gone, including Darren, who had been arrested for possession of a Class A drug and taken away in a police van for further questioning, about both the cocaine and any part he might have played in Amanda's disappearance.

The policemen had initially said they wanted every guest to give their name and address, but I assured them that I could provide them with that information, so they recorded just those of the catering staff and the DJ, who had packed away his unused music and light equipment and departed—but not before he'd been paid, and in cash.

But there was still no sight nor sound of Amanda, and Georgina was getting increasingly frantic.

"So what do we do now?" I asked the policemen. "What if Darren Williamson is responsible?"

"If your daughter hasn't turned up by the morning, we will initiate a search of the local vicinity. You said that Mr Williamson had not been missing from the party for more than forty minutes or so, so he can't have taken her far, not on foot."

"Can't you search now?" I asked. "She may be lying somewhere out there injured."

Or dead, I thought, trying not to believe that.

"We need daylight to be able to search properly," said the policeman. "It is far too easy to miss objects in the dark, even something as large as a human being."

"It's light by half past four," I said.

"We will have a search team here around eight."

I'd be out long before that. In fact, I'd be searching all night.

"How long can you keep Williamson in custody?" I asked.

"Initially, we have twenty-four hours from the time he arrives at the police station." He looked at his watch. "That will be about now, as he's been taken to Oxford. After that we have to charge or release him, or get special permission from a superintendent or a magistrate, to question him further."

"Is he likely to be charged with the drug possession?"

"Almost certainly, especially as he has had a previous conviction, even though that was not for drugs. It will be up to the Crown Prosecution Service to decide. They might recommend he gets charged with possession with intent to supply because he has openly admitted that he supplied cocaine for your daughter's use."

"What will he get?"

"The maximum sentence for possession of a Class A drug is seven years, although he would never get that long, considering the small amount we found on him. But for possession with intent to supply, the maximum is life."

As far as I was concerned, life imprisonment for Darren would be too short.

"So you can keep him while the search is on for Amanda?"

"Almost certainly, but that will be up to my inspector. Depends on how long the search takes."

The policeman stood up to go.

"I'm sorry," he said. "There's nothing more we can do here for now. We'll report everything to our inspector in the morning, and I expect it will then be passed to CID. They'll be here with a search team in the morning."

The two policemen walked out of the kitchen towards the front door, and James went with them.

Georgina looked at me in despair, with tears in her eyes. "Where is our little girl?" she asked quietly.

Where, indeed?

Would Amanda really go off on her own volition during her party? Surely not. But what was the alternative?

I didn't want to think about that and tried to banish such negative thoughts, but the mind is very powerful. As hard as I tried to bury them in my subconscious, they kept popping back to the surface to haunt me.

I had a vivid picture in my brain of Amanda's lifeless body lying naked and bloodied, half hidden in the undergrowth. I shook my head to try and throw the image away, but it persisted and sent shivers down my spine.

How could this be happening to us?

I was finding it hugely difficult to control my own emotions, mostly the terrifying prospect of having lost Amanda forever. What had been one of the best days of my life had suddenly developed into its worst night.

"I'm going out to look for her," I said, fighting to control my voice so as not to make Georgina's distress even worse.

"Where?"

"I don't know, but I can't just sit here doing nothing."

"Then I'll come with you."

"No. You stay here in case the police call. I gave them the landline number because the mobile signal is so poor. I'll take James with me."

"I don't want to be left on my own," Georgina said quickly, the tears now flowing freely.

"All right. James will stay here with you."

"But are you okay to drive?"

"I think so. I've had nothing to drink for the past two hours and not an awful lot before that. I must be fine."

"The last thing I need right now is for you to be killed hitting a tree."

"Then I'll walk. I have to do something. I'll just go around the village. Then I'll come back."

James came into the kitchen.

"I'm going out to search in the village," I told him. "You stay here with Mum."

"I'd rather come with you," he said.

"But your mother needs you here. I'm going up to change."

I had just reached the bedroom when there was a sharp knocking on the front door. I instantly started to go back down, but James beat me to it.

As he opened the door, I was halfway down the stairs, and I could see two uniformed policemen standing there, silhouetted against the headlights of their car.

Georgina came out of the kitchen and saw the same thing.

"Oh God, no!" she screamed, and sat down heavily on the hall floor.

Ever since it had happened to Georgina's parents, when her sister had been killed in a car crash, at just eighteen years old, it had always been our worst nightmare that police would also arrive at our door in the middle of the night. We had discussed it often. Almost always, it meant only one thing.

One of the officers stepped through the door and I now saw that he was one of the two that had been here earlier. He went forward quickly to my wife, who was now lying on the floor, sobbing.

"It's all right, Mrs Newton," he said, crouching down and laying a kindly hand on her shoulder. "We've come to tell you that your daughter is safe and well."

Safe and well!

I sat down on the stairs, and now I was also sobbing—weeping tears of relief.

* * *

"Pangbourne! But that's miles away. How did she get there?"

"We are still trying to establish that," said the policemen.

We were all back in the kitchen, sitting around the table.

"It seems she banged on someone's front door in Pangbourne, asking for help, and the homeowner called 999. We heard the report on our personal radios when we were not that far down the road, so we came straight back to tell you."

"Thank you. Thank you." I said it with meaning.

"Where is she now?" I asked.

"She's been taken to the Royal Berkshire Hospital in Reading."

"Is she hurt?" Georgina's voice was still full of fear.

"Not that I'm aware of," said the policeman. "But it's normal practice for missing persons who are found to be taken straight to a hospital. To check that they are well and that they have not been abused."

"Abused?" Georgina asked.

"Injured or . . . anything."

Raped, he meant, I realised.

"Can we go and collect her?" I asked.

"In due course," he said. "She will need to be interviewed first. If it is believed she's been the victim of a crime, she'll have to be examined by our forensic team for traces of DNA. I assure you, she'll be quite safe overnight in hospital. Security will be provided."

"But we want her home," Georgina insisted.

"Mrs Newton," said the policeman quietly, "I understand your wish to have her back here with her family, but first and foremost, we have to determine her wishes."

"What do you mean by that?" Georgina demanded.

"She's over the age of eighteen, and therefore she is legally an adult. She may have left of her own free will. Perhaps she doesn't want to come back."

"Don't be ridiculous," Georgina said.

But I could see the strength of his argument, even if I didn't believe it.

Surely she would have not left of her own free will without at least taking her phone with her. Unless, of course, she didn't want it to help trace where she had gone.

For the moment, I was just so thankful that she had been found. I could happily wait until the morning to get the answers to the questions of how and why she had disappeared, only to turn up nine miles away.

And there were certainly some pressing questions in my head.

Had she walked to Pangbourne? Or had she been driven?

Walking nine miles in three hours was not particularly difficult for a fit nineteen-year-old. But she'd been wearing a party dress and high-heeled shoes. Or had she stashed a change of clothes and footwear close by, ready for use?

"What was she wearing when she banged on this person's door?" I asked.

"I don't have that information," replied the policeman. "I am sure that all the questions will be answered in the morning."

Probably not all of them, I thought.

"So what happens to Darren Williamson now?"

"He will probably still be detained overnight. Possession of a Class A drug is a serious matter. He'll be interviewed in the morning and may be charged."

"*May* be?"

"If it's his first drug offence, he will likely be released with an official caution."

"A caution? That hardly seems enough punishment for supplying my daughter with cocaine."

"We have no evidence of that. It might have been the other way around. In fact we have no evidence that either Mr Williamson or your daughter took cocaine at all, other than what Mr Williamson said to us earlier, and he might not have been telling the truth."

Now that wouldn't surprise me for a second.

"And accepting an official police caution is a formal admission of guilt and becomes part of the person's criminal record. It's a lot more than just a slap on the wrist."

It didn't sound like it to me.

"Right," said the policeman, standing up. "Time for us to leave."

I walked the two officers through to the hallway and out onto the driveway.

"Do you still need the list of names and addresses of our party guests?"

"That will depend on what your daughter has to say. I'll let you know."

The two officers climbed into their car and drove away, and I went back to the kitchen.

"I want to go to the hospital," Georgina stated determinedly.

"We will in the morning," I said.

"I want to go now. I need to look after my little girl."

"She's not a little girl anymore." I said it quietly and gently. "She's a fully grown young woman."

"To me, she'll always be my little girl," Georgina said, looking across the table. "And I want to see her right now!"

"But even if we do go to the hospital, there's no guarantee the police will let us see her."

"I still want to be close by, in case she needs me."

Even I could see that further argument would be futile. Either I drove Georgina to the hospital or she would drive herself, and I wasn't at all sure that her mind was sufficiently rational under the circumstances. James was certainly in no fit state to get behind the wheel of a car. He was the only one who had continued drinking after the party had come to an abrupt halt, and he still had a can of lager in his hand even now.

"Okay," I said. "I'll take you to the hospital."

"Will you be all right to drive?"

"I'll have to be," I said. "James, you stay here in case the police call again on the landline."

"Why would they do that?" he asked, somewhat slurring his words.

"Just stay here in case they do," I said, resisting the temptation to get cross with him.

"All right," he said, standing up and swaying slightly. "No problem."

If he had any more alcohol, I thought, *he wouldn't hear the phone even if it exploded*.

* * *

We didn't hit a tree, or anything else for that matter, and made it to the Royal Berkshire Hospital in Reading without incident.

I parked in front of the impressive porticoed north entrance and decided not to bother paying the parking charge—surely no one would be checking at three o'clock in the morning.

The only entrance we could find open at this time of night was the Accident and Emergency department on Craven Road.

Even at this hour, the department was quite busy, with at least fifteen people sitting on metal chairs waiting to be seen, a couple of them holding babies.

"We're enquiring after one of your female patients," I said to the young woman sitting behind a glass panel in the reception. "Her name is Amanda Newton. We're her parents."

The receptionist typed something into her computer before looking up at us through the glass.

"She's no longer here in A&E. She's been taken upstairs to the general admissions ward."

"Can we see her?" I asked.

"Visiting times are from two o'clock in the afternoon until eight o'clock in the evening," the receptionist replied unhelpfully.

"But we have come here especially," Georgina pleaded. "Amanda went missing from her home, and she was found and brought here by the police."

She looked at us, as if deciding. "I'll give the ward duty nurse a call."

We waited as the call was made. I could hear that it was ringing, but it was quite a long while before it was answered.

The receptionist turned away from us as she spoke, so I couldn't make out what was being said on either side. After a couple of minutes, she turned back, holding her hand over the phone mouthpiece.

"Your daughter is in a side room under protection. She's not permitted to receive visitors."

Georgina burst into tears and begged. "Please, can we see her?"

"It has been a very emotional evening," I explained. "Please ask the nurse if it would be possible to see her just for a moment, even if it's just through a window or through a crack in the door. So we can reassure ourselves that she is safe and well."

The receptionist turned away and spoke again into the phone before once more turning back to us.

"The night duty nurse is seeing what she can arrange. But she would have to find someone from security to come and collect you, and it might take a while. If you still want to wait, go and sit over there." She pointed across at some of the metal chairs.

"Thank you," I said.

We went over to the seats.

"I need to go to the loo," Georgina said, walking off towards the ladies.

As I sat down, my phone rang.

I looked at it. *No Caller ID* had appeared on the screen.

Who on earth could be calling me at this hour?

"Hello," I said slowly, answering.

"Is that Chester Newton?" asked a funny-sounding voice, all high pitched and squeaky, as if using an electronic voice changer or a swazzle, like Punch in a *Punch and Judy* show.

"Yes," I said warily. "Who is this?"

"See how easy it was for me to take your daughter," said the squeaky voice. "In the future, you will do as I say, or next time she'll come home in a body bag."

CHAPTER

7

"**A**RE YOU ALL right?" Georgina asked, coming back from the ladies. "You look like you've just seen a ghost."

"I'm fine," I said, waving a hand at her. "I'm just tired."

"Mmm, me too." She yawned and sat down next to me.

I didn't tell her about the phone call—of course I didn't. It would have sent her into a wild panic—as it had me.

Was it real or just a prank? Had the person on the other end of the line, man or woman, really taken Amanda from our home and deposited her in Pangbourne? And, in particular, was the threat to kill her next time real? What did the person want me to do? What did he or she mean by *"In the future, you will do as I say"*? Had I not done something they had asked for in the past?

My thoughts were interrupted by the arrival of a man in black trousers and a white shirt, with *Security* emblazoned across each black epaulette. He also had an identity card hanging on a lanyard around his neck.

"Mr and Mrs Newton?" he asked.

"Yes," I replied.

"I'm Justin from hospital security. Please come with me."

We stood up and followed him through two sets of double doors to a bank of lifts.

"The police have given instructions that no one should speak to your daughter other than the medical team," Justin said formally as the lift doors closed behind us. "Anyway, she's fast asleep. She has been sedated."

"Sedated? Why?" Georgina asked.

"You will have to ask the doctors that. It seems she was quite agitated when she was brought in."

"Just seeing her will be great," I said, trying to be positive.

He pushed the button for the fourth floor, where we followed him down a brightly lit corridor to the general admissions ward. He placed his identity card against a small device on the left-hand wall, and the door opened automatically towards us.

"You will need to be quiet now," Justin said in a whisper.

We nodded.

He led us around a corner to a side room where another similarly dressed security guard was sitting on a chair outside the door. He stood up.

"Your daughter is in here," Justin said. "We will open the door for you to see her, but you must not go in or make any noise. Do you understand?"

"Yes," we whispered together.

He opened the door and stood aside.

The ceiling light was dimly lit, and in its glow we could see Amanda lying asleep on her back in the bed, her long blonde hair spreading out over the pillow on either side of her head. She looked quite calm but, at the same time, somehow very vulnerable.

"Oh, my darling," Georgina cried softly. She tried to move forward into the room but Justin, the security man, put out his hand to block her.

"Sorry," he said firmly. "No one is allowed in here." He pulled the door shut. "My colleague will show you out now. We are changing shift."

"Thank you," I said to him. "It is good to see her being so well looked after."

We were escorted back to the A&E department.

"I want to stay," Georgina said. "So I'm here when she wakes up."

"My love," I said. "We have to go home and get some sleep ourselves. We will be no use to Amanda if we are so tired we can't keep our eyes open."

"But she might need me."

"The hospital staff will look after her. And the police will want to interview her before we can see her anyway. Come on—let's go home. We can come back in the morning."

She didn't want to—I could see that—but she eventually allowed me to steer her out to our car, which unsurprisingly didn't have a parking ticket on the windscreen.

* * *

James was still not in bed when we arrived home, but he was fast asleep.

All the lights were still on throughout the house, and he was snoring gently on the sofa in the sitting room. I picked up a throw from the footstool and placed it over him.

"Let him be," I said to Georgina. "He's going to have quite a hangover in the morning."

As was I, but not from drinking.

Georgina had dozed all the way home from Reading, but my mind had been sharp and awake, and asking questions.

Who had phoned me? What did they want me to do?

And—perhaps the most pressing of the questions I was trying to answer—should I report the call to the police?

Part of my brain said, *Of course you must because it's a police matter.*

But another part said, *No, you mustn't because it might put Amanda in danger.*

The man—I thought of the caller as a man because I doubted that a woman would have had the strength to carry Amanda away—hadn't actually told me not to call the police. Was that because he was confident of not being identified even if I did?

Georgina and I went to bed, turning out the light at half past five, when the sun had already been up for more than half an hour, and was shining brightly against our bedroom window.

Even though I had been awake now for over twenty-four hours, I couldn't sleep, endlessly tossing and turning as I tried to get the squeaky voice out of my head.

I must have eventually gone to sleep, because I was awakened by my phone ringing on my bedside table. In trepidation I picked it up. The screen showed me the time was eight-thirty. It also gave me the name of the caller— Owen Reynolds. Relieved, I answered it.

"Morning, Owen," I said.

"Morning, Chester. I hope I'm not too early." Eight-thirty was positively late for a trainer who would be up at five o'clock every day. "Did your party go well?"

"It was definitely one I will never forget," I replied. "What can I do for you?"

"Eleanor and I are having a bit of a bash here at five o'clock this afternoon, to celebrate the Derby win. It's mostly for my stable staff and some neighbours from our village, but we thought it would be nice to also invite the owning syndicate, and yourself and Georgina, of course. Potassium will also parade. But I need the syndicate members' telephone numbers to invite them."

"No problem," I said. "I'll email them over to you."

"Great. Could you also bring the trophy with you, for display?"

"I'll see what I can do."

"Great," he said again. "See you later."

He disconnected and I lay back on the pillow, holding my mobile. The last thing I really wanted to do was to drive over to Owen's yard and be full of bonhomie, but it came with the territory.

I continually needed more and more syndicate members, as those I had were becoming older, and some had dropped off the list altogether, either through death or because they couldn't afford horse ownership in their retirement.

Winning the Derby was the best marketing tool I could have ever asked for, and much of it would be done by word of mouth from the existing syndicate. Hence I needed to be there to press their flesh and get across the message that it was Victrix that gave you wings, at least with the horses.

Owning racehorses is all about dreaming.

Most owners—nay, almost all of them—lose money. Certainly, no one does it to make a fortune. Buying a racehorse, whether it be outright or with others in a syndicate, is to buy into a certain lifestyle.

Make no mistake, I was in the luxury-goods market. Owning racehorses isn't cheap, but it is a price that some are prepared to pay to live the high life. And occasionally they strike it rich—like owning the winner of the Derby.

It was the slot-machine logic. Everyone knows that the casinos have fixed the systems so that, over time, slots never pay out as much cash as they consume. That's why they're known as "one-arm bandits." But still people play them. Partly for the thrill of the gamble but also in the knowledge that, maybe this time, they will hit the jackpot.

And the Las Vegas casinos absolutely love it when someone actually does win a million dollars of their money on a giant slot machine. They know that, with the publicity such a win generates, tens of thousands more punters will flood through their doors to try their luck.

So here I was, hoping for the same thing.

Potassium's win in the Derby, and the publicity it would generate, should have prospective syndicate members queuing at my door, chasing the same dream.

Hence, I would go to Owen Reynolds's stable yard at five o'clock, although whether I could convince Georgina to come with me was another matter. She hadn't wanted to do much recently. She blamed her hormones, as she had done for most things for quite a long while now. "It's the menopause," she would say, as if that was the excuse for everything, as indeed it might be. And *pause* was certainly the right word. Our whole lives together as a married couple seemed to be "on pause."

I looked across at her, and decided to leave her sleeping. She could do with the sleep, something else she often couldn't get enough of because of the hormones rampaging through her body. We would hear soon enough if there was any news from the Royal Berkshire Hospital.

I threw on a T-shirt and a pair of shorts and went downstairs.

James was still on the sofa in the sitting room, but he was just about awake, sitting up and holding his head.

"Morning, James," I said. "How's the hangover?"

"Don't ask," he replied. "Did you see Amanda?"

"Only briefly."

"Did she tell you what happened?"

I shook my head. "She'd been sedated. But I hope to hear from her soon."

Or from the police, I thought.

I went through the kitchen and to my office, to send Owen the email with the Potassium syndicate members' telephone numbers. I was sure none of them would object to me sharing their personal information—not under the circumstances.

I sat at my desk for a while, answering the mass of congratulatory emails I had received from a large number of people, especially from members of my other syndicates, who seemed genuinely happy that a Victrix horse had won the Derby, even if it wasn't the one they actually owned shares in.

As I was just finishing, someone rang the front door bell.

I had installed one of those security systems that showed a video on my mobile phone of who was there. I could also talk to them.

"Hello," I said, looking at the image of a woman in her thirties, standing on the porch.

"Is that Mr Newton?" she said. "Mr Chester Newton?"

"Yes," I replied.

"I'm Detective Sergeant Christine Royle of Thames Valley Police." She held up her police warrant card to the camera so I could read it. "Can I come in?"

"Just a minute."

I rushed through the kitchen and the hallway to the front door.

DS Royle was not alone. Standing by her car was a younger man.

"This is DC Abbot."

I showed the two of them into the house, then through into the kitchen, where we sat at the table.

"Have you spoken to my daughter?" I asked.

"Indeed, we have," said the detective sergeant. "We've come straight here from the hospital."

"Is she all right?" I asked with concern.

"She was fine when I left her," the DS replied. "She's now resting."

"What did she say happened?"

"That's the problem. She told me she has no memory of anything that occurred yesterday evening. The last thing she can remember is getting dressed for your party. She claims to have no recollection of how or why she ended up in hospital. I am hoping that some of her memory might return later. But blood tests have shown she has both cocaine and ketamine in her system."

"Ketamine? Isn't that a drug used by vets on horses?"

"It's also an anaesthetic for humans and is widely used for relieving acute pain due to injury. But it's also taken illegally by some people as a recreational drug. And it can make people do the strangest of things, sometimes totally out of character. Mr Newton, are you aware that your daughter is a drug user?"

"I wasn't. Not until last night when her boyfriend admitted that they had both snorted some cocaine before the party."

"And ketamine?"

"Not that I was aware of," I said. "But I wouldn't put anything past Darren Williamson. Why don't you ask him? He was arrested here last night for possessing cocaine. The officers said he'd been taken to Oxford."

"He has since been released with a caution," the DS said.

"When?" I asked.

"In the early hours, after your daughter had been located. There was no reason to detain him any longer. There's been a major disturbance in Oxford City Centre overnight, which involved rioting and looting. It always seems to happen when the weather is hot and people drink too much. Anyway, numerous arrests were made, and Mr Williamson was released to make room in the cells."

At this point Georgina walked into the kitchen in her dressing gown.

"I thought I heard voices down here," she said. "What's happened?"

"Nothing," I said. "Amanda's fine. These people are detectives. They've come to ask us some questions about last night."

The detective sergeant stood up. "I'm DS Royle and this is DC Abbot. I assume you are Mrs Newton?"

"Yes," said Georgina. "I am."

"I've just been telling your husband that your daughter has no memory of the events of last evening. At least, that's what she's been telling us."

"Don't you believe her?" Georgina asked sharply.

"Should I have any reason not to?" asked the DS.

"None," Georgina replied emphatically.

She would always defend her daughter.

The detective took a notebook from her jacket pocket and opened it. "Could you both please give me an account of events last evening, in particular, prior to your daughter going missing? Especially anything unusual."

I wondered if winning the Derby counted as *unusual*.

I went through everything I could remember, from the time I had arrived home from Epsom until the moment I had been unable find Amanda for the speeches. I also described the actions taken afterwards to try and find her.

"Have you anything to add, Mrs Newton?" asked the detective.

"Nothing," Georgina replied. "I think Chester has covered everything."

The detective closed her notebook.

"I will need a list of the names and addresses of all your guests. I believe you told the constables last night that you could provide one."

"Yes," I said. "I have an Excel file. I'll go and print it out."

I went through to my office, printed the list from my computer, and took it back to the kitchen.

"Don't forget to cross off my mother, and also Richard and Sarah Bassett," Georgina said. "They didn't come."

I put a line through their names and then handed the list to the detective.

"You seem to be taking this matter very seriously," I said to her. "Do you really think that my daughter just had a bad drug trip and wandered off, or is there something you're not telling us?"

The DS hesitated. So there was something else.

"I think we have a right to know," I said. "We *are* her parents."

"But your daughter is over eighteen. She's now an adult, able to make her own decisions, and she is also entitled to her privacy, even from her parents. But are either of you aware if your daughter was in the habit of injecting herself with anything?"

"Like what?" Georgina asked, somewhat alarmed.

"Drugs."

"As I told you, we were not aware of her taking any drugs," I said. "Why do you ask?"

The DS hesitated again, as if deciding whether to tell us. In the end she clearly made up her mind to do so. "It would appear that there is an injection puncture mark on her skin."

"Whereabouts on her skin?" Georgina asked.

"On her neck," said the detective. "Close to her jugular vein."

"Her jugular vein!" I said. "How could anyone inject themselves there?"

"You'd be surprised. Some addicts regularly inject into their jugulars when they can no longer find a suitable vein anywhere else."

"But that's ridiculous," I said. "Someone else must have injected her."

"With what?" Georgina asked.

"Ketamine," the DS replied.

"What's that?" asked Georgina, now deeply worried.

"An anaesthetic. Blood tests show it is in her system, and she is also displaying some of the after-effects of ketamine, in particular amnesia and confusion."

"But is she all right now?" I asked.

"She's better this morning, but because of the ketamine, we are now treating her disappearance as a possible abduction."

"Only a possible abduction?" I said. "What other explanation could there be?"

"We are still looking into that."

See how easy it was for me to take your daughter, the squeaky voice had said. *In the future, you will do as I say, or next time she'll come home in a body bag.*

I debated again whether I should tell this police officer about that call.

"Tell me," I said to her casually. "If someone receives a nuisance call with *No Caller ID* shown on their phone, can the police find out who made it?"

She looked at me. "Why do you want to know?"

"No reason," I said. "I just wondered."

"It's technically possible but it's complicated because of privacy laws. And it also depends on the caller's number having been properly registered. Most nuisance callers use unregistered burner phones, which makes it impossible to trace them."

So there was absolutely no point in me telling the detective about the call I'd received from Squeaky Voice. It wouldn't lead to him being traced, and it might put Amanda in greater danger.

"Have you been receiving nuisance calls?" asked DS Royle, her detective antennae clearly quivering wildly.

"No," I said quickly. "But as the owner of yesterday's Derby winner, I'm worried I might. You know. Begging calls and such. I've heard of it happening to others."

"Let us know if it happens, and we'll see what we can do about it."

DS Royle handed me one of her business cards with her direct dial telephone number printed on it.

"Thank you," I said, putting the card in my wallet. "So, when can we collect Amanda?"

"She is free to leave the hospital at any time," replied the detective sergeant blandly. "But it's for her to decide where she goes when discharged. Are you sure she will agree to come home with you?"

"Absolutely certain," Georgina said.

But was there something else the detective wasn't telling us?

CHAPTER

8

GEORGINA AND I arrived back at the Royal Berkshire Hospital at noon, and this time I did pay for parking.

Georgina had packed some of Amanda's clothes and shoes in a bag so she wouldn't have to wear her party outfit home, but that was the least of our worries.

Amanda was not by herself.

Darren Williamson was there ahead of us, and neither Georgina nor I was pleased about it.

"Darren, leave our daughter alone," I said. "I know that you supplied her with cocaine, and it's got to stop."

He smirked at us. "Amanda's old enough to make her own decisions. The law says so. And she's decided to come and live with me, not you."

I stared at him. So that was what the detective sergeant hadn't told us.

"Don't be ridiculous," I said. "How would she be able to afford to live with you?"

"I will provide for her," he said belligerently.

"Doing what?" I said. "By drug dealing? And what happens to her when you end up in prison?"

Amanda had so far been quiet throughout this exchange, but now she put in her two-penny worth.

"I'm old enough to look after myself," she said. "And I want to live with Darren."

"Where?" I asked.

"In his flat. In Didcot."

Georgina, meanwhile, had started crying once again.

"Don't do this to your mother," I said gently to Amanda. "Come on home with us now. We will discuss everything and sort it all out."

"No," she said firmly. "I'm going to live with Darren. He says it's for the best for me to make a decision and then stick with it."

Of course Darren would say that, but only if she decided to do what he'd already decided for her.

"How about all your stuff?" I asked, clutching at any grounds not to let her go.

"I'll collect what I need later in the week."

I was desperate. How could I possibly protect her from Squeaky Voice if she was not even living under my roof?

* * *

I went to Owen Reynolds's yard for his *"bit of a bash"* on my own. I didn't even bother asking Georgina to come with me, telling her that I was going to a meeting with Owen to discuss Potassium's future, rather than to a celebration.

Having a celebration somehow didn't seem to be appropriate under the circumstances, but I couldn't not go. Everyone would expect me to be there and to have brought the Derby trophy with me.

As it turned out, I had, in fact, driven Amanda home—her and Darren sitting side by side on the back seat of my Jaguar 4x4, with Georgina in the front next to me, all of us in an uneasy silence.

Not that Amanda had changed her mind.

When we had arrived back at the house, she had collected a few things from her room, including her mobile phone and charger, and then she and Darren had driven away in her old Ford Fiesta, and without so much as a backward glance.

Who will now pay the tax and insurance on that car? I'd thought.

But I knew the answer.

I would. As I always had.

I didn't believe that Amanda had the slightest idea how much money it took just to live. At home, she had no bills to pay and had food placed on the table in front of her for every meal. Hence, I was confident that she would soon be back, but keeping her safe in the meantime was my main worry, not just from Squeaky Voice but also from Darren and the drugs.

* * *

There was a carnival atmosphere at Owen Reynolds's stable yard in East Ilsley.

The whole place was decked out in bunting, and there was even a brass band playing on the grass circle in the centre of the stable courtyard, which was driving Owen's two black Labradors crazy. They chased each other's tails round and round the band like demented things, barking loudly.

Owen had said the event was largely for his stable staff and people from the village, but as I pulled my Jaguar into the yard, I could see most of the owning syndicate members were also present, some of them with their families.

"Hey, Nick," I called out to Nick Spencer, the property lawyer syndicate member. "Could you come and give me a hand?"

He came over, and between us, we lifted out the half-metre-wide Derby trophy from the car boot. It depicted three silver horses racing around on undulating circular silver turf, and it needed both of us to carry it over to the table that Owen had prepared.

"Do we get to keep this?" Nick asked, breathing heavily.

"Sadly not. This is a perpetual trophy. We have to give it back next year—unless we can win it again."

"So do we get to keep anything?"

"We get to keep the prize money," I said with a grin. "Unless you'd like to use yours to buy shares in more Victrix horses."

He laughed.

On the two previous occasions that my syndicated horses had won major honours, in races worth more to the winner than a quarter of a million pounds, I had used some of the ten per cent of the prize money retained by the company to produce miniature replicas of the race trophy for each syndicate member, suitably engraved.

I might do the same again, but it would probably have just one small horse on it rather than the three. It would be an expense well worth it for the goodwill generated. Anything to bring the members back to my door to buy shares in next year's crop of yearlings.

The remainder of the withheld prize money would go towards the entry fees for future races. Those with the highest purses, such as the ones we would now consider for Potassium, were expensive to enter, often running to more than ten thousand pounds—the Champion Stakes at Ascot was nearer twenty—far more than I could justify paying from the syndicate fees alone. But with luck we'd win it all back again in the prize money, and with interest.

"Did you have a good night?" Nick asked with a laugh.

"It was certainly one to remember," I said, trying to smile back while not thinking about what Amanda and Darren might be up to together in his flat. "How about you?"

"We got thrown out of racecourse hospitality at seven thirty by Security." He laughed again. "By then, no one was fit to drive, so we piled into the Derby Arms pub across the road from the course and went on celebrating. Claire and I rolled home in a taxi at midnight, but we only live in Esher. God knows how some of the others managed. I'm totally amazed they've all made it here today. I came by train to Newbury, then a taxi, because my car is still in the car park at Epsom." He laughed once more.

Some of the other syndicate members drifted over to have a closer look at the trophy they had only been able to view at a distance yesterday.

One of them, Bill Parkinson, was still wearing his morning-dress striped trousers, white shirt, and braces from yesterday. He saw me looking at them.

"Slept in the car," he said, smiling. "Haven't been home yet to change."

It had clearly been an eventful twenty-four hours for all of us.

*   *   *

Potassium made his appearance at a quarter to six, parading around the stable yard proudly wearing the 'Derby Winner' blanket adorned large with the race sponsor's logo.

As the horse was walked around the quadrangle, he carried his bold head high, as if he knew that he'd done something special and was the star of the show. Then his jockey, Jimmy Ketch, appeared, again wearing the royal blue and white vertical striped silks and a white cap. The band struck up the tune "Congratulations," and everyone cheered.

As if by magic, trays of champagne glasses appeared, and we all drank a toast to Potassium, our Derby winner.

Next, Owen made a short speech thanking his stable staff for all their hard work, and his neighbours in the village for their support and encouragement. He finished by saying how proud he was, at last, to be able to refer to his establishment as a "Derby-winning stable" after more than twelve unsuccessful previous attempts to capture the "big one."

As I listened to him, I realised that it wasn't just *my* enterprise that had needed the boost.

"Where will Potassium run next?" shouted Bill Parkinson.

Owen looked across at me standing to one side. He waved me over to join him.

"Chester and I will have to discuss that," Owen said. "I've already provisionally entered him for the Prix de l'Arc de Triomphe at Longchamp in October. Initial entries for that closed last month. Then there's the King George and Queen Elizabeth Stakes in July or the International Stakes at

York in August. Entries for those close fairly soon. And of course there's always the Champion Stakes at Ascot in October and—who knows?—maybe a crack at the four-million-dollar Breeders' Cup Turf in America come November." He smiled. "There's a lot for Chester and me to decide in the coming days."

"What about Royal Ascot?" asked Nick Spencer loudly.

"That's definitely something else for Chester and me to look at," Owen replied.

"Don't we get any say in it?" shouted Bill Parkinson with a touch of irritation. "After all, we are the flipping owners of the horse."

"Of course you get a say, Bill," I replied calmly. "In fact, it would be great if all the syndicate members could send me an email during this coming week with your suggestions for where Potassium should run next and then for the rest of the season."

But Bill Parkinson must have known, as I did, that the syndicate agreement stated very clearly in black and white that it was *I* who had the final say of where Victrix horses ran, after due consultation with their trainers. I might take some account of the members' preferences, but syndicate ownership was not a democracy, so it would be me alone who'd make the decisions. And those decisions would be based solely on what was best for the horse, and to give him the best chance of winning, not on whether it would be nice to have Royal Ascot owners' badges, a weekend in Paris or a trip to the United States.

Not that all Derby winners raced again anyway.

Several have been retired to stud straight after their Epsom success, the most recent being Pour Moi, the 2011 winner; and back in the nineteenth century, two horses, Middleton and Amato, both won the Derby on their first and only appearance on any racecourse, although that will never occur again as horses that haven't raced at least once before are no longer eligible to run.

Potassium was taken back to his box, and the party began to wind down.

"I'm putting on a barbecue later for my staff, after evening stables," Owen said to me quietly. "You're welcome to stay."

"Thanks," I replied, "but I'd better be heading back home. Georgina's not feeling very well. That's why she isn't here."

"Oh, I'm sorry to hear that," Owen said. "Give her my best."

It was easier for me to tell him a white lie rather than to give him the true reason for Georgina's absence, which was that my wife was close to an emotional breakdown after her daughter had first gone missing and then reappeared only to go and live with a most unsuitable older man who provided her with illegal Class A drugs.

I was tempted to stay on for the barbecue, but I knew that staying later would only cause more problems with Georgina in the long run.

One of Owen's stable lads helped me return the Derby trophy to the boot of my Jaguar, before I set the vehicle's nose back north, towards home.

But I drove without enthusiasm.

Whereas I had once arrived back each time with eagerness and excitement, I did so now with trepidation and dismay, knowing that there would always be some sort of crisis waiting for me inside.

And today was no exception.

"WHY HAVE YOU been so long?" Georgina wailed as I walked into the kitchen.

"I haven't been long," I replied, somewhat miffed. "As it was, I turned down an invitation to stay for a barbecue, in order to be back here for you."

"But James is being nasty towards me," she said.

"In what way?"

"He keeps telling me to pull myself together and to stop crying."

He had a point, I thought.

"Okay," I said. "I'll have a word with him. Where is he?"

"Up in his room."

With a sigh, I climbed the stairs and knocked on James's bedroom door. He didn't immediately shout "Come in," so I waited, and after a few moments, he opened it.

"Can I have a word?" I asked.

"What about?"

"Mum says you've been giving her a hard time."

"That's rich," James said. "It's her that's been giving me a hard time."

"Why?"

"For playing music. She said it was inappropriate. God knows why. It's not as if Amanda's still missing. She's just gone to live with her boyfriend, and I don't blame her. Life in this house is rubbish at the moment. In fact, I'm also going back to Bristol in the morning. Gary's collecting me."

"I thought term had ended for the summer," I said.

"It has for me, but not for Gary. Medical School term goes on for longer. But I'm going back anyway. It's more fun there. There's another three weeks to go on our lease, and Gary and I need to find a flat for next year."

"Can't you stay where you are?"

"No chance. Five of us shared this year, but we are both fed up with that. We're going to find a place for just the two of us. That's provided I've passed my exams."

"When do you find that out?" I asked.

"I get the results at the end of this week. That's another reason for going."

"Don't you get them online?"

"Yeah. But if there's a problem, I'd be able to talk to my tutor."

"Do you think there might be a problem?"

"Maybe. Maybe not. Mathematics isn't easy, you know. I'll have to wait and see, but I should have worked harder than I did." He pulled a face. "But as long as it's all okay and we sort out a flat, Gary and I might go away for a bit in August. Italy possibly, or Spain. Definitely somewhere in Europe."

"How can you afford that?" I asked.

He laughed. "I can't really. That's why we're only going to Europe. We have a little money saved, and we're planning to hitchhike and camp. If our cash runs out, we'll just have to find some work in bars or restaurants."

"Don't you need a visa to work in Europe these days?" I asked.

"Not if you're paid in cash." He smiled. "A couple of our mates went to Italy last year and they said there were plenty of jobs available if you're prepared to work very late in the nightclubs. Or you could always give me a sub. Especially after yesterday at Epsom." He smiled again.

I laughed. "Trust me. There's absolutely no chance of that if you're going to be nasty to your mother. So go down and make peace. It's not her fault that her hormones are up the creek."

"But her hormones have been up the creek for years. Don't they have a paddle?"

We laughed together—for the first time in a very long while.

He wasn't really a bad kid. Not always, anyway.

*   *   *

On Monday morning I was at my desk, as usual, by seven thirty, having made myself a cup of coffee in the kitchen on the way through.

I glanced through the digital version of the *Racing Post* on my computer, to see if there was any news I needed to know—there wasn't—and then set about contacting the eleven trainers of the Victrix horses.

Entries for most horse races have to be made by noon, six days before the race, or five days before those on Saturdays. Only for the most valuable races, such as Group 1 races like the Derby, did entries close at least a month or more earlier.

Having entered a horse, it was possible for me to look online at the list of other entrants, discuss them with the trainer, and decide if we wanted the horse to run. If so, we had to declare it as a runner by ten AM two days before the race, and advise the name of our jockey by one PM the same day. If we decided against or if we failed to declare in time, the horse wouldn't run, and the entry stake money would be forfeited.

With currently forty horses under Victrix management, there were decisions to be made almost every day about entries and declarations.

I normally spent a couple of hours each morning at my desk, phoning or emailing the trainers. Many of the calls or emails were short, just confirming an entry or declaration, which would then be actioned by the trainer; while others would be much longer as we discussed future strategy for a given horse.

On average, a flat racehorse will take part in six or seven races each year, but many run as often as ten times, and the record is more than twice that. It is often the case that the better the horse, the less it races—maybe only three or four times a year, but that is not always true.

Frankel ran fourteen times in three years, winning every one, and the great Australian mare, Black Caviar, won every one of her twenty-five races over a four-year period—including travelling halfway around the world to land the Jubilee Stakes at Royal Ascot. And another stellar Australian mare, Winx, ran forty-three times over five years, winning thirty-seven of them— the last thirty-three in a row—amassing an incredible fourteen million pounds of prize money.

My syndicate members obviously liked their horses to race as often as possible, and preferably on Saturdays. That gave them more chance to go and watch their horses run, and I tried to accommodate their wishes where I could, provided it was the best thing for the horses.

Consequently, there were Victrix horses running somewhere every week—sometimes two or three of them on a single day—and finding the perfectly rated race for each horse, at an appropriate distance and carrying a favourable weight, such that it maximized its chance of winning, was like a game of three-dimensional chess. And of course, everyone else was doing exactly the same to try and make their horse the winner.

I employed two female assistants to help me, both working remotely on computers in their own homes. Every day, they would update the detailed spreadsheets, one for each Victrix horse, to ensure that entry deadlines weren't missed, and all bills were paid on time. And every morning I would receive an email from each, showing me what I needed to do on that day. I was nominally their boss, but it was clearly they who bossed me, and I couldn't imagine how I could now operate without them.

At ten past nine, I called my final trainer, Owen Reynolds, when I knew he would be back in his own office after an early summer morning spent on the gallops.

"How was the barbecue?" I asked.

"Great," he replied. "But a few of the lads had sore heads this morning, especially for first lot at five thirty."

"How is Potassium today?"

"He ate up really well last night. He just had a short loosening canter this morning, but he seems great."

"Good. So what's next for him?" I asked.

"Depends on whether we want to stay at a mile and half, like the Derby, or drop down to a mile and a quarter."

"After Saturday's close shave, I'd be happier at a mile and a quarter, especially against older horses."

"Me too," said Owen. "Shame, really. I've always wanted to win a King George and Queen Elizabeth Stakes or a Prix de l'Arc de Triomphe. Not to mention the Breeders' Cup Turf. All those are a mile and a half." I could hear him sigh down the line. "So, are we then agreed that the plan is to go for the International Stakes at York in August and, provided that goes well, the Champion Stakes at Ascot in October? Both at a mile and a quarter."

"How about the Breeders' Cup Classic instead of the Champion Stakes?" I said. "That's also a mile and a quarter, and winning at York would give him automatic free entry to the Classic, and the Americans will even pay the travel costs for both the horse and connections."

"Let's not get ahead of ourselves," Owen said with a laugh. "We'll only consider the Breeders' Cup if, and after, he wins at York. And remember, he's never run on a dirt track before—always on turf."

"It's a long time from now until the International Stakes in the second half of August. Are we ruling out Royal Ascot completely? The St James's Palace Stakes is over only a mile, but it might suit him."

"He's not entered for that. Entries closed at the beginning of May, and I think we decided against at the time. Maybe that was a mistake."

Or an oversight, I thought.

The Group 1 St James's Palace Stakes was run on the first day of Royal Ascot, in the third week in June, in just fifteen days' time.

"We could always supplement him."

A supplementary entry was made only five or six days before a big race, when normal entries had closed early, and it was a very expensive way of getting a horse into a race late.

A normal entry for the St James's Palace Stakes cost £8,125, paid in three separate tranches—£2,845 to enter in early May, £3,250 unless scratched by the end of May, and £2,030 on confirmation by noon six days before the race. Supplementary entry, however, cost a whopping £46,000.

A supplemented horse would have to finish in the first three just to recover its entry costs. But, if it won, it collected more than three hundred and sixty thousand in prize money, so it might be worth it.

"We have some time to think about that," Owen said. "We'll see how he recovers over the next week. And we could always consider the Eclipse at Sandown at the beginning of July, or even the Sussex Stakes at Goodwood—that's also only a mile—and he's provisionally entered for both of those."

"Okay," I said. "Let's make a decision on the St James's Palace next week. Meanwhile, enter him for the International, and let's keep him in the others for now, other than the Arc. And we'll also definitely skip the King George."

"I agree," said Owen.

We went on to discuss the three other Victrix horses in his yard, but those conversations were somewhat mundane in comparison to that of Potassium, including into which race to enter a late-developing three-year-old gelding called Dream Filler at the upcoming Saturday evening meeting at Lingfield. Our choices were either a Class 5 Novice Stakes, over seven furlongs, or a mile-long Class 6 Handicap—prize to the winner £4,100 or £3,250, respectively.

We opted for the Class 6 Handicap as the better chance for a win, a mere nine steps down the race-quality ladder from the Epsom Derby.

Such were most of my discussions and decisions with trainers.

Potassium was the exception, not the rule.

After speaking with Owen, I took DS Royle's business card from my wallet and called her on her direct line.

"DS Royle, Thames Valley Police," she said, answering at the first ring.

"Good morning, Detective Sergeant," I said. "This is Chester Newton, Amanda Newton's father. I am calling to see if you have made any progress with your investigations."

"I'm afraid I have nothing more to tell you since yesterday. Clearly, we are delighted that your daughter turned up safe and well, with no signs of any form of abuse."

"What about the injection in her neck?" I asked. "Is that not a form of abuse?"

"Minor abuse, I agree. But I really meant that there was no evidence that she had been sexually abused."

"Have you searched through any CCTV from Pangbourne that might show how she arrived there?" I asked.

"No," replied the detective. "That would take many man-hours to collect and then to examine."

She didn't exactly say out loud that she didn't think it would be a good use of her limited resources, but her tone certainly implied that.

"Have you made any house-to-house enquiries in Pangbourne?"

"No."

"Are you, in fact, still investigating Amanda's abduction?"

"Her case remains open," she said. "But I have more pressing enquiries to make elsewhere at present. Perhaps you might have heard on local radio that there were further serious disturbances in Oxford last night, and a critical incident has now been declared by the chief constable." She paused. "Now, if you will excuse me, Mr Newton, I have to go and interview a man whose home was set ablaze by the rioters and whose wife is still unaccounted for."

She disconnected.

I suppose I couldn't really blame her for her choice of priority.

I finally put my phone down on my desk at a quarter to ten.

I then sent emails to the syndicates for those horses that the trainers and I had agreed today to enter for races over the coming weekend, or to declare to run in two days' time, to give the members the maximum time to arrange to attend or not, and to apply through Victrix Racing for entrance badges.

I prided myself on the amount of time I spent communicating with all my syndicate members, either by phone or email. I wanted each of them to feel that they were as involved with the horses as if they had wholly owned them individually, and I was sure it was one of the chief reasons for my success. It was certainly a major factor in attracting so many repeat Victrix shareholders year on year.

I stood up and stretched.

Very often, it would now be nearly time for me to be off to the races to watch a Victrix horse in action during the afternoon, but this day I was attending the evening meeting at Windsor, so I wouldn't have to leave until after four o'clock.

My phone rang and I looked down at it.

No caller ID was displayed on the screen, and my heart missed a beat.

I picked the phone up and slid my finger across the screen to answer it. "Hello."

"Is that Chester Newton?" asked the squeaky voice.

"Yes," I replied angrily. "What the bloody hell do you want?"

"You will enter Potassium into the Ascot Gold Cup."

"What?"

He repeated. "You will enter Potassium into the Ascot Gold Cup."

I almost laughed. "Don't be ridiculous."

"You will do as I say."

"I can't. Quite apart from the fact that entries for that race closed a month ago, it is reserved for horses aged over four, while Potassium is only three."

The Ascot Gold Cup was also run over two and a half miles, twice the distance Owen and I considered appropriate for our horse.

There was a long pause from the other end of the line, and then whoever was there disconnected without saying another word.

I stood there holding my phone.

I was clearly dealing with an idiot—but he still might be a very dangerous idiot.

10

THERE WAS A party atmosphere at Windsor races on Monday evening, which was just as well because, in spite of winning the Derby just two days earlier, I was in need of a lift.

James's departure back to Bristol had been fraught.

Gary Shipman had arrived at our house in his car at eleven o'clock.

"Morning, Mr Newton," he said when I answered the front door to him. "Thank you for Saturday night."

"Yeah, well, it was not quite what we'd planned," I replied.

"No. But I'm glad everything turned out all right in the end."

James came bounding down the stairs with a holdall over his shoulder while Georgina came rushing out of the kitchen. She had tears in her eyes, and she grabbed hold of James's arm, begging him not to go.

"I have to, Mum," he said with obvious embarrassment at the scene that was playing out in front of his best friend. "I can't stand it here. You're both driving me crazy."

She didn't like that. *Crazy* was a word we tried to avoid using in this household at present, especially anywhere around Georgina.

James unhooked her fingers from his arm and walked out the door.

"Bye, Dad," he said, pulling the door shut behind him.

Georgina sobbed as if in grief.

"Stop it," I said, trying unsuccessfully to control the anger in my voice. "He's only gone to Bristol, for goodness' sake."

"But I've lost both my babies."

"They're not babies," I said. "They're adults. And you must learn to let them go with a smile on your face, or they will never come back."

It did little to console her.

"Look," I said, "why don't you come to Windsor Races with me this evening. It will take your mind off things."

She looked at me. "You and your bloody horses."

"It's my job. You used to enjoy going racing."

"Well, I don't anymore."

So I went to Windsor on my own, and to be honest, it was a relief.

Whereas Georgina had once pandered to the Victrix syndicate members, she had recently become something of a liability.

At Cheltenham in March—the last time she had been to the races with me—she had not held back from openly criticising their horses, their dress sense, and anything else that came into her mind, and all of it in their presence.

When I'd remonstrated with her about it on the way home, she had just waved a dismissive hand, as if she didn't care about the potential damage to my business.

* * *

The theme of the Windsor race evening was the 1960s, and there was an abundance of flared jeans, tie-dyed shirts, multicoloured bandanas, and Jesus boots on display by both sexes, even though I was personally sporting a sand-coloured linen summer suit.

A Beatles tribute band blasted out the Fab Four's greatest hits both before and after racing, Babycham was being drunk by the lorryload, and the main greeting spoken by people of all ages was "Peace, Man!"

But the racing itself was far from as it was back in 1960.

Modern methods were employed, including the use of starting stalls, large TV screens for the crowd to watch, and the bookmakers' on-site computers generating instantly printed betting slips, to say nothing of the scanning of the microchips inserted in all the horses' necks to check for "ringers," and the rigorous, routine urine dope testing of all the winners for illegal stimulants.

The Victrix-owned horse I had come to see was a three-year-old bay colt called Balham, due to run in the fourth race at seven-fifteen, the Class 3 Windsor Sprint Series Qualifier, over six furlongs.

This was his first outing of the season, but he had shown considerable promise as a two-year-old, winning one race and placing in his other two runs before an injury had cut short his season. If things went well tonight, I had hopes of him competing in the prestigious Class 2 bet365 Handicap at the Newmarket July Festival.

As always, I had emailed the Balham syndicate owners with the details, and I knew from the replies that at least six of the twenty shareholders were planning to attend, some with their wives, husbands, or children.

All racecourses looked after the owners of the horses running in their races, affording them complimentary entry, a free meal, and subsidised drinks. Windsor was no exception, providing an excellent facility with balconies on each side overlooking both the parade ring and the track.

They appreciated, as we all did, that racing couldn't continue without owners prepared to invest their money into bloodstock, and to pay the training, race-entry, and other fees. Up to eight owners' badges were available for each horse declared to run, with further badges on offer for larger syndicates, although those had no free meal attached.

It was the job of one of my assistants to liaise with both the syndicates and the racecourses to ensure the maximum number of our members could make use of the badges on offer, and to ensure that everyone had their turn.

As usual, I had agreed to meet my syndicate members in the Owners and Trainers' Restaurant before the first. I didn't need to be here to supervise the preparations for the race—the trainer would do all that. My job, as always, was to be the Victrix PR front man. The members would expect me to be here to welcome them and to give them any inside information I might have about the horse.

Many of them liked to have a bet on their horses—mostly a small wager just for fun—and the size of the stake might be affected by my report on how the animal had been performing in its training and my evaluation of its chances.

The racing regulations clearly state that an owner is allowed to bet on their runner, or indeed on any other, but they are not allowed to "lay" their own horse, that is, they are not allowed to take bets from others—in effect betting that their horse will lose—such as is now possible on the online betting exchanges like Betfair or BETDAQ.

Similarly, trainers can bet on any horse, even those in their care, but are not allowed to "lay" their own, or instruct anyone else to do so on their behalf, or to receive any of the proceeds of any such bet.

There are also restrictions on anyone involved in any way with a horse contacting directly or indirectly with betting organisations, particularly against passing on insider information to bookmakers about the likely chances of their horse in any given race.

Overall, the racing authorities have a very peculiar love–hate relationship with bookmakers and the betting companies. While they recognise that gambling revenues are the lifeblood of the sport, and without legalised betting, horseracing as we know it would not exist, they are also aware that betting can invite corruption.

Their prime concern is to maintain probity and trust within the sport. Consequently, they have to weave a middle path, allowing owners and trainers to bet—but not jockeys—while attempting to maintain the integrity of the races.

Bookmakers and online betting companies also pour tens of millions of pounds into race sponsorship, not only to support the goose that lays their golden eggs but also as a form of advertising to the punters.

Balham was trained by Richie Mackenzie, a young up-and-coming trainer from Newmarket, whom I had spotted as a potential Victrix trainer as soon as he had acquired his licence, and it had been a fruitful choice. He now had five Victrix horses in his ever-expanding string, and he was building a new stable block at home to house yet more.

As with my other trainers, I had spoken to Richie this morning. He had also agreed to meet me in the Owners and Trainers' Restaurant, forty minutes before the first race, but he was there ahead of me, chatting to the syndicate members.

One of the side benefits of syndicate membership were the stable visits I regularly arranged for members to visit their horses at home and to watch them at exercise on the gallops. Trainers were usually very good at accommodating members, and feeding them with bacon rolls, and there had been a stable visit to Richie's yard only a couple of weeks ago, so some of them were already well acquainted.

"So, Richie," I said after all introductions were complete, "does Balham have a good chance this evening?"

"I would say so," he replied. "He's been working well at home. But he's been off a racecourse since last August because of the injury to his hock. That's all cleared up now, but he might still be a bit race rusty. On the plus side, his handicap rating is generous, and I'd say that he is definitely worth an each-way bet."

An each-way bet was not only a bet for the horse to win but also one to place, that is for it to finish in the first three. The place bet may not win you much, but it might cover your loss of stake on the win bet, that's if he came in second or third.

There were murmurs of approval from the syndicate members.

"Do we have any idea what his starting price will be?" asked Derek Berkeley, one of my most long-standing members.

"I expect him to start at about six-to-one, maybe thirteen-to-two if we're lucky," Richie said. "Kennedy Curse is the top weight, but he will likely start as favourite, having won easily at Newmarket last month. He might be as short as nine-to-four or even two-to-one, but he's giving us ten pounds in the handicap, and I reckon he's been overrated."

Handicap races were those in which the weight a horse carried on its back was determined by a rating given to it by the official handicapper, based on its previous performances—the better the horse, the higher was its rating, and so the more weight it carried. The aim was to give every horse an equal chance of winning, to make the races highly competitive, ideal for encouraging the public to go racing and gamble on the outcome, something the racecourses desperately wanted.

Five of the seven races at Windsor this evening were handicaps, the other two being novice races for inexperienced young horses.

"So will you be backing Balham?" Derek asked Richie pointedly.

Richie laughed. "I'm backing him with my reputation."

Everyone else now laughed, but it was more of a nervous titter than an outright guffaw.

"Right," said Richie. "I also have a runner in the second race that needs my attention. Don't forget, Balham is in the fourth, at a quarter past seven. I'll see you all in the parade ring beforehand."

Richie walked away with the thanks of the syndicate members ringing in his ears, and then, as one, they turned their attention to me.

"So what do you think?" Derek asked.

"I agree with Richie," I said.

"So will *you* be backing him?"

"Yes, I will," I said quickly. "As Rickie recommended, I'll have a small each-way bet."

And it will be a small bet, I thought, because I hated losing. I was staking too much on the success of Victrix horses as it was, without adding to it with my hard-earned cash.

I left my syndicate members in the restaurant to enjoy their free steak-and-kidney-pie supper while I went down to the weighing room, not so much to see anyone in particular as to be seen. It was good for business.

"Hi, Chester. Well done with Potassium on Saturday," said a man coming out of the Press Room.

"Thanks, Jerry," I replied.

Jerry Parker worked for the *Racing Post*, the sport's dedicated daily newspaper.

"Maybe I should do a feature about you," Jerry said.

"Anytime you like," I said, smiling.

"Do you have anything running this evening?" he asked.

"Balham in the Sprint Qualifier."

"Any chance?"

"Fair to middling," I said. "He's coming back from injury."

"Good luck. And I'll be in touch about that feature."

"Thanks."

Jerry hurried away and I went on smiling. A feature in the *Racing Post* was just the sort of publicity I had hoped for after the Derby win.

"So what are you so happy about?" said a booming voice, bringing me back from my daydreaming.

Bill Parkinson, a member of the Potassium syndicate, was standing a few yards in front of me, and he was no longer in his morning-dress striped trousers.

"Hi, Bill," I said. "What brings you here?"

"I'm a guest at the charity dinner." He pointed over towards the River-bank Restaurant marquees on the far side of the parade ring.

"Which charity?" I asked.

He looked somewhat perplexed. "I'm not sure. Something to do with cancer, I think. They seem to think I might bid at their auction."

"And will you?" I asked.

He laughed. "Depends on what they're selling. I have a bit of spare cash after Saturday, but most of that is already spoken for." He looked at his watch. "I'd better be getting back as the auction will be starting soon, and I should at least be there for it."

I watched his back as he strode away.

Bill Parkinson was a brash outspoken man, originally from Birming-ham, who had run a highly successful chain of video rental stores right across the south of England before the introduction of online streaming of films by Netflix had quite suddenly and catastrophically put him out of business. Such had been the rate of takeover by internet downloads from rented DVDs that Bill's video-rental company had gone from having over two hundred busy and successful stores in January 2013 to total closure, compulsory liq-uidation, and bankruptcy just nine months later.

I knew this because Victrix is required to make background checks on all its syndicate members to ensure they meet the racing authority's defini-tion of a "fit and proper" person, and to ensure that money-laundering regu-lations are adhered to.

Fortunately for Bill, the bankruptcy of his company didn't apply to him personally, which was lucky for me too, because the British Horseracing

Authority regulations clearly state that any person or entity that is subject to any form of insolvency proceedings is banned from having any legal or beneficial interest in a horse running in any race.

I went back to the Owners and Trainers' Restaurant for some steak and kidney pie, and to watch the first two races, and then, during the third, I wandered over to the saddling boxes to wait for Richie Mackenzie and Balham to arrive. On my way, I stopped at one of the Tote betting desks and wagered ten pounds each way on him because I knew that Derek Berkeley would check.

I didn't always go and watch the Victrix horses being saddled, but I liked to if I could.

With great respect for the horsemanship—or rather the lack of it—of most of my syndicate members, it was my general rule that they should go directly to the parade ring rather than try to watch their horses being saddled. A large group of people, each of them jostling to get a better view, could easily upset the animal at a time the trainer and I were doing our best to keep it calm.

However, my general rule didn't apply to me as I felt an extra pair of calming, helping hands could be useful, especially if the horse was frisky or skittish.

On this occasion, Balham was far from that, appearing somewhat lifeless.

"Is he all right?" I asked Richie. "He seems half asleep."

"Don't worry," he replied. "He's always like this at home. He'll soon wake up when he gets out on the track."

I stood back and watched Richie go to work.

While the stable lad stood in front of the head, using the reins to hold the animal still, Richie first placed a square nonslip chamois leather cloth over the horse's back. Next went on the saddle pad, then the weight cloth was placed on top of that, above the withers.

A weight cloth is a synthetic or leather purse-like device with pockets for holding lead sheets to bring the total weight the horse has to carry up to the correct amount—that's if the jockey and his saddle together are lighter than is required.

Next to go on was a black number cloth with the horse's racecard number boldly printed in large white figures on each side, then finally the jockey's saddle itself, with its attached stirrup irons, all secured in place by a wide girth connected to two buckles on either side of the saddle and tightened around the horse's body.

As a final safety measure, in case the regular girth or buckles were to fail, Richie placed a webbing overgirth around the whole lot, tightening it under the belly.

"There," Richie said. "That should do him."

He gave the horse an affectionate wake-up slap on its rump as the stable lad led him out of the saddling box and across to the parade ring. Richie and I followed behind and met up again with the syndicate members, who were already standing in a group on the grass.

"So, did you back him?" Derek Berkeley asked me bluntly as I arrived.

"Of course." I briefly waved my Tote ticket at him, but with my thumb strategically placed over the stake amount.

We were soon joined by our featherweight jockey. He was wearing the Victrix colours.

This race might have just been a Class 3 handicap at a Monday evening meeting at Windsor, rather than the Group 1 Derby on Epsom Downs last Saturday, but I never tired of the feelings of pride and nervous anticipation that the sight of the royal blue-and-white-striped silks gave me.

There were eleven runners in total in this race, and I studied each one of them in turn.

In spite of still appearing rather lethargic, Balham looked well, with a nice shiny coat, but so did Kennedy Curse, as did most of the others.

Richie gave our jockey a leg up onto Balham's back, and while he was being led out onto the track, the syndicate members and I went back to the Owners and Trainers' Restaurant to watch the race itself.

Windsor Racecourse is like a squashed figure eight surrounded on three sides by the meandering River Thames. It has a long straight down the middle, with a loop at either end. The six-furlong start was at the far end of the straight from the grandstands, way away to our left, partially hidden by a slight curve in the running rails.

I watched on the big screen in front of the grandstand as the horses were taken behind the starting stalls and loaded. Balham had been drawn in stall number one, closest to the far-side running rail.

"They're off," called the racecourse commentator as the starter dropped his flag and the gates snapped open. This race was over only half the distance of the Derby, and it was, as its name suggested, a straightforward sprint from the start to the finish, lasting a mere seventy seconds.

The eleven horses broke in an even line. Balham had clearly now woken up as he made the running along the rail over the first couple of furlongs. I watched the screen as Kennedy Curse cruised up on his outside, taking over the lead by a head. But as the race progressed into the final furlong, those extra ten pounds of weight on his back compared to Balham's began to take their toll as he came under pressure from his jockey, and I knew he would be beaten.

And he was. But so was Balham.

One of the other runners, one that was carrying even less weight, came up late on the outside to pip him on the line in a thrilling finish—but ultimately not a thrilling result, at least not for my syndicate members, all of whom had been totally convinced we were going to win.

Overall, I was quite encouraged by Balham's run after such a lengthy injury layoff, but it was a group of very glum-faced owners that I led down to the space reserved in the unsaddling enclosure for the second.

"Ah well," said Derek Berkeley with resignation. "Let's hope for better luck next time."

Yes, indeed, I thought. We had lost only by a nose, the same margin by which Potassium had won the Derby. Some you win, some you lose. Such are the fine margins between victory and defeat, joy and despair. But I know which of the races I would have rather won.

The syndicate members went to the bar to drown their sorrows while I made my excuses and decided to go home, stopping only briefly to collect my meagre winnings from the Tote and to have a quick chat with Richie to congratulate him on getting Balham safely back to the racecourse after his injury.

"So do you still fancy having a tilt at the bet365 Handicap next month?" he asked.

"What do you think?"

"It depends on what happens to his rating after today," he said.

Every racehorse the world over is given an official handicap rating every Tuesday.

"We may have to wait now until next week to see if this result changes it. But we can easily wait until then before making any decisions."

"All right, let's do that," Richie said. "But thanks for coming. Sorry I didn't manage a win for your team."

"Maybe next time," I said.

The fifth race was in progress as I walked out to the car park.

Only when I was sitting inside my Jaguar, with the engine started, did I notice that there was a piece of paper tucked under one of the windscreen wipers.

Bloody advertising, I thought.

All too often these days, someone puts flyers on the windscreens of all the cars in the car park during racing, advertising everything from vehicle maintenance to exotic holidays.

I got out of the car again to remove it.

It was a plain white piece of paper, folded in half, but it wasn't an advert.

I unfolded it. There was some writing on it in black capital letters. Three short lines of text:

I AM WATCHING YOU
DO AS I TELL YOU
OR ELSE

11

I STARED AT THE three lines of text for several long seconds, then spun right round on my heel, searching for someone who might be watching me at this particular moment.

Of course there wasn't anyone, or if there was, I couldn't see them.

I slowly climbed back into the car and put the note down carefully on the front passenger seat.

Who could be doing this? And why?

I sat for quite some time, mulling over these two leading questions without coming up with a single satisfactory answer to either.

A third question floated into my mind.

What could the person tell me to do that was so important?

And I had no answer to that one either.

I looked across again at the black words and wondered if any fingerprints could be lifted from the paper. But that would involve telling the police, and was I willing to do that?

Yet another question I was unable to answer.

Eventually, I restarted the car and set off for home, driving automatically while my conscious mind was still preoccupied with other matters.

* * *

As usual, Georgina was in another panic when I walked into the house at a quarter to ten.

"I can't contact Amanda," she squealed. "I've tried her phone multiple times all evening, but all I get is a voice that keeps telling me that her number is not recognised."

I took my own phone out of my pocket and called Amanda's number.

"This number is not recognised," said a disembodied electronic voice. "Please check and try again."

"How about Darren's phone," I said.

"I've tried that," said Georgina. "It rings but he's not answering, and I'm worried. What if she's gone missing again?"

"I'm sure she's fine," I said. "Darren would tell us if something was wrong."

"But I wouldn't trust that boy to tell us anything."

Georgina had a good point.

"Her phone is probably out of order," I said. "I'll sort it out in the morning." I yawned. "I'm tired now and I'm going to bed."

My wife wasn't happy.

"Don't you think we should drive over to Didcot and check?"

"No, I don't. The last thing Amanda would want is her parents turning up late at night to check up on her. She's no longer a child. Leave it until the morning. If we still can't contact her tomorrow, I'll go and see her."

I started to go upstairs, leaving Georgina, still unhappy, standing in the hallway with her hands on her hips in frustration.

"I'll go on my own then," she said.

"Do you even know where Darren lives?" I said, stopping halfway up.

"No," she said. "But I'll find it."

I only knew where Darren's flat was because I had picked Amanda up from there a few weeks ago, but I'd never been inside.

I could tell what Georgina was doing. She was blackmailing me into going with her because I could hardly allow her to simply wander around Didcot all night, looking for Amanda on her own.

"Oh, all right," I said, irritated. "Give me a minute."

I went up to the bedroom and changed out of my linen suit into jeans and a lightweight sweatshirt before rushing down again, but even though I'd been really quick, Georgina was already out in my car, waiting for me, and she was holding the piece of paper I had carelessly left lying on the front passenger seat.

* * *

"Who is watching you?" Georgina asked quietly, as I drove out of the driveway through our white gates.

"I've no idea," I said. "I found that under my windscreen wiper in the car park at Windsor racecourse when I went out to come home. Probably just some idiot prankster having a laugh."

"*Or else* what?"

"Exactly." I laughed. "It's nonsense. Ignore it."

"You should report this to the police," Georgina said seriously.

"You must be joking. What do you think they would do about it? I'll tell you. Absolutely nothing. They're not even investigating Amanda's abduction anymore. I was told as much by that lady detective on the phone this morning. I'm quite surprised she even bothered to come out to see us after Amanda turned up unharmed, and un-raped."

"Un-raped?"

"That's what they were doing the forensic tests on her for. Checking to see if there was anyone else's DNA where it shouldn't have been."

"Oh," muttered Georgina, clearly upset by the thought.

I drove on in silence.

It was exactly three and a half miles from our house to Didcot railway station, and Darren's flat was close by to that, above an Indian takeaway in a small parade of shops, half of which were boarded up and covered with graffiti. And the takeaway had clearly seen better days too, with red paint flaking off the name board above the window. But it was still open at twenty-five minutes to eleven at night, although there didn't appear to be many customers about.

"That's it," I said, pointing. "The flat above the Raj Tandoori takeaway. His front door is to the left."

Georgina screwed up her nose in horror when she saw where her daughter had chosen to live rather than in our lovely detached four-bedroom village house.

"You go," Georgina said, choking back tears. "I'm not sure I'm up to it."

I climbed out of the car, walked over to Darren's front door, and banged on it loudly with my fist. I then took a step back and waited.

Nothing happened, so I went over and banged on it again.

The door still wasn't opened, but the window above my head was.

Darren stuck his head out and looked down. "What the fuck do you want?"

"Is Amanda all right?" I asked.

"Of course she is," he said. "Why wouldn't she be?"

"We have been unable to call her."

"I changed her phone number. She doesn't want to speak to you."

"I would like to hear that direct from her, not just from you."

His head disappeared inside, and presently Amanda's replaced it.

"Go away, Dad," she said.

"Your mother is worried about you," I said, waving towards where Georgina was still sitting in the car. "She's been trying to call you."

"I'm fine. Now go away. You're only making things worse."

Amanda's head withdrew, and in turn, Darren's appeared again.

"You heard her. Now, piss off."

"Tell Amanda to call her mother."

The window was shut with a bang. I stood staring up at it for several long seconds, forlornly hoping that Amanda would reappear and ask to be taken home. But she didn't.

I went and climbed back into the car.

"Now what?" I asked.

"Can't we report him to the police?" Georgina asked.

"What for?"

"For kidnapping my little girl."

"But it is Amanda's choice to live with him," I said in exasperation. "You heard what she said yesterday. And the law states that she's now an adult who should be capable of making her own decisions."

I started the car and drove us home in silence.

However, there was one thing Amanda had said that really worried me. *You're only making things worse.* Did that imply that things were already not good? Otherwise, how could my presence have made them *worse*?

I knew that Darren's behaviour was controlling—he had already shown that—so was he keeping Amanda in his flat against her will? Was she actually too frightened of him to leave?

There had been far too many examples shown on the news of young women being murdered by their controlling and jealous boyfriends when everyone else was asking, "Why didn't she just walk out and leave him?" But it wasn't usually that easy. Trying to leave might have been what caused the murder in the first place.

*   *   *

It was almost midnight by the time I switched out my bedside light, not that my thoughts had any intention of allowing me to go to sleep.

I tossed and turned for at least a couple of hours, wondering about who was watching me, and why, as well as how I could get Amanda out of Darren Williamson's flat and back home to her mother.

Georgina had sobbed all the way home and had then proceeded to cry herself to sleep.

I knew from experience that it was best just to leave her to her own demons and not try to soothe her with banal platitudes about how everything would turn out all right in the end. She would have simply accused me of not knowing what I was talking about—and she might well have been correct.

I, too, must have drifted off eventually, as the next thing I knew, I was being awakened by the alarm going off on my phone.

I sleepily reached out to stop it, not wanting to believe that it was already six-thirty, not when I felt I had been asleep for only five minutes.

But it wasn't six-thirty. It was still dark outside.

And it wasn't the alarm that was going off—my phone was actually ringing.

I was instantly wide awake.

I leapt out of bed, picked up my phone, and took it with me into the bathroom, so as not to wake Georgina.

No Caller ID was displayed on the screen.

I turned the phone to silent mode, and the sound of the ringing stopped, but it went on vibrating in my hand.

I moved my finger over the slider but then decided against answering it.

Instead, I turned the phone off completely and went back to bed.

I was damned if I was going to dance to Squeaky Voice's tune.

12

H E RANG ME again at nine o'clock, when I was between calls to the trainers.

"Don't you ever call me again at night," I said. "In fact, don't ever call me again at any time."

"I'll call you whenever I like," said the squeaky voice. "And you'd better answer."

"What do you want?" I asked.

"You will enter Potassium into the King George and Queen Elizabeth Stakes at Ascot in July."

At least he had done his homework this time. The King George and Queen Elizabeth Stakes was for horses three years and older, so Potassium was eligible.

"Why?" I asked.

"Just do it," said the voice, with a touch of irritation.

"No."

"You will do as I say." His irritation was greater.

"The trainer and I consider that the race is too long," I said. "Why would we enter our horse into a race we don't think it can win?"

"You will enter it anyway. But it will definitely not run."

"If I have no intention of running the horse, why would I bother to enter it in the first place? It would be a total waste of the entry fee."

Which, at over five grand, was not cheap.

"If you value your daughter's life, you will enter Potassium in that race."

And with that, he hung up.

I sat there for some time, simply holding my phone.

Why would Squeaky Voice want me to enter Potassium in a race and then not run him?

It had to be because of ante-post betting.

To bet on a horse ante-post meant to bet on it before the day of the race. All bookmakers and betting shops take ante-post bets, but only on the big races, such as the King George and Queen Elizabeth Stakes.

From the bettors' perspective, the advantage is that the offered odds are usually longer, that is, they offer a better rate of return if the horse wins. However, the major disadvantage is that if your horse doesn't even run, for any reason whatsoever, you lose your stake.

For some races, such as the Grand National, the biggest betting race of the year, bookmakers quote ante-post prices on some horses even before the race entries close—often several months before. Betting on them that early might be at higher odds, but it can be really risky. If your chosen horse isn't even entered for the race, you still lose your stake.

If Potassium was entered for the King George and Queen Elizabeth Stakes, he would almost certainly be the favourite, irrespective of the fact that Owen and I thought the race was too far for him. After all, he had won the Derby, and that was also over a mile and a half.

If Squeaky Voice was a bookmaker, he could offer higher odds on Potassium than the other bookmakers and rake in every ante-post bet he could, in the sure knowledge that the horse wouldn't be a declared runner, so he'd never have to pay out on it winning. The same was true for anyone laying the horse on the internet betting exchanges.

With hundreds of millions of pounds being staked on a race as big as the King George and Queen Elizabeth Stakes, only a small slice of the action could prove to be extremely profitable. Except, of course, it was strictly against the rules for anyone to know ahead of time that the horse definitely wouldn't run, and yet still to take bets on it.

Even if Squeaky Voice was not a bookmaker, nor did he lay horses on the internet exchanges, knowing for sure that Potassium definitely wouldn't be a runner was also an advantage. Odds of the other horses would be higher simply because Potassium was entered for the race, so any bets made on them would be at a fraudulently inflated price.

I looked up the closing date for entries to the King George and Queen Elizabeth Stakes. It was in a week's time.

So what did I do?

Entering Potassium for the race might get Squeaky Voice off my back for a while. But on the other hand, acquiescing to his demands would likely get him always coming back for more.

And did I really believe he would carry out his threats to kill Amanda?

If not, could I not just call his bluff? But if I was wrong, and he did harm or kill her, how could I ever forgive myself?

I called Owen Reynolds.

"Are we being a bit hasty," I asked, "in not entering Potassium for the King George and Queen Elizabeth Stakes in late July?"

"I've actually been thinking the same thing myself," Owen replied. "It's such a high-value race. Only the Champion Stakes and the Derby are worth more. But I'm also worried what it might do to his reputation if he runs but doesn't win."

"That shouldn't stop us entering him. We won't have to make the next decision to run or scratch until after Royal Ascot."

"Okay," he said. "As long as you're happy to pay the entry fee, I'll make sure he's entered before next week's deadline."

"Fine," I said. "Go ahead."

Somehow, the fact that Owen was also very keen to enter him made the decision easier, and I could tell myself that it wasn't simply because of the threats from Squeaky Voice.

"How about Dream Filler at Lingfield on Saturday?" Owen asked. "Shall I declare him to run?"

"Have you looked at the other entries?"

"There are sixteen in total. Dream Filler is fifth in the weights at nine stone seven pounds. Top weight is nine eleven."

"What do you think?" I asked.

"Go for it," he said. "He should have a good chance. But Jimmy Ketch will be riding at Haydock, so I'll book Tim Westlake. He often rides for me when Jimmy's unavailable."

"Fine. I'll let the syndicate members know their horse will be a definite runner."

We briefly discussed the progress of the other two Victrix horses in his yard and made plans for them to be entered the following week into races at Brighton and Newbury, before disconnecting.

I leaned back in my chair and was quite angry with myself. Wouldn't it have been best to tell Squeaky Voice to get stuffed and to have stuck to my original decision? But he had somehow managed to abduct Amanda from the middle of her own birthday party, and who was to say he couldn't abduct her again?

And then how angry would I be with myself?

* * *

I went to Newbury races on Wednesday afternoon to watch a Victrix three-year-old run in a Class 4 Fillies' Handicap over seven furlongs.

I always liked to have runners at Newbury if I could manage it. Firstly, it was the closest racecourse to my home, so my travel was easy, and second, many of my syndicate members were also fairly local or lived to the west of London, which was just a simple trip down the M4 motorway. Add to that the fact that ten of the Victrix horses were also trained nearby, and it was clear that Newbury was a popular choice with many.

And it was certainly popular with those of my syndicate members present on this day because the Victrix filly romped home to win by two lengths, and at odds of six-to-one.

"You're on bloody fire," the *Racing Post* journalist Jerry Parker said to me with a smile in the unsaddling enclosure. "Let's do that feature next week. I'll call you tomorrow to arrange a time. I'll come to your place if you like."

"That would be great," I replied.

*   *   *

On Thursday morning, after the ten o'clock deadline, I logged on to the racing administration website and checked the declared runners for the Class 6 handicap at Lingfield. Of the original sixteen entries, nine had been declared to run, including Victrix's Dream Filler, which was now only third in the weights.

I did a quick scan of the other eight, checking their previous form, and came to the conclusion that Dream Filler, having dropped down a class from his previous races, would quite likely start as the bookies' favourite. That didn't worry me too much, although I would have preferred it to be otherwise.

I always felt that being the favourite, as Potassium had been in the Derby, somehow placed extra pressure to fulfil that favouritism. It is more noticed by the public if the betting favourite fails to win, even though only about a third of all races are actually won by favourites, which must mean that two-thirds aren't.

My phone rang.

I looked at the screen: *No Caller ID*.

I debated with myself whether I should answer but, in the end, decided that I should.

"Hello," I said tentatively.

"Hi, Chester. Jerry Parker here. Is now a good time to talk?"

I breathed out a sigh of relief. "Yes, Jerry. Go ahead."

"How does Monday suit you for my feature interview?" he asked. "I could come to your place mid-morning. I'll bring a photographer."

"Sounds good," I replied, "but there's not much to photograph here. Wouldn't you rather meet at Owen Reynolds's yard in East Ilsley? You could get a picture of me with Potassium there."

"Great idea. Shall we say eleven o'clock at Owen Reynolds's place on Monday?"

"Fine," I said. "I'll tell Owen we're coming. I'm sure he'll be delighted."

"Good. See you then."

We disconnected and I put my phone down on my desk, but it rang again almost at once—*No Caller ID.*

I answered it immediately thinking that perhaps it was Jerry calling back. But it wasn't.

"Dream Filler will run on Saturday, but it won't win," said the squeaky voice.

"Clairvoyant now, are you?" I said sarcastically.

"You will make sure that it runs but doesn't win."

"And how on earth do you think I can do that?" I asked.

"You will find a way."

He hung up and I remained sitting there, holding the phone, for several long minutes.

Forcing me to enter Potassium into the King George and Queen Elizabeth Stakes was one thing—most people would expect that to happen in any case—but demanding that I stop a horse from winning a race was something totally different.

And how could I do it anyway?

CHAPTER

13

FRIDAY WAS ANOTHER bright summer morning, but this particular day was special. Nineteen years ago, our much-loved daughter had arrived in the world at twenty past two in the morning.

Georgina and I had desperately wanted a daughter to complete our family, but we had no idea what sex the baby would be until she had popped out after a relatively easy labour—much easier than that for James two years previously.

Mother and baby had spent three nights in hospital as little Amanda had developed postnatal jaundice and she had needed to be kept in an incubator under a special lamp, so I, as the proud dad, had taken toddler James in to meet his little sister.

I remembered it as being a very happy time.

My new Victrix Racing business had been expanding rapidly, and we'd had more than our fair share of initial success, while Georgina and I had begun the search for our new forever home. But here and now, nineteen years later, those happy days seemed to have deserted us.

When I had finished speaking to the trainers at ten o'clock, there had still not been a birthday telephone call or a text message from Amanda to her mother, and we still had no idea of her new number. Needless to say, Darren was not answering our calls.

"We must go and see her," Georgina said tearfully when I went back into the kitchen.

"No, we must not," I replied firmly. "You heard what Amanda said the other night. We would only make things worse."

Georgina looked at me. "How could things get worse than this?"

Little did she know.

* * *

I hadn't originally planned to go to Lingfield races on Saturday evening, expecting to spend the afternoon at Haydock watching one of Victrix's northern trained horses run in the Group 3 John of Gaunt Stakes, but events changed all that.

The post in our village normally didn't arrive until well into the afternoon, and Friday's was no exception. I was in the kitchen making myself a cheese sandwich for a late lunch when I heard the letters drop through the slot in the front door.

I went to collect them.

As always there was the usual unsolicited junk mail offering a free gift if I were to visit a newly constructed local retirement home, some clothes catalogues for Georgina, and a couple of utility bills. There were also three envelopes addressed to Amanda that I assumed were birthday cards, but it was the plain white envelope with my name and address written on it in bold, black, capital letters that particularly caught my eye.

I used a knife from the cutlery drawer to slit open the end of the envelope, and then I withdrew the single sheet of paper from inside. Written on it in the same bold, black, capital letters were just two lines:

DREAM FILLER WILL LOSE
I KNOW WHERE SHE IS HIDING

I studied the front of the envelope. A single first-class stamp had been franked with three wavy lines alongside some printed words that showed that it had been through a sorting machine at the Royal Mail Swindon Mail Centre at precisely 16:19 and 50 seconds the previous afternoon.

There was nothing else to show where it had been posted, or by whom.

I stuffed the paper and the envelope into my trouser pocket.

Who could be doing this? Did I really believe his threats?

But could I afford not to?

So, on Saturday morning, I called the northern trainer of my Haydock runner and apologised for not being able to be there for the John of Gaunt Stakes after all, and set off southeast for Lingfield in Surrey instead.

The one-mile Class 6 Handicap for three-year-olds was the first race on the card, due off at 5.35, and I wanted to be there a good hour and a half beforehand, even though I had little idea of what I was going to do, if anything.

I had some mad idea of perhaps claiming in the parade ring that Dream Filler was lame and shouldn't be allowed to race. Being withdrawn was not what Squeaky Voice had said he wanted—he'd said the horse should run—but it might be better for him than the horse winning.

The traffic on the M25 was lighter than normal, and I arrived at Lingfield Park Racecourse at quarter past three, more than two hours before the first race. I parked in the car park across the road from the main entrance, and I was so early that I had to wait fifteen minutes before the gates were opened.

Lingfield Park had always been one of my favourite racecourses, and I could well remember being brought here as a child by my father.

That had been before the installation of the first British all-weather racetrack at Lingfield in the late 1980s. Since then the building of a new grandstand, a hotel complex, and other developments have transformed the racecourse into one of the most popular in the country, with some sixty-seven race days throughout the year.

Many of the summer evening fixtures had music acts playing after racing on a stage set up on the paddock lawn, and I noticed from the racecard that today would be one of those, with a well-known band performing. It was the racecourse's way of attracting more people through the turnstiles, especially the young, who would come by train from London to Lingfield station, conveniently positioned adjacent to the racecourse.

I had called Owen Reynolds before I left home, to tell him I was coming and that I would meet him in the saddling boxes before the first race. In the meantime, I wandered around, enjoying the June afternoon sunshine.

As always when at the races, I was wearing a jacket and tie, this time a lightweight, blue-checked sports coat and a yellow tie, but it was so hot that I took the jacket off and slung it over my shoulder.

I may have looked to anyone else as if I was relaxed and enjoying myself, but my mind was spinning as I tried to work out if there was anything I could do to stop Dream Filler from winning.

I convinced myself there was nothing.

I could hardly offer Tim Westlake, Dream Filler's jockey, a backhander to lose the race on purpose—he would simply report me to the authorities, and then my world would begin to crumble around my ears. The penalties for attempting to fix a race, whether successful or not, were intentionally severe to deter anyone from trying it.

Never mind the potential criminal fraud conviction and likely prison sentence that would follow, the worldwide racing authorities would almost certainly ban me for life from being a syndicate manager and from ever setting foot on a racecourse or in a registered training stable anywhere in the world. Any mitigating pleas of threats or coercion would simply be swept aside.

No, I would just have to hope for the best that, on this occasion, Dream Filler would be one of the two-thirds of favourites that didn't win.

But what about next time?

* * *

About forty minutes before the first race, Dream Filler was led into the pre-parade ring.

He had probably been at the racecourse for at least a couple of hours and would have been settled into the racecourse stables to recover from the journey from East Ilsley. On arrival, the horse's identity would have been checked by a racecourse official by taking a scan of the microchip embedded in his neck—to ensure he was actually the horse the trainer claimed him to be, and not an imposter.

I leaned on the white rail of the pre-parade ring and watched him being walked round, led by one of Owen's stable staff. He looked sound, well, and eager for the race. Some horses just knew what being at a racecourse meant, and Dream Filler was clearly one of those, looking around him and savouring the building atmosphere as more and more racegoers arrived.

Owen showed up carrying Tim Westlake's saddle, saddle pad, and weight cloth. They would have been weighed, along with Tim himself, to check that together they matched the nine stone and seven pounds as decreed by the handicapper, plus the three-pound allowance given for the jockey's safety vest.

The safety vest, or back protector, is mandatory for all jockeys to wear under their silks, so it is weighed, whereas an approved racing helmet, known as a skull cap, is also compulsory equipment but is not weighed.

Owen would have collected the saddle and other things from Tim in the weighing room in order to put them on the horse. Now he walked over to one of the vacant saddling boxes and waved for the stable lad to bring the horse over.

I went over to join them.

"Do you think he looks a bit lame?" I asked. "Front nearside leg?"

"Really?" Owen said. "I thought he was fine. We'd better check."

He put the saddle and associated equipment over the half-height wooden partition between the saddling boxes and told the lad to take the horse back out to the pre-parade ring. I slung my jacket over the partition next to the saddle and followed them.

Owen and I watched as the lad led him around a couple more circuits.

"He looks absolutely fine to me," Owen said.

And he did.

"I still think we should get a vet to check him over," I said. "Just to be sure. He looks all right now, but I still feel he was favouring that leg earlier."

Owen sucked air through his teeth in frustration, but I suspect he felt that if I was concerned, then perhaps he should do as I'd asked. After all, I was the syndicate manager for by far the best horse in his stable yard, and he surely wouldn't want to rock that particular boat.

He would also know that if something were to happen to the horse in the race, after a vet had cleared him to run, he, Owen, couldn't be held responsible.

"If you insist," he said with clear irritation. He turned to the stable lad. "Keep him walking round. I'll fetch the parade-ring vet to have a look at him."

Every racecourse has a designated veterinary surgeon standing by for any such eventuality, and Owen went rushing off towards the weighing room to find him or her.

I went back into the saddling box and waited.

Presently, Owen returned with a man in a green uniform with "Racecourse Veterinary Surgeon" embroidered in yellow on his left breast. I went to join them. Together we watched as Dream Filler was led first towards us and then away again. The vet then felt all four legs of the horse, running his hand down the back, over the tendons, checking to see if there was any heat in them, which might indicate an injury.

"Nothing," announced the vet, standing up straight. "He's as sound as a bell. Clearly fit to race."

"Thank you," I said. "It's much better to be safe than sorry."

"Absolutely," said the vet. "No problem." And with that, he walked away towards the weighing room.

Owen resisted the temptation to say, *"I told you so."*

"Right," he said instead. "Let's get this horse saddled before I'm fined for him being late into the parade ring."

We all hurried back to the saddling box, and Owen busied himself with applying the tack while I collected my jacket. Finally all was ready, and the stable lad took the horse through into the main parade ring. Owen and I followed on behind, to meet up with the syndicate members.

"Sorry about that," I said to Owen as we walked side by side. "I'm glad he's fine."

"As you said," he replied, "it's better to be safe than sorry."

But nevertheless, I could tell he wasn't very happy at my insistence on having a vet check the horse in spite of his own expert opinion that all was well.

To be fair, neither was I.

* * *

The syndicate members went to watch the race from the section on the grandstand steps reserved for owners and trainers while Owen and I remained in the parade ring to follow it on the nearby big-screen TV.

"I think we'll have this," Owen said to me with a smile. "I reckoned that Ferguson colt was the only other real danger to us, but he's been sweating up badly in the ring, with bulging eyes, as if he was having a panic attack. That will drain a lot of his energy. I now think he has no chance against us."

And the bookmakers clearly agreed with him. They all made Dream Filler the clear favourite, and he was quoted on some boards as short as two-to-one to be the winner.

I felt sick.

Today at Lingfield was what the racecourse described as a "mixed" meeting, insofar that some races were run on the all-weather artificial surface and others on the lush, green, grassy turf.

The opening three races were to be run on the all-weather track, and for this first one, the starting stalls were positioned at the one-mile start, which was at the beginning of the back straight.

I watched on the screen as the nine horses were each loaded into their allocated stall.

"They're off!" called the racecourse commentator as the gates flew open.

Tim Westlake tucked Dream Filler in behind the two early leaders, up against the inside running rail, and he was still third as the field made its way around the long bottom turn into the finishing straight.

Now he eased the horse out slightly wider to give him a clear view ahead. Very smoothly, Dream Filler drifted up alongside the other two and then seemed to have a fresh turn of foot to leave them in his wake, while the Ferguson colt was going nowhere.

Dream Filler won the race by three lengths from his nearest challenger, without ever truly exerting himself, and part of me wondered if the Class 5 race would have been the better option after all.

"Dream Filler will lose. I know where she is hiding."

Oh God!

14

O WEN WAS OVER the moon.

"I told you," he said, beaming. "Never in doubt."

I smiled at him, at least on the outside. "Well done."

The two of us walked the short distance to the unsaddling enclosure while I reflected on what might happen now.

The syndicate members were already waiting for us and gave a great cheer as their horse was led into the place reserved for the winner.

"Champion. Champion," said one of them, grinning from ear to ear.

In racing, having a winner was the important thing, irrespective of the class of the race or the size of the purse, and there were multiple high fives and back slapping going on amongst the jubilant owners.

Tim Westlake, also smiling, dismounted and removed his saddle, the sweat dripping in a stream from his head.

"Don't forget to weigh in," Owen said to him firmly, and he went off towards the weighing room as the horse was washed down with several buckets of cooling water.

"Horses away," called an official and our still-steaming hero was led away, back to the racecourse stables for a well-earned rest before the journey home.

The public address system suddenly emitted a triple-tone alert, the signal that there would be a Stewards' Enquiry, followed by an announcement reminding racegoers to retain all betting tickets until after the result of the enquiry was known.

"What's that all about?" Owen said sharply. "It surely can't affect the winner—he was too far in front for there to have been any interference."

But the public address wasn't finished. "Would the trainer Owen Reynolds or his representative report immediately to the stewards' room."

Owen looked at me and shrugged his shoulders before rushing off.

"What's happening?" asked one of my syndicate.

"I've no idea," I said. "But the result will not be made official until after the enquiry."

"Does it mean we won't keep the race?" asked another.

"Let's just wait and see."

The syndicate members began to disperse, and I sauntered over towards the weighing room and met Owen coming out. His face was puce with rage.

"I don't bloody believe it," he said to me.

"What?"

"Dream Filler has been disqualified and placed last."

"Why?"

"They say the jockey weighed in two pounds lighter than he weighed out."

"How could that happen?"

"God only knows. I told them it must have been them that made the mistake, weighing him out wrong, but they refuse to believe it. They say they have CCTV to prove it."

"So how *did* it happen?" I asked.

"Tim told them that he might have lost the weight in sweat. It is a very hot day today. He claims he's been sweating profusely under his safety vest and skull cap, but the stewards say that the rules clearly state that the maximum weight loss allowed for sweating is only one pound, not two. To add insult to injury, they've also fined me £750 and given Tim a three-day riding ban. They said it's the standard punishment, irrespective of who is to blame. I tell you, I'm bloody furious about it, and I intend to appeal."

"I'd better go and tell the syndicate," I said. "They're not going to be happy."

But I didn't need to tell them because, at that point, the triple-tone alert sounded again through the public address, followed by another announcement.

"Here is the result of the stewards' enquiry. The Clerk of the Scales lodged an objection to the winner on the grounds that the rider weighed in light. After due consideration, the Stewards have disqualified Dream Filler and placed him last."

There was a loud groan from the betting public, many of whom had invested heavily on the favourite. There was also some anger, much of it directed towards Owen Reynolds and Tim Westlake.

To assist the official handicapper in his job to rate each racehorse each week, the British Horseracing Authority calculates a performance figure for every horse in every race at every racecourse. They work out how much less weight each losing horse would have needed to carry for it to have finished in a multiple dead heat with the winner.

Clearly the length of the race also matters, as the less weight would have to be carried over a greater or lesser distance. For example, the Grand National is four and a quarter miles long, so a decrease of one pound in weight carried all that way has more effect on a horse's finishing position than the same pound less when carried over only five furlongs.

Many years of statistical study have shown that, on good ground, a one-horse-length difference in performance in the Grand National is the result of a 0.7-pound difference in weight carried, whereas in a five-furlong sprint the same one-horse-length difference will only be produced by a weight difference of 3.4 pounds.

Dream Filler's race had been over one mile on the all-weather surface. For such a race, the official handicapper considers that one-horse-length difference in performance is equivalent to 2.1 pounds in weight. So, even if Dream Filler had been carrying two pounds more over the whole race distance, it would have made less than a single horse-length difference to his finishing position. But he had passed the winning post three lengths ahead of his nearest rival.

He would have won anyway.

No wonder that Owen Reynolds and the punters were furious.

But rules are rules, and no one sticks to them as rigidly as the stewards in horseracing. So Dream Filler, clearly the best horse in the race on the day, was considered to have finished last, and all bets on him lost, even though the handicapper would still rate him next Tuesday as if he had finished first but only by two lengths instead of three, making it more difficult for him to win next time out.

It certainly didn't seem fair.

* * *

To my surprise, the syndicate members were quite laid back about the disqualification when I went to see them in the Owners and Trainers' Bar.

"We still had our moment of excitement," one of them said with a laugh. "And it isn't as if the prize money was very big anyway, especially not when you've divided it amongst the twenty of us." He laughed again.

"It's Owen Reynolds and the jockey who I feel sorry for," said another. "It doesn't seem fair on them to lose money."

Personally, I didn't know how to feel. Outwardly, I shared Owen's frustration at the stewards' decision, but deep inside I was absolutely delighted.

"Dream Filler will lose."

And ultimately, he had lost. In fact, he had been officially placed last.

I watched the second race on the TV in the bar and then decided that, as I had no further Victrix runners and also no intention of remaining to listen to the band, it was time to go home.

As I made my way out to the car park, there was still a steady stream of people arriving. With five more races on the card still to be run, plus the band playing afterwards, there was plenty more to enjoy, even if they had missed the most dramatic moment of the evening.

I tossed my blue-checked sports coat into the boot of the car.

As I did so, two flat grey pieces of metal slid out of its pockets—the two one-pound lead weights that I had removed from Dream Filler's weight cloth as Owen had been fetching the parade-ring vet.

* * *

I sat in my Jaguar for quite some time, hating myself.

Was I totally crazy?

Yes was the right answer.

It had taken me twenty-four years to establish Victrix Racing as the preeminent syndicate ownership company in British racing, and I could well have destroyed all of that by one grossly stupid act.

I went hot and cold at the thought that I could have so easily been exposed. No one had questioned the weight cloth. Tim Westlake hadn't shouted that he remembered having added x number of pounds to it before the race only to find x minus two pounds in it afterwards.

Perhaps he didn't know exactly how many lead pieces had been required to bring the weight of him plus his equipment up to the necessary nine stone and seven pounds. He was one of the lighter jockeys, so there would have been quite a few.

That would all have been done using the lead weights supplied by the racecourse and the pre-scales made available in the jockeys' changing room. Tim would then have presented himself to the Clerk of the Scales to be officially weighed out. But did he get the weight cloth ready by himself or had it been done by somebody else, such as a jockey's' valet?

I didn't like to think that investigations might be still ongoing.

I started my Jaguar and drove out of the car park, concerned that I had better leave before someone came looking for the missing lead.

I didn't recall much of the journey back to South Oxfordshire, but I did take a slight detour into Goring-on-Thames and parked on the High Street. I climbed out of the car and opened the boot.

The two lead weights had "1 lb" and "Lingfield" stamped into their surface. I picked them up and walked back onto the bridge over the river.

I walked to the centre, over the deepest part, and looked down into the abyss, both physical and metaphorical. I considered putting the two weights into my trouser pockets and throwing myself into the muddy water below, to sink to the bottom and drown.

It would be the honourable thing to do.

Instead, having checked no one was about, I dropped the weights alone into the depths and then walked back to the car.

I felt wretched.

Honesty and integrity were the bedrock on which all horseracing was built. Without it, the public could have no confidence in the purity of the results and wouldn't be prepared to wager their hard-earned cash. Sure, everyone has heard stories of how so-and-so fixed this or fixed that and made a killing off the bookies. But, nowadays that's all they were—stories.

I told all my prospective syndicate members that modern racing was straight, and they should have no concerns that they were getting into something dubious, dishonest, or corrupt. Yet here I was, the evil villain, who had torn up the racing rule book. What I had done was against everything I had ever stood for.

So, of course I felt wretched.

But the question I was now asking myself was *What are you going to do about it?*

*   *   *

When I opened the front door, there were four of them standing outside— Owen Reynolds, Tim Westlake, and Detective Sergeant Christine Royle, together with her sidekick DC Abbot, who he was shaking a pair of handcuffs at me.

Strangely, Tim Westlake was still wearing the Victrix silks, and Owen Reynolds was holding a long pole with a large dripping net at the end, within which I could just make out the two Lingfield one-pound weights.

"What do you want?" I asked.

"You," they all replied in unison.

"Go away," I shouted, but they advanced towards me through the door. Then I saw lots more people behind them—syndicate members.

"Did you back him?" Derek Berkeley shouted.

Bill Parkinson was there in his morning-dress striped trousers, and Nick Spencer, the property lawyer in his top hat, and there were many others I recognised as they all pressed forward through my front door.

"Go away," I shouted, but they took no notice, forcing me down onto the floor and lying on top of me so I couldn't breathe.

"No. No! *No!*" I shouted.

I woke up with a start. Someone was shaking me hard by the shoulder.

"You're shouting in your sleep," Georgina said.

"I was having a nightmare," I mumbled back to her.

"And a bad one by the sound of it."

Georgina rolled over onto her side of the bed, and I lay on my back, in the dark, sweating and breathing heavily, thankful that the ordeal was over.

It had indeed been a bad nightmare, but it had seemed so real.

Was that because my whole life, asleep or awake, was currently a nightmare?

Winning the Derby felt like it had been months ago, not just one solitary week.

Perhaps that had been a dream too.

CHAPTER

15

THE WEEK BEFORE Royal Ascot is a quiet one as far as British horseracing is concerned. Sure, there are plenty of meetings—thirty-three in total, with seven of them on the Saturday—but not a single Group race is run at any of them.

Contrast that with the nineteen group races over the five days of the Royal meeting, eight of them being Group 1, the races for the very best of the best, and the most valuable.

"So what do we do?" Owen asked when I called him on Monday morning at ten past nine.

"About what?" I asked, slightly concerned.

"About Potassium?" he said.

I breathed out. "What about him?"

"I've entered him for the King George and Queen Elizabeth Stakes—entries close tomorrow—but are we going to supplement him for the St James's Palace Stakes? If we do, it has to be done before the deadline of noon this coming Wednesday."

"Remind me how much is it to supplement him?" I asked.

"Forty-six grand."

It was a huge amount of money, but there was enough in his Victrix winnings pot.

"Have you looked at the other entries?" I asked.

"I certainly have," Owen replied. "There are fifteen still in, and all the usual suspects are amongst them. But are we frightened of any of them? I don't think so. They will be more afraid of us. Once they know that

Potassium has been supplemented, I reckon quite a few will decide not to declare at the two-day stage."

"Has he recovered enough from the Derby?" I asked.

"I think so. He had a full gallop this morning with not any signs of stiffness. He's in great shape and raring to go, and there will be seventeen days between the two races. That's more than enough. And it would then give him almost five weeks to prepare for the King George—that's if we go for that rather than the International."

"So you think it's worth supplementing him?" I said.

"Yes," Owen said. "I do, but it's not my money."

Over the years, Victrix Racing had had four previous winners at Royal Ascot, but none of them had been at Group 1 level. Potassium might be the best chance I would ever have to change that.

"Okay," I said. "Let's do it. Will Jimmy Ketch ride him?"

"He certainly will. He's been on about it to me for days. He'll be delighted."

We briefly discussed plans for the other Victrix horses in his yard, but he said nothing about Dream Filler's run at Lingfield the previous Saturday. That was in the past, and Owen was always one to look only to the future.

"So, this week, you have Moisturiser in the six-furlong maiden tomorrow at Brighton, and I'll declare Hameed as a runner in the two-year-old novice stakes at Newbury on Thursday. Will you be at either?"

"Not at Brighton," I said. "But I'll definitely be at Newbury."

"I'm not going to go to Brighton either," he said. "My travelling head lad will sort Moisturiser out there. But I'll definitely be at Newbury on Thursday to watch Hameed. He's an exciting prospect. He's come on really well at home since his first race at Goodwood last month, and I think he'll have a very decent chance. Right, I must go now. I'll see you later."

"Eh?"

"At eleven o'clock, remember? You're coming here with a journalist to have your photo taken with Potassium for the *Racing Post*."

"Oh yes," I said. "Thanks for reminding me. See you later."

He disconnected, and I sat at my desk, feeling like a fraud.

How could I simply go on as normal after what I had done? And also have a feature in the *Racing Post*?

The only thing I deserved to feature in was a list of upcoming criminal trials.

My fearful nightmare of Saturday night had reoccurred on Sunday, with Dream Filler also appearing, filling my own dream as he kicked his way through the front door of my house.

Perhaps I should send an email to the members of all my syndicates explaining that I couldn't continue as their syndicate manager, giving them the reason.

But it would be professional suicide, and bad as I felt, I was not quite yet at the suicidal stage.

My phone rang: *No Caller ID.*

I stared at it.

Maybe it was Jerry Parker calling to tell me he'd be late arriving at East Ilsley.

It wasn't.

"Hameed will run, but he will lose on Thursday at Newbury," said the squeaky voice.

"Bugger off," I replied, and hung up.

He called back immediately.

"You will do as I say," he squeaked.

"No, I won't," I replied. "I did what you asked before, but not anymore."

"How much do you value your daughter's life?"

How much did I value my own?

* * *

"Just a couple more," the photographer said.

He took at least six.

"Now just move slightly to the right."

I did.

"That's fine. Now look at the horse."

I did that too. Snap, snap, snap, snap, snap, snap.

"Now at me."

I turned my head, and he snapped another string of six shots.

I wondered if he would ever stop unless I told him to.

"I think that will have to do," I said finally, my face sore from all that forced smiling when I didn't feel particularly happy.

The young photographer looked crestfallen. But he must have taken over a hundred photos in the past ten minutes. Surely *one* of them must be good enough. Probably the first one he took.

I handed Potassium back to his stable lad, who had been waiting patiently to one side, out of camera shot.

Jerry Parker had also simply stood by and watched.

"He's very keen," Jerry said quietly to me as the photographer went to pack away his equipment. "He'll learn. Now, where can we talk?"

"Owen said we could use his stable office."

The interview lasted almost an hour, covering everything from the formation of Victrix Racing right up to the Derby win.

"Why do you think you have been so successful?" Jerry asked.

"Luck," I replied. And he laughed.

"There's nothing lucky about choosing the right horses to buy. That's surely the key."

"Indeed it is," I agreed. "And I do spend an age studying the new crop of yearlings each year at the sales. I seem to have a good eye for what I want, and at the right price. I'm obviously not in the market for the most expensive ones, but I like to think that I can see a moderately priced horse with real potential, and one that my trainers can get the best out of."

"That seems to have been the case with Potassium."

I smiled at the memory of the Newmarket yearling sale when I'd bought him.

"The horse that went through the sale ring immediately ahead of Potassium had gone for over two million, and I think I got lucky with that. He seemed to slip through next almost unnoticed. I'd been prepared to go a little higher and was pleasantly surprised when he was knocked down to me for just a hundred thousand."

We went on to discuss how I chose the trainers for each horse and my daily routine. Finally, he stopped and switched off the recording he'd been making on his phone.

"Thank you," he said. "That was great. Very interesting. The feature should run in the paper either this Saturday or one day next week, depending on the space available with Royal Ascot."

We stood up and moved towards the door of the office.

"So, tell me," he said casually, as if as an afterthought, "what happened to Dream Filler on Saturday at Lingfield?"

"The whole thing was ridiculous," I said. "He was clearly the best horse in the race, and the stewards placed him last."

"Yes, I know," he said. "But why did the jockey weigh in light?"

His journalistic instincts were in full force, hoping for some insight or revelation.

"Owen thinks they must have made a mistake when they weighed him out."

"Don't they have CCTV to check for that?"

"They said they did, but I never saw the footage. Tim Westlake claims he might have easily lost two pounds during the race. It was a very hot afternoon, and I saw his skull cap after the race. It was soaked with sweat, and of course none of that sweat gets weighed."

"It still seems very odd to me," Jerry said.

He looked me straight in the eyes, and I was worried that he could see right through them into my guilty conscience.

"It's the first time it's ever happened to a Victrix runner," I said, turning away. "And I sincerely hope it's the last."

It certainly would be the last time that I'd do anything so stupid.

*　*　*

"I'm so angry I could spit," Georgina said when I got home.

"What about now?" I asked, doing my best to keep the frustration out of my voice.

"Amanda."

"What's she done?"

"She turned up here just after you went out."

I wondered if she had been watching and waiting for me to go.

"What did she want?" I asked.

"Money."

"And did you give her any?"

"No. I told her that she could have all the money she wanted, but only if she came back to live at home instead of staying in that awful flat with that horrible boy."

I bet that hadn't gone down well. Amanda was a very headstrong teenager, and she wouldn't have taken kindly to such an ultimatum from her mother.

"She told me that I didn't understand what it was like to be young these days, what with all the pressures on them. I told her to get used to the real world."

"What did she want the money for?" I asked.

"She didn't say."

For drugs, I thought gloomily.

I could tell that Georgina was upset, but this time, anger had displaced the usual tears.

"And she also wouldn't give me her new phone number. Said she didn't want to speak to me. So I told her that was just fine by me."

The tears were closer now.

"She'll soon see the error of her ways," I said, trying to be comforting. "You watch. She'll be back home before you know it."

And I prayed it wouldn't be in a body bag.

16

NEWBURY RACES WAS very sparsely attended on Thursday afternoon, almost as if the public were also taking a rest before the big five days ahead at Royal Ascot that started the following Tuesday.

Hameed's race, the Class 3 Novice Stakes for two-year-olds, was the second race on the card, over a straight six and a half furlongs.

As usual, I had emailed all the syndicate members and had arranged to meet those attending before the first race in the Owners Club, situated close to the West Entrance.

The lawyer, Nick Spencer was amongst them, as he also owned a share in Hameed.

"Hi, Chester," he said jovially as I arrived. "The atmosphere's a bit different here today compared to that at Epsom on Derby day." He laughed.

"But let's hope for the same result," I replied.

"Do you think we have a chance?" he asked.

"Owen believes we have a good one. He says the horse has come on well at home since coming second at Goodwood last month."

"Worth a punt then?"

I looked up Hameed's probable starting price, as printed in the racecard. It stated that his likely price would be four-to-one, second favourite.

"Maybe worth a bit each way," I said. "But don't stake your house."

"I'd never do that. I'm a lawyer, remember. All lawyers are cautious by their very nature." He laughed again.

I remained in the club to have some lunch with him, and we watched the first race on the racecourse's closed-circuit TV network.

The pre-parade ring at Newbury is right next to the Owners Club, and immediately after the race, we wandered outside to watch Hameed being walked around.

"Looks great, doesn't he?" Nick said.

"Splendid," I agreed.

Some young horses grow in spurts, with different rates front and back, leaving them sometimes looking rather gawky and ungainly, but there was nothing awkward about Hameed. He moved in a smooth easy manner like a well-oiled machine.

When Owen Reynolds appeared carrying Jimmy Ketch's saddle, pad, and weight and number cloths, I remained leaning on the white rail and resisted the temptation to go anywhere near the saddling box.

I did not want to jog free any hidden memory Owen might have of me being left alone with Dream Filler's weight cloth for a full three minutes while he had fetched the parade-ring vet at Lingfield.

To that end, I had also chosen not to wear my blue-checked sports coat, opting instead for a more formal dark suit. And I certainly had no intention of repeating my wrongdoing of last Saturday.

This race was a novice stakes, not a handicap, so all the male horses, the colts, were to carry an equal weight of nine stone seven pounds, while the three females, the fillies, each had a five-pound allowance, carrying nine stone two pounds.

Horseracing is one of only a very few sports where males and females regularly compete against each other. Sure there are some races specifically for one gender or another, such as the Oaks at Epsom for fillies only, or the St James's Palace Stakes at Ascot for colts only, but most races are for both male and female horses racing together, and each can be ridden by a male or female jockey.

However, everything in racing is not quite equal between the sexes. Although no special allowance is made for a female jockey, female horses carry less weight than their male counterparts in the same race, even in the major ones like the Epsom Derby, where the allowance for fillies is three pounds.

The allowance is designed to give the girls an equal chance of winning against the boys, but even so, in the first two hundred and forty-four runnings of the Derby, only six fillies have ever won it, the most recent being back in 1916.

Owen finished saddling Hameed, and then he and his stable lad led the horse out of the saddling box and across into the main parade ring. Nick and I, together with the other members of the owning syndicate, walked over to join them.

There were twelve runners in total, and the connections were soon joined on the grass by the twelve jockeys, their vivid silks brightening up what had become a rather gloomy afternoon under a cloud-filled sky.

Jimmy Ketch, in the blue-and-white-striped Victrix colours, touched the peak of his white cap with his riding whip, as a deferential greeting to the owners, before Owen gave him some last-minute race instructions.

"He was rather slow out of the stalls last time out at Goodwood," Owen said to him. "There he gave the field a couple of lengths start, so keep your wits about you this time, and jump off fast. Otherwise, use your initiative as to whether to make the early running, and do your best."

"Yes, guv'nor," Jimmy replied.

An official rang a bell to indicate that it was time for the jockeys to mount, so Owen and Jimmy walked over to intercept Hameed. The trainer gave the jockey a leg up onto the horse's back. Jimmy gathered the reins, put his feet into the stirrups, and was led out onto the track with the rest.

I decided I wanted to be alone to watch the race, so I left the others and walked through between the Hampshire and Berkshire Stands onto the lawn, close to the winning post, from where I could watch the race on the large-screen TV set up across the track from the grandstands.

Hameed will run, but he will lose on Thursday at Newbury.

I wasn't sure how I felt about the impending result. I had done nothing to affect it either way. Like everybody else, I would just have to wait and see what happened.

* * *

True to his instructions, Jimmy Ketch jumped Hameed quickly out of the stalls as the gates swung open, so much so that he was a length or more up after just the first two strides.

The field of twelve raced close to the far side running rail and was quite tightly bunched as they passed the five-furlong pole, with Hameed just still having his head in front.

At the halfway stage, four of them were beginning to drop back out of contention, having struggled with the fast early pace, but Hameed was still there, in the lead by a neck.

Having passed the two-furlong pole, Jimmy asked his mount for its final effort, pushing hard with his hands and heels, and giving the horse a gentle reminder down the shoulder with his whip. Hameed immediately responded, going a length and a half clear, but one of the others came back at him, and in spite of Jimmy's best efforts, they were caught with just a few yards to go.

The judge called for a photograph to determine the winner, but from my position on the finish line, I could tell that Hameed had been beaten into second place.

In spite of not being sure beforehand if I'd wanted him to win or not, I now found that I was hugely disappointed that he hadn't. And mostly, I realised, it was because I didn't want Squeaky Voice believing that I had made the horse lose on purpose.

*   *   *

Life at home in the Newton household hardly improved over the weekend.

If it was not one crisis, it was another.

I was just beginning to think that we had weathered the Amanda anxiety, when Georgina's mother called early on Sunday morning to tell her that her father had taken a turn for the worse overnight.

"We really should go up there to help her," Georgina said to me, clearly distressed. "Mum's finding it very hard to cope with him on her own."

"Shouldn't he be in hospital?" I asked.

"Neither of them wants that. They think that if he goes into hospital, he'll never come out again."

And they were probably right. He'd been unwell for at least the past year, and he'd been gradually going downhill for months. I thought it was only a matter of time now, and not too long a time at that.

"I can't go at the moment," I said. "Royal Ascot starts on Tuesday, and it's the most important five days of my whole year. Not only is Potassium running on the first day, but I also need to be there all week. I've arranged meetings with prospective syndicate members for this autumn's yearlings."

I could tell that Georgina wasn't very happy about that.

"You go on your own," I said. "You can take a train to Leeds and get a taxi from there. I'll be fine here by myself."

I knew Georgina didn't like us to be apart at night, but that was mostly because she was nervous sleeping alone in our house, and she had especially been so when the children were small. Consequently, I had always tried to come home each night, even if I'd been racing way up in the north.

But if she went to stay with her parents, she wouldn't be alone, at least not in the house, even if she were in bed.

"Are you sure?" she asked. "I'll only go for a couple of days, maybe three."

"I'm perfectly sure," I said. "And I won't feel under pressure to get back here early from Ascot. It's the perfect solution. You go and pack a bag, and I'll look up the train times."

She hesitated for a moment, as if debating with herself. A decision was suddenly made, and she turned and went upstairs to pack a small suitcase while I sat at the kitchen table with my laptop.

According to Trainline, the quickest route from Didcot to Leeds on a Sunday involved first going into London Paddington, then taking the Tube to King's Cross, and finally catching a train from there to Leeds.

"There's a train leaving Didcot in half an hour," I shouted up to her. "Is that okay?"

"Fine," she shouted back. "I'm almost ready."

"I'll buy the ticket online and send it your phone."

I dropped her at Didcot station at a quarter past ten and watched her safely through the ticket barriers on her way to the platform.

The display indicated that the 10.20 train to London was on time, but nevertheless, I waited until it arrived, and then departed.

"What will you do for food?" Georgina had asked on the way to the station.

"I'll be fine," I'd replied. "Perhaps I'll pop into Tesco on my way home to get something."

"You could look out for Amanda."

Indeed I could.

Looking out for Amanda was very high on my agenda.

* * *

Amanda was not working in Tesco when I went in, or at least she wasn't sitting at any of the tills.

I had been unable to resist the temptation of driving slowly past the Raj Tandoori after dropping Georgina at the station, but there was nothing to see. The takeaway was closed, as were all the windows in the flat above.

I hadn't stopped to knock on the flat front door. Amanda would make her own decision, and in her own time. I was sure that continually pestering her would make the process longer, not shorter.

I bought a couple of microwavable ready meals, along with some sourdough bread and two bottles of red wine, and then drove home.

Coming back through my own front door felt like a release.

I had the house completely to myself, and I suddenly didn't have to worry about upsetting my wife. I could leave dirty dishes in the sink, fail to make the bed, or leave my shoes haphazardly strewn in the hallway, and no one was going to tell me off about it.

It wasn't until this actual moment that I realised how much I normally spent my time tiptoeing around on the proverbial eggshells, just in order to have a quiet life.

Now, I walked through the hall into the kitchen, shouting and swearing out loud, like Colin Firth in his portrayal of King George VI in *The King's Speech*. I knew it was strange behaviour, and slightly risqué, but I didn't care. I shouted loudly again all around the house, this time using the very rudest words I knew.

And no one complained or told me to be quiet.

But then my phone rang: *No caller ID.*

My moment of unbridled joy was instantly cut short.

I answered it but said nothing.

"Chester Newton?" said the squeaky voice.

"Leave me alone," I shouted, and hung up.

He rang back almost immediately, but I didn't answer.

He tried twice more, but each time, I just left my phone lying on the kitchen table unanswered.

The phone went beep. A text message had arrived and was shown as a notification on the home page.

Potassium will lose on Tuesday.

I stared at it.

Not if I can bloody help it, I thought.

And had Squeaky Voice made his first mistake in sending me a text?

Texts were always traceable somewhere, but not, I supposed, if he'd used a burner phone. Time would tell.

CHAPTER

17

I WAS ALWAYS EXCITED on the first morning of Royal Ascot, but this year, my excitement was tinged with apprehension and worry, and not only because Potassium was running in the St James's Palace Stakes but also because of the text message I'd received from Squeaky Voice, telling me the horse must lose.

I spoke to Owen earlier than usual, at eight o'clock, and he reported that all was well with the horse and that it had just left the yard in a horsebox to get to the course early to avoid the usual dreadful Royal Ascot traffic jams.

I had plans to leave in good time for the same reason.

I also spoke to Georgina. She had called me on Sunday afternoon to tell me that she had arrived safely at her parent's house in Harrogate. During that first call, she had been very upset by her father's worsened condition, but he had recovered somewhat over the last couple of days, and he was now eating again.

"I know I said I'd only be here a few days, but having seen how he is, I think I should stay for the rest of the week," she said.

"That's fine," I replied. "I'll be at Ascot all this week anyway."

"Mum is totally exhausted. She can't cope on her own, so I've arranged with a care agency for someone to come in every day for an hour or so in the mornings, to help her get Dad washed and to clean out his oxygen equipment. But they can't start until Thursday, and I'd like to be here for the first day or so to see what they do and how it goes."

"Does your father need to be in a care home, even if he's not in hospital?"

"It may come to that. I'll talk to Mum about it. But they've lived here together for so long, it would be a great wrench."

Georgina sounded good. She had always been confident in dealing with other people's problems. It was just trying to deal with her own that left her an emotional wreck.

"I don't suppose you've heard from Amanda," she said.

"No, I haven't."

"Neither have I." She sighed down the line. "I can't even let her know that her grandfather is so ill."

"Is he actually dying?" I asked. "I mean imminently?"

"I really thought he was going to pop off on Sunday afternoon when I arrived, but he's rallied since. He's even started telling his dreadful jokes again." She laughed.

It was good to hear her laugh.

"Tell him to watch the 4.20 at Royal Ascot today on the television," I said. "Potassium is running. You could watch it with him."

"Okay," she said with a happy note. "We will."

"Great. Take care."

"You too."

We disconnected.

It was true that while I was still greatly enjoying my time at home on my own, I was beginning to miss her a bit, and I had caught myself feeling quite lonely on a couple of occasions, especially in the evenings.

* * *

In spite of my early start, I was still caught up in some of the race-day traffic.

Horseracing has been staged at Ascot for over three hundred years, since Queen Anne first recognised the potential for building a racecourse on Ascot Heath. But I am quite sure that the original designers of the course, and of the surrounding roads, never envisaged that up to seventy-five thousand people would now descend on this part of Berkshire for each of the five June days of Royal Ascot.

Hence the traffic jams.

Over the years I had tried to find the perfect approach to the racecourse during the Royal meeting, investigating the very smallest of back roads in the hope of bypassing the queues. On a map, my route to the course would appear akin to spaghetti in its winding, but it meant that I would sit for only about ten minutes in traffic, just to get across the final roundabout, rather than the hour or more that some would wait if using their satnavs.

I parked my Jaguar in Car Park 2, across the road from the racecourse.

I checked again that my named Royal Enclosure badge was securely pinned to my morning coat's left lapel.

I didn't actually need to purchase a Royal Enclosure badge if I didn't want to. As the syndicate manager of a runner in one of today's races, I received a complimentary owner/trainer badge that gave me access to the Queen Anne Enclosure, which included the parade ring.

However, many of the people I arranged to meet were members of the Royal Enclosure, and I felt that it put me at a disadvantage to have to ask them to come out to join the lesser mortals in order to speak to me. Hence I believed the expense was justified, and I put it through the company accounts.

The Royal Enclosure was first established in 1822 when a separate area was designated for the sole use of King George IV, to entertain his personally invited guests. Since then the clientele has expanded somewhat, although everyone entitled to purchase Royal Enclosure tickets is still sent an annual stiff invitation card by the reigning monarch's representative.

The Royal Enclosure has always had a very strict dress code.

Today, gentlemen have to wear black, grey, or navy-blue morning dress, a waistcoat, a tie (but not a bow tie), socks that cover the ankle, black shoes (but not sneakers), and a black or grey top hat.

Ladies must be in what Ascot calls "formal daywear," which includes a dress or skirt that falls to just above the knee (or longer) and that has shoulder straps with a minimum width of one inch, or a trouser suit of matching material and colour. See-through, strapless, off-the-shoulder (one or both), and halter-neck dresses, as well as visible midriffs, are all definite no-nos. A hat (not a fascinator) that has a solid base with a diameter of at least four inches must also be worn at all times.

In addition, fancy dress, novelty, branded, or promotional clothing of any type is not permitted anywhere on the racecourse (unless you're a jockey).

The dress code is rigorously enforced, not least by the Yeoman Prickers, the sovereign's Ascot ceremonial escort, dressed in their forest-green velvet livery coats and top hats, both trimmed with gold braid, as they have been since they were first introduced by Queen Anne.

I collected my owner/trainer badge for the day plus my parade-ring pass for the fourth race from the collection desk, but I didn't make my way directly through the turnstiles into the enclosures. Instead, I walked down the High Street on the outside the racecourse, and into the entrance to Car Park 1.

I had an invitation to a prerace picnic lunch in the most sought-after and exclusive picnic site on the planet.

"Come early," Nick Spencer had said. "Claire and I will be setting up from about nine o'clock."

I looked at my watch. It was ten minutes to eleven. Five and a half hours to Potassium's race time.

I walked down the rows of parking spaces looking for Nick Spencer. He had told me the row and number, and I had written it down, but I had carelessly left the piece of paper at home on the kitchen table.

Row G, I thought I remembered.

Parking berths in Car Park 1 for Royal Ascot were all numbered and reserved, with the spaces often passed down through the generations. The longer you or your family have had it, the closer you were to the racecourse entrance, and any spaces becoming available were as rare as snow in the Sahara.

And picnics here are not of the "rug on the beach" variety.

Oh no.

Folding dining tables and chairs were set up on the grass, with starched white tablecloths, flowers in vases, silver cutlery, best cut glass and fine china, and even the occasional candelabra. Lavish spreads of smoked or poached salmon, foie gras, cold sliced rare roast beef, coronation chicken, and multiple salads were on offer, accompanied by the finest wines and champagne, served in some cases by a butler wearing a tailcoat and white gloves.

It was definitely the Rolls-Royce of all car-park picnics, with plenty of vehicles of that marque also on display, many of them vintage or classic models. It was as far removed from a wet winter's afternoon racing at Bangor-on-Dee as was possible to imagine.

Unquestionably, it was a day to see—and to be seen.

I found Nick Spencer in Row G, or rather, he found me.

I was about to call his mobile when I heard him shouting.

"Chester, over here!"

I walked over to join him and saw that a few other members of the Potassium syndicate were amongst his guests. I looked at them and wondered if any of them were Squeaky Voice, but I more or less dismissed the thought almost as soon as I'd had it.

Why would any of them want Potassium to lose today?

A Class 6 handicap at Lingfield or a Class 4 Novice Stakes at Newbury were one thing—they were both only worth a few thousand pounds to the winner—but here, today, was quite another.

The prize money awarded to the victor of the St James's Palace Stakes was over three hundred and sixty thousand pounds, to say nothing of how a triumph today would further enhance his value at auction as a future stallion.

Even with about ten per cent of that prize going to the winning trainer, and seven per cent to the winning jockey, plus the remainder being divided amongst the twelve syndicate members, it would still take a lot of betting on others, or laying of Potassium, to match the personal financial reward we would each acquire from our horse winning the race.

So how could Potassium losing it be a benefit to any of us?

"Come and meet my American guests," Nick Spencer said, breaking my line of thought. He took me by the arm and steered me over to a group of three people I didn't recognise, one man and two women.

"Chester Newton," Nick said, "meet Herb and Harriet Farquhar, and . . ."

He tailed off.

"Toni Beckett," said the lady on the left, the attractive one with the blonde shoulder-length hair, who I took to be in her early forties. "That's Toni with an *i*." She drawled it out, Southern style. "It's short for Antonia."

"Yes, of course," Nick said, not seemingly embarrassed in the slightest by his forgetfulness.

I shook their hands.

"Chester, here, is our syndicate manager," Nick said. "He keeps us all in order." He laughed. "Herb owns a beautiful horse farm just outside Lexington, Kentucky."

I nodded in approval. "I've been to the yearling sales in Lexington," I said.

"Buy anything?" Herb asked sharply.

I smiled at him. "Not on that occasion, but I might in the future."

"Chester has a great eye for a horse," Nick said. "He bought Potassium at the sales for only a hundred thousand guineas, and look what's happened to him since. He's now worth millions."

Thankfully, he didn't mention some of the other horses I had bought for roughly the same money, which had then turned out to be fairly useless in comparison.

"What's a guinea?" Toni asked.

"It's an old British measure of money," I said. "A little over a pound. Horses are still sold in guineas at Newmarket. On present exchange rates, a guinea is about one and a third American dollars."

She raised her eyes to the heavens as if to imply that we were all crazy.

"Who'd like a drink?" Nick said, and he turned away to fetch a bottle.

Herb and Harriet drifted off after him, leaving me standing alone with Toni Beckett.

"Do you work on the horse farm too?" I asked.

"Oh no. I run the ticketing division at Keeneland Racetrack in Lexington. Mr and Mrs Spencer came over for our Spring Meet in April, and they stayed with Mr and Mrs Farquhar. I managed to get them all Clubhouse hospitality tickets for the races. This is a sort of thank-you for that."

"Have you been to Ascot before?"

"Never. This is my first trip to England. I caught the red-eye over, Sunday night."

"Are you here at the races all week?" I asked, noting that she had a five-day Royal Enclosure badge pinned to her yellow dress.

"Just for four days," she said. "I have to fly home Saturday, to be back at work Monday morning." She pulled a face.

"Will you be with Nick Spencer for all four days?

"Oh no. Just today. Mr and Mrs Farquhar have invitations from other friends for the rest of the week, and I will just tag along with them. We're in someone's private suite tomorrow, and then guests of something called the Ascot Authority on Thursday. I can't remember where we are on Friday." She smiled. "I just know it's going to be a busy week."

Nick came back with two glasses of champagne.

"Here you are," he said, handing one to each of us. "We will sit down to eat at a quarter to twelve. That will give us plenty of time to finish and get in to watch the Royal Procession at two o'clock."

"Royal Procession?" Toni said.

"The King and other members of the royal family ride down the racecourse in open carriages, and then under the grandstand to the paddock. It's very grand and most people go to watch."

"Open carriages? Doesn't anyone take a pot shot at them? If our president did that, he'd be killed inside five minutes." She laughed. "The last one to ride in an open-topped car was shot dead in it, in Dallas back in the sixties."

"But we all love our royal family," Nick said.

"Yeah," Toni replied. "But it only takes one nutcase with a gun."

"I'm sure security is tighter than it looks," I said. "Let's have another drink."

But she was right.

And what lengths would Squeaky Voice go to in order to prevent Potassium from winning?

Surely not that.

He'd probably have more chance if he shot the horse.

CHAPTER

18

I WAS PLACED BETWEEN Claire Spencer and Toni Beckett for lunch.

"So do you think we'll win?" Claire asked.

"I hope so," I replied. "This race is much shorter than the Derby. It's actually quite unusual for a horse to drop back to a mile having raced previously over a mile and a half, but Potassium has good pace, and I think that the mile will suit him just fine, probably better than the longer distance."

She smiled at me. "We have more champagne on ice in the boot of the car, just in case."

I was on my third glass already.

No more, I told myself. Not only because I would be driving home later but also because I needed to have all my wits about me in case I was needed to help Owen get Potassium ready for the race.

Toni was deep in conversation with the man on her other side, another member of the Potassium syndicate. Strangely, it made me think of the argument between Amanda and Darren at our party. Then I realised that was because I was also fed up with all the attention she was paying to the other man rather than to me.

I shook my head slightly, as if to tell myself not even to think about going there, but the thought persisted.

* * *

Lunch wound up at about a quarter past one after a spectacular feast, finished off with fresh strawberries and lashings of cream.

"I'm stuffed," Toni said next to me. "I'm not sure I can even stand up."

But she managed it.

"Now for the real reason we're all here today," I said. "The racing."

But I was quite sure that some of the people around me in the car park had no intention of going into the enclosures to watch the horses. For them, the car-park picnic was *the* point of the day, and nothing else mattered. Indeed, the four hours or so it took to run the seven races was simply a chance for them to have a little snooze before the eating and drinking started again afterwards.

"Thank you so much for a fabulous lunch," I said to Nick and Claire. "Nick, I'll see you in the parade ring later. Claire, I'm so sorry I don't have a paddock badge for you."

"No problem," she said. "But I'll get in there somehow if we win."

"You bet," I said with a laugh. "I must dash now as I've arranged to meet Owen Reynolds at half past one."

"Please come back after racing," Nick said. "Either to celebrate a win or to drown our sorrows. We'll be here until late either way."

"That's very kind," I said. "Let's wait and see how we get on."

I turned to go.

"Can I come with you, Chester?" Toni asked suddenly. "I promise I won't be a nuisance, and it would be nice to be shown around by someone who really knows what's going on."

I smiled at her. "I'd be delighted to show you around, but we'll have to go right now."

"I'm ready," she said.

We both hurried over to the enclosure entrance, queued for a minute to get through, and then went on through the Royal Enclosure Gardens, past the temporary restaurants and London club members' tents and bars, towards the weighing room, where I had arranged to meet Owen.

I tried to take her along the horse walk under the bridge into the parade ring, but we were stopped by an official wearing a dark suit and a bowler hat, who asked to see our badges.

I showed him my owner/trainer badge.

"And for the lady?" he asked.

"She's with me," I said, trying to move on.

"Sorry, sir," the man said firmly but politely, blocking the way. "If the lady has no badge, she cannot gain entry. You know the rules."

"Yes. Sorry."

The security was indeed tighter than it looked.

We retraced our steps and went up the steps onto the upper level. People were already beginning to congregate around the parade ring in anticipation of the arrival of the royal family, but I found a space on the rail, near the steps down to the weighing room.

"You stay here," I said to Toni. "Don't move or you will lose your place. I have to go and briefly see the trainer of our horse, but I will come back here to join you."

"I'll stay right here," she said, gripping the rail with both hands.

I rushed down the steps, hoping that Owen wouldn't be late.

I wondered why I had bothered to arrange to meet him.

But I knew the answer. Because meeting up with my trainers before racing was what I usually did. It made me feel comfortable to know that everything was in order with the horses and there was no panic going on over forgotten colours or broken tack. Indeed, I always kept a set of Victrix silks and a spare bridle in the boot of my car, just to be on the safe side.

Perhaps I could have phoned him instead, but calls were often not easy to make on a racecourse, especially one as crowded as it was today. Getting a signal could be difficult with so many people making calls, sending texts, and sharing photos all at the same time, and the background noise of people talking or music playing through the public address system was a problem, even if you were able to get through. Face to face was always better anyway—I was then able to read their body language, which often told me more than their words.

Thankfully, Owen was there ahead of me.

"Everything all right?" I asked.

"Absolutely fine," he replied. He appeared very relaxed, which was an encouraging sign. "Jimmy has rides in the first two races, the second for me in the Coventry, so we'll get an accurate assessment of the going. It's officially 'good,' which suits us perfectly."

"Great," I said. "I'll see you later then. In the saddling boxes."

I went back up the steps to where I'd left Toni. The whole place had filled up noticeably, even in the few minutes I'd been away, and I had some difficulty getting to her.

"I've been trying to save you some room," she said as I squeezed in beside her. "But everyone keeps pushing forward." She said it in a manner that implied that she could hardly believe that gentlemen in full morning dress and ladies in elegant frocks plus equally impressive millinery could act so much like a football crowd.

"Thank you anyway," I said, personally quite enjoying the sensation of being pressed so close to her body.

I looked again at her Royal Enclosure badge with *Mrs Antonia Beckett* written on it in black ink.

"Is there a Mr Beckett?" I asked.

"Not anymore," she replied, turning her head and looking straight at me. "Is there a Mrs Newton?"

"Yes," I said. "There is."

"Huh, there would be." She looked away. "Goddammit. All the men I fancy these days are hitched."

So she did fancy me.

I turned and faced forward, towards the parade ring, so that she wouldn't see me blush beneath my top hat.

By the time two o'clock approached, there was not a single space to be found anywhere around the parade ring that provided any sort of view of where the Royal Procession would pass.

We watched on the big screen at the far end of the parade ring as, at two o'clock precisely, the first of four open-topped landau carriages made its way through the Golden Gate at the end of the straight mile.

"Which one is the King in?" Toni asked.

"The front one. The one that the four Windsor Greys are pulling. The other three are pulled by Cleveland Bays."

"Do they come all the way from Windsor Castle in those?"

"They did once upon a time, but these days they come most of the way in a fleet of cars and then get into the carriages just a short distance from the racecourse."

We watched on the TV as the procession made its sedate passage down the centre of the racetrack, with the horses trotting. Each carriage was driven by two postilion riders wearing their special Ascot livery of scarlet, purple, and gold jackets with black peaked riding hats, all inspired by the royal racing silks.

They were accompanied by red-uniformed outriders and followed by four mounted police officers. More police were stationed on foot every twenty yards or so down each side of the course.

"Who are the other people?" Toni asked.

"The Queen is sitting next to the King, and more members of the royal family are in the carriages behind. The other people with them are their guests. They will all have had lunch at Windsor Castle. It's a massive honour to be invited to ride in the Royal Procession."

"Have you ever?"

I laughed. "No. Nor likely to be. Although I have been in the royal box. I was invited in for a drink after one of my horses won a race here a few years ago."

"So you've met the King?" She sounded impressed.

"I actually met him two weeks ago, at Epsom, when Potassium won the Derby. But I also met Queen Elizabeth the Second here at Ascot."

I could see that she thought that even more impressive.

We watched the screen as the procession was shown slowing to a walk, and then it turned in to the tunnel under the grandstand that, later, the horses would use to access the track for the races. After another minute or so, the King's carriage appeared at the end of the parade ring to our right, to rapturous applause from everyone around us, and then made a complete circuit of the ring, to give everyone a good view.

Finally, the carriage stopped just below where we were standing, and we were in the perfect position to see the King and Queen step down and from it, to be met by the waiting dignitaries.

The royal party disappeared from sight into the grandstand at the lower level, and I breathed a small sigh of relief. No one had taken a pot shot at them.

"Wow!" Toni said. "That was neat. I've never seen one of our presidents up that close. Does it all happen again in reverse when they leave?"

"No. They go back to Windsor Castle by car. But the procession will happen again tomorrow and every day until Saturday, although with different guests."

Some of the crowd remained to watch the horses parade for the first race, but many of them dispersed to secure a viewing point in the grandstand.

"Come on," I said. "Let's go and find some seats."

I boldly took her arm and steered her across the parade-ring concourse into the huge steel and glass grandstand. She didn't object.

We took the long escalator up to the fourth level and went out to the seats at the front reserved for Royal Enclosure badge holders. Most were already full, but we managed to find a couple free, side by side, in the second row.

"The first race is called the Queen Anne Stakes," I said to Toni. "It's always the opening race of Royal Ascot and is named after Queen Anne, who started horseracing here back in 1711."

"In 1711?" She was amazed. "But that was even before the United States was created."

"It certainly was, and Ascot is not the oldest racecourse in England—not by a long way. That accolade belongs to Chester, where horseracing has been held continuously since 1539. That's more than eighty years before the *Mayflower* sailed to America with the Pilgrim Fathers."

"Chester knows all about Chester." She laughed.

"I think my dad actually named me after Chester racecourse. He was mad about his racing. And especially about its history. When I was a kid, he used to quiz me all the time about all the racecourses—you know, their dates and such." I sighed. "I suppose I should be grateful that I'm not called Epsom or Ascot." I sighed again.

"When did he die?" Toni asked, correctly reading the cause of my sadness.

"Years ago," I said.

I paused briefly, but then I decided to go on.

"I was only fifteen. He and my mother owned a boat on the River Thames. A cabin cruiser. They had it for years. When I was a boy, we used to holiday on it every summer, chugging up and down the river. I absolutely loved it, jumping off with the ropes and working the locks." I smiled at the memory. "Then, one day, Mum and Dad decided to go out for a short jaunt when I was at school, and the boat blew up."

"Blew up?"

"Yeah. An investigation later worked out that there had been a leak in the fuel system, which had caused a large petrol and air vapour mix to accumulate in the hull, under the floorboards. When my dad went to start the engine, the vapour exploded. Killed them both instantly."

"Oh my God, how awful." She had tears in her eyes.

"I'm sorry," I said quickly. "I shouldn't have told you. I didn't mean to upset you."

I really didn't know why I had told her.

I never told anybody.

Georgina knew, of course, but no one else. I'd never even spoken about it in such detail to my own children, yet here I was telling the whole story to a complete stranger.

"I'm very grateful that you did tell me." She put her hand gently on my arm. "So what then happened to you?"

"My grandparents collected me from school later that afternoon, and I went to live with them."

"Do you have brothers or sisters?"

"No, just me."

"I'm so sorry." She stroked my arm.

"Thank you," I said, putting my hand on hers to stop it moving. "But you don't need to be. It was a long time ago."

"Are your grandparents still alive?"

"Oh no. They're also long gone. But they lived until I was in my early thirties. And they were both at my wedding."

Now there were tears in my own eyes.

Thankfully, any further conversation on the matter was interrupted by the arrival of the twelve horses for the first race, appearing from the tunnel beneath the grandstand, their silks brightly contrasting with the lush green turf.

"Can we go have a bet?" Toni asked.

"We'll lose our seats if we do. You can't reserve them. Let's have one on the second race."

The Queen Anne Stakes was run over a mile, just like Potassium's race, but in this case it was the straight mile, as opposed to being on the round course that would be used later. And this race was for horses aged four and over, of either sex, while Potassium's was restricted to three-year-old colts.

The runners made their way slowly to the start, way off to our far right, close to where the King's carriages had entered the course less than half an hour previously.

"In the States," Toni said, "the horses always race past the grandstands from left to right as you look out, yet here they'll be going the other way. It's very confusing. Like all your stupid cars driving on the wrong side of the road."

I laughed. "In this country, which way the horses go varies from race-course to racecourse. At some they go one way, and some the other."

"But I'm sure they go from left to right at Royal Ascot in the film *My Fair Lady*. I love that film. It's one of my favourites. *'Come on, Dover! Move your bloomin' arse!'*"

She shouted it out loud and received some very strange looks from those around us, just as Audrey Hepburn had done in the film.

I was so enjoying being with Mrs Toni Beckett that I was forgetting all my other troubles, but that didn't last for long.

The phone in my trouser pocket vibrated for a moment.

I took it out and read the home screen notification.

Remember, Potassium must lose. Fix it.

"What's that?" Toni asked.

"Nothing. Just someone wishing me luck for later."

I quickly stuffed the phone back into my pocket, hoping desperately that Toni hadn't read the message.

CHAPTER

19

I WATCHED THE FIRST two races, with Toni Beckett, from the seats on level four, even having a small bet on the second, which sadly lost.

I had told her to back the horse Owen trained, and it had finished eighth of the twenty-two runners, out of the money in more ways than one.

"I'm sorry," I said. "I'm not a very good tipster."

"So should I bet on Potassium?" she asked.

"His price will be pretty short," I said. "Probably best to keep your money in your purse."

"Don't you expect him to win?"

Had she seen the message?

"I hope he wins," I said. "But I never expect anything in racing. And I'm afraid I have to go now, to start getting the horse ready for the race. You can come with me if you want, but you will have to stay well away from the horse, and I don't have a paddock pass for you to use."

"That's fine," she said. "I may just wander about on my own for a while. I'm used to doing that. I'll see you later, back in the car park with Mr Spencer."

I stood up to go.

"Good luck," she said.

"Thanks."

I left her sitting there alone in the grandstand seats.

Why was I worried that she was cross with me for leaving her?

* * *

Potassium looked magnificent as he was led around the pre-parade ring, his well-groomed coat shining brightly in the afternoon sunshine.

There were only eight runners in the St James's Palace Stakes. So Owen had been right about Potassium's supplementary entry frightening some of the competition out of the final declaration. The connections of the others must have decided to find an alternative race to run in rather than go up against the Derby winner.

Owen appeared with Jimmy Ketch's saddle and waved the lad to bring Potassium over to one of the saddling boxes. I went to join them but stayed out of the box because Owen had brought his assistant with him to help.

I watched as the two of them went about their business, not forgetting to fit the weight cloth securely under the saddle. In this race, all the runners carried the same weight, nine stone two pounds, plus the allowance for the safety vest.

It was a true test to find the best three-year-old colt over a mile.

Satisfied that all was in order, and with the horse's racecard number six showing clearly behind the saddle, Owen told his assistant and the stable lad to take Potassium through to the main parade ring while he walked on behind.

I went over to join him.

"All good?" I asked.

"Perfect," he replied, totally relaxed.

And I found I was relaxed too. All that nervousness I'd experienced on Derby day at Epsom had not reappeared here. I realised it was because Potassium had already proven himself as a great horse. A win today would be the icing on the cake, but the cake was already assured, whatever the outcome. As long as he came home sound, I'd be happy.

Not that I didn't want him to win.

I did. Desperately.

Most importantly, I didn't again want Squeaky Voice believing that any loss was prearranged by me on purpose.

Nick Spencer was already in the parade ring, standing in a group with six other syndicate members, including Bill Parkinson, with me making up the maximum of eight paddock passes I had managed to acquire.

"All set?" I asked, joining them.

They all nodded, some of them showing obvious signs of nerves.

"Gentlemen, we are going to enjoy this," I said. "Potassium has already done more than we could have asked of him. He's an Epsom Derby winner. No one can ever take that away from him. If he wins today, then that would be great. If he doesn't, well, he will have another day in another race."

They all smiled at me, and some of the tenseness seemed to go out of their shoulders.

In a while, Jimmy Ketch joined us, wearing the Victrix silks.

"No time to waste in this race," Owen said to him earnestly. "It's only a mile, so we want a strong pace from the off, to sap the finish out of the sprinters. So jump him out of the stalls, and don't be afraid of going immediately to the front. But don't go mad. Keep enough in reserve to kick on again just before the two-furlong pole, after you've completed the turn into the final straight."

"Yes, guv'nor," Jimmy said.

The bell was rung, and Owen took Jimmy over to Potassium and gave him a leg up onto the horse's back. There was now no more he could do.

As always when there was a large crowd, I stayed in the parade ring to watch the race on the large-screen TV. In the past, I had tried to get through to the owners' viewing steps, only to be thwarted by the crush from seeing the race at all.

What is known as the "round course" at Ascot is, in fact, triangular with rounded points, and the one-mile start was at the apex farthest from the grandstand, close to that part of the course known as Swinley Bottom.

Who Swinley was is a mystery lost in time, but the Bottom refers to the lowest part of the racecourse, some seventy-three feet below the finish line. It was the original site of a kennel established by Queen Anne to house the royal pack of hounds, known as the Buckhounds.

Potassium had been drawn in stall number two, and I watched on the big screen as he and the other seven runners were loaded without fuss.

"And they're off in the St James's Palace Stakes," called the race commentator through the public address system as the gates snapped open.

Jimmy did as he was told and jumped Potassium out of the stalls fast, and he built a three-length lead in the first twenty strides. As they settled down, Potassium hugged the inside rail, going the shortest distance, and by the time he started the long turn into the finishing straight, he had extended his lead to five lengths, and the rest of the field were well spread out behind him, chasing hard.

Two of the other runners began to close round the turn, but Jimmy had indeed kept a little in reserve, and he kicked again as they straightened up, stretching the lead once more.

Within the last furlong, Potassium's stride began to shorten as he tired, and the others started to gain on him. Then, in the last hundred yards or so, he began to paddle, with his head going up and down, but he had established enough of an advantage, and he managed to keep going, passing the winning post still a length to the good.

No need for a photograph this time. The result was clear for all to see.

"First number six," called the judge.

That's all I needed to hear.

The celebration in the parade ring around the winners unsaddling enclosure started even before the horse appeared, with most of the rest of the syndicate somehow having bypassed the men in bowler hats to gain entry, many of them with wives and partners in tow, all of them laughing and smiling.

It was moments like this that made up for all the disappointments, and in horseracing, there were lots of those.

Claire Spencer had made it in too, and she beamed at me.

After a few minutes, and accompanied by a fanfare from the trumpeters of the Household Cavalry, Potassium and Jimmy Ketch arrived through the tunnel into the ring and were led into the space reserved for the winner.

I went in there with them as everyone cheered.

Jimmy dismounted, removed his saddle, and then posed for press photographs with Owen, me, and the horse, with the other syndicate members waving madly in the background.

Jimmy then went off towards the weighing room, carrying his saddle and other equipment, including the weight cloth. Now all he had to do was weigh in at the same weight as he'd weighed out. Only then could the trophy presentation begin.

"Horses away," shouted an official.

Potassium was led out, back towards the racecourse stables, now wearing his new rug with "Royal Ascot—Winner The St James's Palace Stakes" emblazoned on both sides.

"Weighed in. Weighed in," was announced over the public address, and there were no triple tones indicating a Stewards' Enquiry.

We had won. It was now official.

The forty-six-thousand-pound supplementary fee had been well spent.

As we waited for the presentation party to arrive, both Owen and Jimmy were interviewed by ITV racing. Then the cameras switched onto me.

"Well done, Chester," said the interviewer. "So what's next for Potassium?"

For the media, it was always about *what's next* rather than *what's past*.

"We're not quite decided yet. He's entered for both the Eclipse at Sandown and the Sussex Stakes at Goodwood, and we're also looking at the International Stakes at York in August."

"How about the King George VI and Queen Elizabeth Stakes back here next month?"

"He's been entered for that too," I said with a smile. "A multitude of riches. But we'll have to see how he recovers after today."

The presentation party was now ready, and I collected the St James's Palace Stakes perpetual silver trophy from a senior member of the royal family on behalf of the winning syndicate, while Owen received a silver cup, and Jimmy a silver photo frame.

As we stood on the presentation platform for yet more press photographs, I could see someone in a yellow dress waving wildly from the viewing steps to my left.

It was Toni Beckett.

I waved back, smiling broadly.

*   *   *

The *Racing Post* journalist, Jerry Parker, was waiting for me outside the weighing room when I went to sign for the trophy.

"The Victrix Racing feature will run in the paper this Thursday," he said. "When we knew Potassium had been supplemented for The St James's Palace, we held it back, to see what happened in the race. I'll now write the last bit."

"Thanks," I said. "I hope it's all good."

"Of course," he said with a smile, but there was something about the way the smile failed to reach his eyes that slightly worried me.

The celebrations by the other syndicate members were still going on when I came out with the trophy in its box.

"Everyone is invited to join me in car park for a victory party," Nick Spencer said loudly.

There were still three races to be run, but I reckoned that none of this lot would see any of them. And I couldn't blame them.

"How about you, Chester?" Nick asked. "Are you coming?"

"I'll be there a little later," I said. "I need to secure this first." I held up the trophy box.

"Bring it with you," Bill Parkinson said loudly with a laugh. "We can fill it with champagne and pass it around."

"Best not to," I said. "It's survived more than a hundred years, and I'd hate for us to be the ones who lost it."

"But it's ours for now," Bill said quite belligerently. "We're the owners of the horse." He turned to the other members. "Come on, let's have a vote. Who wants the trophy taken to the car park?"

"Bill, stop being naughty," I said sharply. "You know perfectly well that, although prize money is shared, trophies remain the responsibility of Victrix."

"Spoil sport."

Was I?

Once in the past, I had taken a trophy out to a celebration in a race-course car park, only for it to get run over by a reversing car. This one was far more valuable—and I was the one who'd just signed for it.

"Okay," I said. "But just for a little while."

Before they all get too drunk, I thought.

Owen was still standing there with them.

"Are you coming?" I asked him.

"I may later," he said. "But I doubt it. I have a runner in the last anyway. And there's usually a drinks party in the trainers' car park after racing. I normally go to that for a single beer before heading home. It's far too long a week for me to get plastered on the first day."

I agreed. Like him, I would be here every day. There were two more Victrix runners to come, one on Thursday and the other on Saturday, although neither was trained by Owen, and I also had a possible new Victrix trainer to meet, as well as some prospective new syndicate members. Potassium's win should now make those conversations a little easier.

I'd already spent many hours on the telephone speaking to bloodstock agents and breeders about their yearlings that would be going to the sales in the coming autumn. I'd even been to see quite a few, and I had started making up my list of interest.

Potassium's Derby win, plus his one today, might allow me to raise my sights somewhat, perhaps to spend a little more money on a horse at the sales than I had in the past, in order to secure the ones I really wanted for next year.

Provided, of course, that Squeaky Voice hadn't destroyed my business by then.

20

THE ST JAMES'S Palace Stakes hundred-year-old silver trophy was indeed filled with champagne and handed around, each of the twelve syndicate members, including me, taking it in turns to raise it up like the winning captain of the FA cup, and then drinking from it, as everyone else cheered.

Nick and Claire Spencer had broken out the reserve bubbly from the boot of their car, but there was no sign of the American trio.

"Where are your American friends?" I asked Nick casually after the trophy drinking had finished.

"They're having afternoon tea with the American ambassador in one of the private boxes. He's also from Kentucky and is a good friend of theirs. Seems he's regularly bought horses from their farm. But they'll be along later. Herb told me the ambassador has to leave before the last to get back for some sort of diplomatic function this evening."

"How did you meet Herb and Harriet?" I asked.

"I acted for them when they bought an apartment in a lovely new block in Knightsbridge, overlooking Hyde Park. About six years ago now. We became friends, and Claire and I have since been out to their place a couple of times."

"Do you think it's worth me talking to them about joining a syndicate?"

Victrix Racing already had several overseas members, including two that lived in the United States.

"You can if you like, but I doubt that they will. They have a whole string of racehorses in the U.S. And they breed most of them themselves."

"But you can never have too many racehorses," I said with a laugh.

The phone in my trouser pocket beeped and vibrated once.

"Excuse me," I said to Nick, taking the phone out. "I need to take this."

I walked a short distance away so that no one else could see the screen.

There was just one text notification showing.

Do not defy me. You were warned what would happen.

I turned around quickly to look back at the syndicate members, checking to see if any of them had their phones out.

They hadn't, and the thoughts from earlier returned: Why would any of them have wanted Potassium to lose? What advantage would it give them?

But if it was one of them, they would have surely ensured that they put their phone away as soon as they had pushed "Send."

I put my own phone back in my pocket and walked quickly back to Nick.

"Sorry," I said. "I have to leave now. Something's come up at home."

I packed the trophy back into its carrying box, made my excuses to the rest of the syndicate members, and hurried out of Car Park 1.

I almost ran down the High Street to my Jaguar, placed the trophy box in the boot, along with my coat and top hat, and jumped in.

I could feel the panic rising in my throat, and I almost turned out onto the road right into the path of another car.

I slammed on the brakes just in time.

Calm down, I told myself. *It won't help to kill yourself in a car crash.*

Although maybe it would.

* * *

I didn't go home. Instead, I pulled up opposite the Raj Tandoori.

I went and banged on the front door of the flat above, but there was no answer. So I went back to the car and waited and waited and waited.

Georgina had called me on my phone's hands-free system as I'd been passing Reading.

"Dad and I watched the race together," she said. "It was so exciting. And we watched your interview afterwards. He is so pleased for you."

"Thanks," I said. "How is he doing today?"

"Much the same. Mum's a bit better now she's been able to have a couple of nights' proper sleep after I moved her into the spare room. I've gone back into the bed I slept in before we were married. It feels very strange. And Mum keeps asking me what she will do if he dies, or rather *when* he dies."

Not come to live with us, I hoped.

But Harrogate was a very long way away from south Oxfordshire, and after the early death of her sister, Georgina was their only child left.

A couple of years ago, we had investigated some sheltered-living bunga-
lows in our village and had even put her parents' name down for one, but
there was a long waiting list—waiting for the current residents to die off.

Getting old was no fun, but it was probably better than the alternative.

"Are you going to Ascot again tomorrow?" Georgina asked.

"Every day," I replied. "We have more runners, one on Thursday and
another on Saturday, but I don't really expect those two to win. I'm running
them more because the syndicates are desperate for Royal Ascot tickets."

"I can't think of anything worse."

"But you used to love to go."

"No, I didn't. I only went because you wanted me to. It was always too
damned hot—or raining—and I hated wearing all those bloody hats, and as
for the shoes! They always hurt like hell by mid-morning."

I was surprised by her forcefulness.

"Well, you should be thankful you're in Harrogate then," I said. "It was
hot and crowded at Ascot today, and according to the forecast, it will be even
hotter tomorrow and again on Thursday, for the Gold Cup."

"You're welcome to it."

Her attitude distressed me.

I wondered if Georgina was also sensing that our marriage was beginning to crumble around our ears. Did she mind? Or might it be a relief to her
too?

What was it she really wanted from her life? Was my presence a necessity
or a luxury? Or both?

Or neither?

And what did I want from my life?

Could we go back to how it had been, or should we go forward into
uncharted waters, either together or separately?

All I knew was that something *had* to change. I didn't want to go on as
we had been recently, not for the next twenty-five years or so.

*   *   *

Nothing was moving outside the takeaway—nothing that I was interested in
anyway. A steady stream of customers came and then went again, clutching
their white plastic bags of food. I reckoned the last thing anyone would want
on such a hot June evening would be a vindaloo or a madras, but perhaps
they were just having a korma.

By nine o'clock, there was still no sign of Amanda or Darren.

I climbed out of the car to stretch my legs, walking up and down the
road a few times, before going once more to the flat front door. No one had

come in or gone out since I'd arrived, but I banged on the door again, never-theless. Again, no one answered my knock, nor did anyone open any of the windows above.

I went back to the car once more and climbed in.

Where were they?

Perhaps I should have gone straight to Tesco to see if Amanda was work-ing. Maybe she'd only just gone in when I arrived and was working the night shift at the twenty-four-hour store. That would mean she wouldn't be back until the morning.

What would I do then? Stay here all night?

Should I call the police?

But what would I say to them?

"My daughter's life has been threatened."

"Who by?" they would ask. *"And how do you know?"*

Then what would I say? Would I tell them about the phone calls from Squeaky Voice and show them his texts?

"And why didn't you tell us about this immediately you received the first threatening phone call? Or on the days you received the other calls or the texts? And how did you make Dream Filler lose? What did you do with the weights you removed from his weight cloth?"

"You are now under arrest for race fixing."

I shook my head to dispel the thoughts.

There was clearly no way I could ask the police for help.

* * *

Amanda and Darren arrived back at a quarter to eleven, by which time I had convinced myself they weren't coming. Even the Raj Tandoori was getting ready to close for the night, and I was about to go home.

I saw them walking towards me along the pavement on the opposite side of the road to where I was parked. I didn't immediately get out of the car, in case they saw me, turned around, and briskly walked away.

I let them get to within about ten to fifteen yards from their front door before I climbed out of the car.

"Amanda," I called across the road. "Can I have a word with you please?"

"I thought I told you to piss off," Darren said aggressively. "She doesn't want to talk to you."

I ignored him.

"Amanda, it's about your grandfather."

I saw her hesitate, and then she walked over the road towards me. Dar-ren started to follow, but she told him to wait.

"What about Grandpa?" she asked gravely. "Is he all right?"

"Mum has gone up to Harrogate to be with him, and with Granny. Grandpa wasn't at all well on Sunday, but he's perked up a bit since then. But we have no way of contacting you if anything does happen, because you won't give us your new telephone number. So I've been waiting here all evening for you to come back to tell you. Please call Mum. And will you give us both your number?"

She took her phone out of her pocket but hesitated again.

"Darren says I'm better off without either of you."

"Then Darren is a fool," I said. "Why don't you come with me now, and we'll call Mum on the way home. I'm sure she'll still be up."

She half turned and looked back at Darren, who was waiting by the front door, and there was almost a look of fear on her face, rather than adoration.

"No, Dad. I'm staying here."

She turned to go.

"Look," I said, grabbing her by the arm to stop her, "I'm worried about you. Someone took you away from our party, and they could do it again. You will be much safer at home, where I can look after you."

She pulled herself free from my grasp.

"I'm quite safe here. Darren will look after me."

Short of picking her up and bodily throwing her into my car, there was nothing more I could do.

"Be very careful," I said urgently. "Please don't go out on your own, especially at night."

"Dad, stop it," she said. "I'm quite old enough to look after myself. Go home."

"Not until you have rung your mother."

"I'll ring her in the morning."

"Then please call my phone right now, so I have your number. If Grandpa dies, I will need to call you."

She hesitated once more and glanced back over her shoulder.

"Is it on silent?" she asked, almost in a whisper.

I took it out of my trouser pocket and made it so.

"It is now."

She touched her screen a few times, and my phone began to vibrate. I didn't answer, and she stopped the call.

"Thank you," I said quietly, adding the number to the "Amanda" contact in my phone.

"But, please, don't call me unless you absolutely have to." It was almost a desperate plea. "Now go home."

I waited while she walked back across the road, and the pair of them went in through the door. As a parting gesture, Darren stuck two fingers up at me just before he closed it.

Charming, I thought.

I was almost as concerned about Amanda's safety at his hands as I was at those of Squeaky Voice.

21

T HE WEATHER FORECASTERS were absolutely correct. Wednesday morning again dawned bright and sunny, and the mercury was predicted to
climb several degrees higher than it had yesterday.

I didn't sleep particularly well, not least because I had eaten so late.

I hadn't picked up the last curry of the night from the Raj Tandoori.
Rather, I had made myself some sourdough toast at home, liberally spread
with chicken liver pâté. And I'd had a glass of red wine to help wash it down.

I should have been so happy.

Victrix's star horse had proved again that he was a true champion, winning yet another Group 1 race. But I worried about what the consequences of
that win might be for me, and for my family.

I was really pleased that I'd managed to see Amanda, but also disappointed I hadn't convinced her to come home with me.

In the morning, I spent the usual couple of hours in my office, speaking
with the trainers.

The office had obviously been built on as an afterthought, subsequent
to the construction of the main house, but it had been done before we
bought it.

It was a single-storey extension and one of the main reasons I had liked
the house so much in the first place. It allowed me to somehow feel that I
could escape from the rest of the family and concentrate on my work without
disturbance.

"How's Potassium today?" I asked Owen, the last trainer on my list.
"Did he get home all right?"

"No problem, but he's clearly tired. He was a bit unsteady coming off the box last night, and he didn't eat up very well. He's just going in the walker for half an hour to dispel any stiffness in his legs. Other than that he'll have a quiet day today and only a gentle canter tomorrow."

"How about you?" I asked. "Did you have a good evening?"

"Quiet," he said. "I had a beer with a few friends in the trainers' car park after racing, then came straight home. I was in bed before nine."

I wished I had been as well, but there again, I hadn't had to get up this morning at sunrise.

"Are you back at Ascot again today?" I asked.

"I suppose so, but I'm not looking forward to it much in this heat. And I won't be getting there very early. I have only one runner, Silvia's Choice in the Royal Hunt Cup, and that's not off until five o'clock. There are thirty declared runners, so I suspect it will be the usual cavalry charge."

The Royal Hunt Cup was a handicap, run over the straight mile. It was one of the biggest gambling races of the whole week, and the bookies usually had a field day, with plenty of long-odds winners in the past.

"Does yours have a chance?" I asked.

"They all have. The race is a bloody lottery. Silvia's Choice is drawn right in the middle, and that's not normally good.

"Well, good luck anyway. I'll look out for you later."

We disconnected and I went back into the house to get ready to depart.

* * *

"Was it something I said?"

I turned around.

Today, Toni Beckett was in blue—blue dress and blue hat.

"Did you bring a trunk load of hats?" I asked, smiling.

"Only two. I'm back in the yellow again tomorrow. So what happened to you? I was all ready to party in the car park last night, but you weren't there."

"I had to go home. How was tea with the ambassador?"

"Boring. There was another man there with him, who leered at me all the time. It was creepy."

"I'll try and remember not to leer."

"*You* can leer at me as much as you like," she said, looking me straight in the eyes.

"So where are you today?" I asked, trying to change the subject.

"Where would you like me to be?"

We were standing on the parade-ring concourse, just outside the entrance to the grandstand, and I instinctively turned and looked around me, to make sure that no one I knew had seen or overheard this overtly flirtatious encounter between us, occurring in the most public place on Ascot racecourse.

I turned back to face her.

"I meant, which box are you in today?"

She looked down at the triangular badge pinned to her dress, above the Royal Enclosure one.

"Box 522," she said.

"That'll be nice. The views from the private boxes are spectacular, especially from up on the fifth level."

"I'd rather be having a spectacular view of the rest of you," she said.

I blushed. "Stop it."

"Why? It's only a bit of fun. Although I mean it. Come on—let's go and have some champagne. I don't have to be at the box until twelve-thirty."

I looked at my watch. It was a quarter to midday, and I had made no appointments until after the first race.

"Okay," I said.

I led her away from the Royal Enclosure, down some steps to the Moët & Chandon Champagne Bar, situated near the bandstand. Maybe because I felt there would be less likelihood of running into anyone I knew down there.

"Get a bottle," Toni said as I surveyed the prices.

"I have to drive later," I said.

"Boring!"

I bought a bottle of Brut Imperial for over a hundred quid, but it did come ready opened, and in a see-through acrylic Moët & Chandon ice bucket—but that had to go back to redeem the twenty-pound deposit.

We found a couple of spare seats under a sun umbrella.

"Who are your hosts today?" I asked after I had poured two glasses.

"I don't know. Some rich cronies of the Farquhars."

"And they don't mind that you tag along?"

"Don't seem to. Mr and Mrs Farquhar have sorted out this whole trip for me. It's really kind of them. But I do lots for them back home. They regularly need clubhouse hospitality for their guests at Keeneland, and I fix it for them, at a price of course. They have a reserved box in the grandstand, but our boxes aren't like the ones here. We call those suites. For us, a box is just a small railed-off area with six or eight chairs in it. There's no privacy. And the Farquhars always want a private suite with food and wines when they have visitors."

"You're clearly a useful person to know."

"You can bet on it," she said with a laugh. "And they will expect more of the same from me in the future after this little jaunt."

She took another sip of champagne.

"You should come over for our Fall Meet in October," she said. "I'll sort you out properly."

I was quite certain she would.

"And we also have the Breeders' Cup World Championship weekend at Keeneland this year."

"Do you, indeed?"

Running Potassium in the International Stakes at York in August suddenly seemed much more attractive. It was one of their "win and you're in" qualifiers for the Breeders' Cup Classic. So a win there would secure him a guaranteed berth in the race.

"Tell me more about you," she said.

"Not much to tell, really," I replied. "I'm a workaholic who never seems to take a day off. Horseracing in this country is a seven-day-a-week activity. Apart from Christmas Day and the two days beforehand, there are at least two race meetings in this country every single day of the year. On most days, there are four or five, and on some, as many as eight or nine. There are over fourteen hundred different fixtures over the whole year."

She stared at me in amazement.

"Not that they're all like this," I said, waving my hands around at the grandeur of Royal Ascot. "There'll be over sixty thousand people here tomorrow for the Gold Cup, but there may be fewer than a hundred at a wet January evening meeting at Wolverhampton."

"So why do they bother to hold it?" she asked.

"For the betting shops and the online bookmaking sites. Racing is kept afloat by people gambling on it, and most of them don't go anywhere near the actual racecourses. The government collects a portion of all bookmakers' profits through something called the Horserace Betting Levy. And that money is used to keep racing going."

"But you must do something to relax," she said. "Do you have any hobbies?"

Did I? Not really. Horseracing was my hobby as well as my work. I didn't actually need to be here at Ascot today, but I had chosen to be so.

"Sorry," I said, shaking my head. "It's official. I am totally boring."

"I could change that," she said. "How about another drink later? Maybe in the car park or . . . back at my hotel?"

"You're very forward," I said.

She laughed. "I have to be. I'm only here for six nights, and three of them have gone already."

"What about the Farquhars?"

"They're out to the theatre in London this evening, and I wasn't invited."

How convenient, I thought.

"So are they leaving here early?" I asked.

"They have a driver collecting them at quarter of six."

The last race was not until ten past six, so they should avoid the worst of the traffic, but it would still be tight if their show started at seven-thirty.

"Are you leaving with them?"

I wondered what the hell I was doing, asking such a leading question.

"No. The Farquhars have kindly arranged for me to have my own car back to my hotel, as they are going direct from here to the theatre. I just have to call my driver forty minutes before I need him."

She smiled at me. She seemed to have everything perfectly worked out.

"I'm sorry," I said, bursting her balloon, "but I don't think it's a good idea."

"Damn men!" she said with feeling. "I spend half my life fighting most of them off me because I don't want them, and now, when I absolutely do want one, he has a fit of conscience."

"I'm a married man."

"So what? Tell your wife you've met an important client at the races, and you will be going to dinner with them in London tonight, so you might as well stay over in a hotel. And you'll be home tomorrow—or on Friday—or Saturday."

She smiled at me once again.

And Georgina herself wouldn't be home until at least Saturday.

*   *   *

At twelve-thirty, Toni went off to the private box for lunch while I remained sitting a little longer at the table, having another glass of bubbly and cogitating about what to do.

We had agreed to meet again later.

I would collect her from Box 522 after the big race of the day, the Group 1 Prince of Wales Stakes, and we would watch the next race together from the seats on level four, before she went back to the box for the last two races and afternoon tea.

And then what?

She had made it perfectly clear what she wanted, but she was a long way from home.

What happens on tour stays on tour.

But this was my backyard, my place of work, where hundreds, if not thousands, of the people here today would recognise me. My face had been on the television after the Derby, and again only yesterday, collecting the St James's Palace Stakes trophy from royalty.

I returned the ice bucket to the bar and collected the deposit, then went back up to the parade-ring concourse. It was as good a place as any to see some of the people I quite hoped to run into, but it was very quiet there at this time of day. Everyone was busy having lunch, either in the restaurants or in the car parks, and no one had yet started to arrive for the Royal Procession.

I wondered what Toni would be eating in Box 522.

The standard of the box catering at Royal Ascot is legendary, and I'd been lucky enough to have been invited to savour it quite a few times over the years. And there is also ample fine dining available in the many racecourse restaurants, some with Michelin-starred chefs on duty—provided you had booked your table many months in advance.

However, as I had no box invitations, no restaurant bookings, and no access today to the Owners and Trainers' Dining Room, I opted for sweet and sour pork with sticky rice from the Chinese takeaway in the base of the grandstand, served in a cardboard box, with a choice of a wooden fork or chopsticks.

Conscious that there were three more days of Royal Ascot after this, and I had no time between days to get my morning dress cleaned, I chose the fork.

And very delicious the food was too.

I hadn't realised how hungry I was. I'd had hardly anything to eat since lunch yesterday in the car park with Nick and Claire Spencer, and I'd expended a lot of energy since then, both physical and emotional.

After finishing the pork, I went up to level four and bagged myself a front-row seat for the Royal Procession, and wished I were watching it again with Toni Beckett.

"Well done, yesterday," said the man behind me, patting me on the shoulder. "That Potassium is quite a horse."

I turned in my seat. I'd never seen the man before.

"Thank you," I said. "Yes, he is."

"Will he go for the Arc?" he asked. "I fancy a trip to Paris."

"Probably not this year," I replied. "Do you own any horses?"

"No," he said. "But I've thought about it."

I pulled one of my Victrix Racing business cards out of my inside coat pocket and gave it to him. "If you fancy joining an owning syndicate, give me a call."

"Thanks," he said, looking at the card. "Maybe I'll do that."

The seats filled up fast as two o'clock approached, and right on time, the first of the Windsor Greys appeared through the Golden Gate.

I never tired of watching this.

Horseracing is known worldwide as the Sport of Kings, and here was the King at the races to prove it, carrying on the tradition first started by his great-great-great-great-great-uncle, King George IV, in 1825.

The four carriages made their steady way down the course, and a military band, standing on the grandstand steps, struck up the national anthem as they passed. Then the royal party disappeared from our sight as they went through the tunnel, and on to the parade ring.

I remained in my seat to watch the first race, the Queen Mary Stakes, a five-furlong dash for two-year-old fillies. There were twenty-six runners, and if you blinked, you could miss it, the whole thing being over in less than a minute, after it had taken almost five times that long to load them all into the starting stalls.

I went down to the concourse to meet with my first appointment of the day, a young man from Yorkshire, whom I'd had my eye on for some time as a possible future Victrix trainer. He had a runner later in the afternoon, and he had made a rare excursion south, so here I had a chance to meet him face to face.

I was looking to sign up another northern-based trainer, as I had an increasing number of prospective syndicate members from Manchester and Leeds who preferred to go to stable visits and race meetings close to home.

As arranged, I met him on the small Grundy Lawn near the Owners and Trainers' Bar, and we spent fifteen minutes or so discussing matters. He said he was very keen to add his name to my list of trainers, and we agreed to meet again at the yearling sale in Doncaster at the end of August. In the meantime, I would send to him all the Victrix information for him to study.

I wandered back towards the parade ring and watched the second race on the big TV screen there, but I didn't really notice who won.

I had other things on my mind.

* * *

I knocked loudly on the door of Box 522 after the fourth race.

It was opened by one of the catering staff. I went in.

Most of the occupants were still on the balcony, having watched the race, but there was one man sitting at the table, studying the *Racing Post*. He looked up at me.

"Can I help you?" he asked.

"I've come to collect Mrs Beckett," I said.

"Then you must be Chester Newton," said the man, standing up.

"Yes. I am."

"Mark Gill. It's my box." He came over and we shook hands. "Toni said you would be coming to take her away from us for a race. Do you have a runner?"

"No," I said, "but I want to watch one trained by Owen Reynolds."

"Your trainer of Potassium," he said, smiling. "Great result yesterday."

"Yes, it was. Thank you. Very exciting."

Toni saw me through the glass and came in.

"Are you ready?" I asked.

She smiled and nodded.

"You could both stay and watch the race from here if you like," Mark said. "We're about to have our tea."

I looked at Toni and she nodded again.

"Or would you prefer a drink?" Mark asked. "Glass of champagne?"

I'd probably already had too much alcohol to drive home now anyway.

"A glass of champagne would be lovely. Thank you."

One of the staff poured one and handed it to me.

Herb and Harriet Farquhar came in from the balcony.

"Hi, Chester," Herb said. "Good to see you again."

"And you too," I replied.

We shook hands and I wondered if now would be a good time to talk to him about taking a share in a Victrix horse next year.

But, on balance, I decided that it probably wasn't.

Tea of sandwiches, scones, and all sorts of delicious-looking cake was laid out on the table, and the other box guests came back in from the balcony to take their seats. I went outside with my glass, and Toni came out briefly to join me.

"Have you phoned your wife?" she asked me quietly, straight away.

"Not yet," I said.

"At least that sounds more promising than 'no.'"

"Do join us, Chester," Mark said, stepping outside. "There's plenty of food, and we have just had a huge lunch."

"Thank you," I said once again. And the staff found me a spare chair.

"What's the name of Owen Reynolds's horse in the next?" Mark asked.

"Silvia's Choice. But he doesn't think it has much of a chance."

"But we must have a bet on it," Toni said. She stood up and looked across at me. "Come on. Let's go and make it."

I stood up and followed her out of the box.

"Call her now," Toni said intently when the box door had closed behind us.

"I will. Later. Don't rush me."

I placed a ten pounds each-way bet on Silvia's Choice at the Tote desk, and then we went back into the box to watch the race.

"You'll find this interesting," I said to her as we took two of the seats outside on the balcony. "It'll be like two separate races happening at the same time."

The thirty runners were loaded into the stalls, which stretched right across the track at the straight-mile start, way off to our right, near the Golden Gate.

When the stalls snapped open, the field immediately split in two, with one half running down the near rail, and the other half over on the far one.

It was the race commentator's nightmare to try and decide which side was in front. And the jockeys had little idea either.

But whichever side was in front, Silvia's Choice was not going to win. The horse faded badly in the last couple of furlongs and was well beaten.

In the end, the leading horse on the far side edged out the one on the near side by about half a length, but neither of the jockeys was sure which of them was the winner, nor were most of the crowd until the judge made the announcement. But Silvia's Choice wasn't one of them anyway.

"Another loser," I said tearing up our Tote ticket.

"Never mind," Toni said. "You might be a winner tonight."

22

"I'VE BEEN INVITED to dinner tonight in London by an American couple," I said to Georgina when I finally made the call. "Their names are Herb and Harriet Farquhar, and they own a stud farm outside Lexington in Kentucky. I met them in the car park yesterday, when we were fellow lunch guests of Nick Spencer. They're over here for Royal Ascot, and they could be very useful contacts if I ever want to expand Victrix into the United States."

It was so easy. Too easy.

"You're surely not going to drive home afterwards," she said.

"No. I'll get a hotel room for the night. You're not at home anyway, and I'll come straight back here again tomorrow."

"What about a clean shirt?" she asked, practical as ever.

"I'll just have to make sure I don't drop soup down it," I said. "Or I'll pop into Marks and buy a new one."

"The hotel might do overnight laundry."

"A new one would probably be cheaper."

"Well, have a nice time," she said. "And don't drink too much."

"Did Amanda call you?" I asked, changing tack.

"Yes, thank God. She called this morning. She even spoke to my father. It perked him up no end."

"Good."

"But she told me not to call her back unless it was an absolute emergency."

"She said the same to me."

I'd already told Georgina about going to see Amanda last night, without saying that I'd spent the whole evening waiting for her.

"I told her not to be so silly," Georgina said. "But she was adamant. She said she'd change her number again if I did."

I could tell that Georgina was distressed by that, but not as distressed as she could be.

"It might be a late dinner," I said. "So I'll call you again in the morning."

"Okay. Sleep well."

We disconnected and I felt terrible.

What was I doing?

I should just tell Toni to forget it, and go home alone, even if I had to order a taxi to get there, but there was something driving me on. Perhaps it was the niggling feeling that life was somehow passing me by, and it was time to try something different.

Something exciting.

* * *

Toni's driver dropped us outside her hotel in Kensington High Street.

"I've never done anything like this before," I said nervously as we walked into the lobby, my top hat in my right hand.

"It'll be quite easy," Toni said, taking my left. "We go up to my room, open the bottle of champagne from the mini bar, get undressed, and then we go to bed. Then we'll have some dinner, and later on, we go to bed again."

How could any man say no to that?

We took the lift to the eighth floor and went along the corridor to room 807.

"Which is Herb and Harriet's room?" I asked, almost in a whisper in case they could somehow hear me.

"Don't be silly," Toni said, laughing. "They're not staying here. They're at the Peninsula. They pick me up on the way past in the morning."

We went into her room. It had one large double bed, a desk and a chair, plus a sofa by the window, but it was the view through that window over the trees of Kensington Gardens towards the city that was the true five-star experience.

"Open the champagne," Toni said, pointing at the mini bar and tossing her blue hat onto the desk. "I'll be out in a moment."

She went into the bathroom while I took off my coat and laid it on the bed. I then took the bottle from the fridge and fumbled with the wire over the cork, my hands shaking.

Finally it popped, and I poured two glasses.

"Do you want yours in there?" I asked.

She didn't answer. Instead, the bathroom door opened, and she came out.

She was stark naked.

"What do you think?" she asked, posing with her arms held up. "Not bad for forty-six. I've still got firm, pointed tits and a flat belly."

Not bad at all, I thought.

I stood there with the champagne glasses still in my hands as she came over and stood close to me. She undid the buttons on the front of my waist-coat and carefully removed it without me spilling a drop.

She pulled my braces to the sides, lifting them over the glasses.

Then she went down on her knees and began to unfasten the front of my trousers.

"Why do these pants have buttons, not a zip," she said, looking up at my face.

"All morning-dress trousers have buttons," I said breathlessly, looking down at her face and at the further delights beyond. "I don't know why."

Did I care?

She finished undoing everything, and the trousers fell down to the floor around my ankles.

"I love a man in boxers," she said. "Or rather, I love a man out of boxers."

She tucked her thumbs over the elastic waistband and pulled them sharply down to join the trousers. It caused a shiver to run through my whole body.

"I'm spilling these," I said in a sort of croak.

She stood up, took the glasses, drank from one, then put them both on the bedside table. Then she unbuttoned and removed my shirt.

Next, she lay down on the bed, on her back, with her knees drawn up and spread wide apart.

"Take me now," she said.

So I did.

* * *

"My God," she said afterwards. "You clearly needed that even more than I did."

We were still lying naked on the bed. I was cuddling her with my right arm, and her head rested on my chest.

"I'm sorry it was over so quickly," I said. "Not enough foreplay."

"Don't be sorry. And to hell with foreplay. I was gagging for it too. It was wonderful."

I stroked her hair.

"Do you do this sort of thing often?" I asked.

"First time in years," she said, but I wasn't totally sure I believed her. "In fact, I've only done it a few times since I got divorced."

"When was that?"

"Seven years ago. I discovered that my husband preferred sleeping with other men—or mostly boys—rather than with me."

"What a silly man," I said.

"That's exactly what I told him as he was handcuffed in our den by the cops."

"You're kidding."

"No, I'm not. He was eventually convicted of having sex with a minor—one boy was only fifteen—and he did jail time in the state penitentiary. But he's out now."

"Do you have any children?" I asked.

"No, thank goodness. So the divorce was easy, especially since he was incarcerated at the time. He couldn't really object."

"But you still have his name, Mrs Beckett."

"No I don't," she said indignantly. "Beckett was always my name, not his. It's just that la-di-da Ascot requires you to put your marriage status down on the ticket application form. I put down 'divorced,' but they still wrote 'Mrs' on my Royal Enclosure badge."

"You should be thankful they let you in at all. For the first hundred and thirty years of its existence, no one who was divorced was allowed to enter the Royal Enclosure. It was not thought proper that the sovereign should have to gaze upon a divorced person."

"Now you're the one who's kidding."

"I'm not. It was only after the Queen Elizabeth's younger sister, Princess Margaret, got divorced in 1978 that divorcees were truly accepted by everyone. Nowadays, I reckon that at least half the people in there have been divorced at some time or another, including the King himself."

She ran her fingers across my tummy, causing more shivers down my legs.

"Do you ever see your ex?" I asked. "Now he's been released?"

"No, thank God. He moved out west. California, I think. He had no choice really, not if he wanted to find a job. His trial was big news at home because the young boy he had sex with was the son of a state congressman. The boy's name was leaked to the press by a political opponent of his father, and then it was all over the local TV stations. Everyone in Kentucky knew about it."

I stroked her hair again.

"You live such an interesting life," I said.

"Not as interesting as yours," she replied.

"But you said I was boring."

She turned her head to look at me. "No. *You* said you were boring. And I've never met a queen. Or a king. Not even anyone royal. That definitely makes you more interesting than me."

I laughed. "Is this a competition?"

My phone started ringing, instantly cutting short my laugh.

The phone was still in my trousers pocket, where it had been when they had dropped to the floor, along with my boxers.

"Ignore it," I said, not moving. "I don't want to speak to anyone."

And certainly not to Squeaky Voice.

The ringing stopped. But then it immediately started again.

"Might that be your wife?" Toni asked. "Checking up on you?"

"I don't care if it's the prime minister. I'm still not answering it."

"So your prime minister also has your number." She laughed. "I think that means I win."

The ringing finally stopped, and we lay there for a considerable time longer, our legs entwined, enjoying being so close to each other. Eventually, she lifted my right hand off one of her firm and pointed breasts, climbed off the bed, and stood up.

"I need to go pee."

She skipped into the bathroom but left the door wide open, and I found even the sound of her urinating was sexy and arousing.

She shortly emerged again, wearing, rather disappointingly for me, a white hotel towelling bathrobe.

"What do you want to do for dinner?" she asked, pouring two more glasses of champagne from the bottle.

"What would you like?" I asked her back.

"The hotel restaurant is very good. I ate there on Monday evening."

"But I've only got my morning dress," I said. "Unless I go down in a bathrobe."

"Room service, then?"

"Perfect."

She gave me one of the champagne glasses and came back to bed with the room service menu, slipping off her robe and dropping it on the floor.

She snuggled her naked body up next to mine, and I couldn't ever remember feeling so relaxed and content as I was at that precise moment.

Such a shame it didn't last.

*   *   *

The two missed calls on my phone were not from Squeaky Voice. They were from James. There was also a WhatsApp text message from him.

Dad, I need to speak to you urgently. Call me back.

I had got up to go to the bathroom and had picked up my trousers so they weren't too creased for the following day. The phone slipped out of the pocket.

All sorts of dreadful scenarios flashed through my head.

Was James calling me because something had happened to Amanda, and she had contacted him?

"I'd better call my son," I said to Toni. "He never rings me unless it's important. I'll do it in the bathroom."

I did close the bathroom door.

"What is it?" I asked when James answered.

"I need my passport."

"I thought you weren't going away until August. So what's the urgency?"

"Now that I know I passed my exams, me and Gary have found a great flat for next year, but the letting agency won't confirm us as the tenants until we can prove our identities. Something to do with bloody money-laundering regulations. I'm really worried they will go with someone else, and we'll miss it. So send me my passport."

"Where is it?"

"In the top drawer of my desk. Go and get it now."

"But I'm not at home," I said. "I'm in London at a dinner. I've just stepped out to call you. I'm booked into a hotel for the night."

"I suppose I'll have to call Mum, then." His tone implied that calling his mother was likely to cause him more trouble than it was worth.

"Mum's not at home either. She's staying with Granny and Grandpa in Harrogate. Grandpa isn't very well."

"When are you back at home?"

"Not until tomorrow evening after racing at Ascot."

"Bloody hell. Then it won't get in the post until Friday at the earliest, and Saturday deliveries are totally hopeless in Bristol."

"Look. As soon as I get home tomorrow, I'll scan your passport and email it to you or to the agency. Ask them if that would be enough."

"Can't you drive it down to me here tomorrow night?"

I thought of the possibility of spending a second night with Toni.

"Ask the agency if a scanned copy of it will suffice for the moment, until we can get the real thing to them. Ask them tomorrow morning, and then let me know."

"Okay. I'll ask them." He paused. "Did you say that Grandpa isn't well?"

"I'm afraid I did," I said.

"But he will get better, right?"

"Darling, I'm not sure. Mum said he was very unwell on Sunday, and she was very worried about him, but he's been a little better since then. Why don't you give Mum a call and ask her how he is? You could even speak to him."

"Okay. Maybe."

"No 'maybe.' Do it now. I have to go now to get back to my dinner. Call me tomorrow when you've spoken to the agency. Bye."

We hung up and I went out of the bathroom, not only to eat my dinner but also to enjoy my special dessert afterwards.

23

"HAVE YOU SEEN the front of today's *Racing Post?*"
Owen almost shouted it down the phone at me when I called
him at eight o'clock.

"What about it?" I asked.

I would normally have glanced through the electronic version of the
paper on my computer by this time of the morning, but my computer was at
home—and I wasn't.

"I should bloody well sue them for libel."

"Why?" I said, somewhat alarmed. "What does it say?"

"The banner headline on the front page reads *'Mystery of the Missing
Weights.'*"

I went cold.

"What does it say under that?"

"It implies that the two-pound underweight Tim Westlake weighed in
after riding Dream Filler at Lingfield last Saturday must have been done on
purpose."

"But that's ridiculous," I said, trying to keep my heart rate down.

"Of course it is, but this bloody man, Jerry Parker, who wrote the article,
claims that Tim Westlake weighed out correctly at nine stone seven, but he
weighed in at nine five, because two one-pound lead weights had been taken
from his weight cloth sometime between the two. It's all total nonsense."

"How does he come up with that crazy idea?"

"Parker claims that the weighing-room manager at Lingfield told him
that two one-pound weights were missing from his stock after Saturday's

racing, and he says that's too much of a coincidence not to be connected with Tim Westlake's underweight."

He wasn't wrong.

"Couldn't they have fallen out during the race?" I said.

"That seems rather unlikely."

"But I've heard of it happening before."

I could remember reading about a handicap hurdle at Catterick when the champion jump jockey, Brian Hughes, lost weights during the race through a hole in the weight cloth, and had consequently weighed in two pounds light. Brian Boranha, the disqualified horse, had also been a fairly short-priced favourite, just as Dream Filler had been at Lingfield.

"Does Jerry Parker specifically name you in the piece?" I asked.

"He names me as the trainer of the horse. He also states that the stewards fined me seven hundred and fifty pounds and that my appeal against that was dismissed last week. Both of which are true. But he doesn't actually accuse me of having done it on purpose. Not in so many words."

"That makes it rather difficult for you to sue him," I said. "But don't worry. It will all soon blow over. You watch—someone will find the weights somewhere out on Lingfield's all-weather track."

Or not.

* * *

"Come back to bed," Toni said when I'd finished making my calls to the trainers.

"What time are the Farquhars picking you up?"

"Ten o'clock."

I looked at my watch. It was a quarter to nine.

"How long do you need to get ready," I asked.

"Half an hour."

"So we have forty-five minutes to play with. Shall I order us some food?"

"Don't be silly," she said, tapping the bed as encouragement for me to lie down. "I'm eating you for breakfast."

* * *

Herb and Harriet Farquhar arrived at the hotel at ten o'clock precisely, and Toni was ready.

"Are you coming with us in the car?" she had asked as we dressed—my shirt not quite too creased or grubby to wear for a second day, and her yellow dress from Tuesday, now dry-cleaned and pressed by the hotel laundry service.

"I think I'll catch the train. Then there'll be fewer difficult questions to have to answer on the journey."

I stood inside the lobby, half hidden behind a pillar, and watched as Toni climbed into the front passenger seat of the Farquhars' private-hire Mercedes.

Even though I knew I would be seeing her later in the day, my body still ached desperately for her.

Georgina had never been fond of oral sex. Indeed, she found the whole idea rather abhorrent, so it had never been on our sexual agenda. But the American lady had no such qualms. Hence, this morning had been a revelation, my mind near exploding, both with ecstasy and the sudden realization of what I had been missing for so many years.

As soon as the Farquhar's Mercedes was out of sight, I walked along to the local underground station, stopping off at a convenience store to buy a copy of the *Racing Post*.

The *"Mystery of the Missing Weights"* headline was printed over two lines in large bold letters, and seeing it there in black and white made me feel quite weak at the knees.

I leaned against a lamppost for support and read the article beneath the headline, from start to finish.

Just as Owen had said, the implication made by Jerry Parker was that the weights had been removed on purpose, without him actually accusing any specific person. I could imagine that a team of *Racing Post* lawyers had spent many hours scrutinizing his text to ensure the paper wasn't opening itself to accusations of libel.

Indeed, the article didn't mention me by name at all, only referring to the owner of Dream Filler as Victrix Racing, and then only in passing.

I suddenly felt very self-conscious, standing there dressed in top hat and tails amidst the scurrying Thursday-morning shoppers on Kensington High Street, reading about something of which I alone knew more than anyone else—far more than I should.

I looked around me, worried that those nearby might detect my unease.

I folded the newspaper in half, front page inwards, and tucked it under my arm before continuing my trek to the station.

I took the Tube to Waterloo, and from there I caught a very congested train to Ascot.

The Thursday of the royal meeting, with the running of the Gold Cup, was always traditionally the busiest day of the week, although, since the expansion of Royal Ascot from four days to five in 2002, to mark Queen Elizabeth II's Golden Jubilee, the Saturday crowds have steadily grown and are now the largest.

Not that you could imagine that any more people could squeeze aboard this particular train. Not only was every seat taken, many of them with an occupant plus another sitting on their lap, but every available square inch of floor space was packed with men in morning dress or smart suits, and women in their colourful finery, all of them ready for Ladies Day at the races.

Fortunately, I had arrived at Waterloo just after the previous train had departed, so I was one of the first to board the next one, so I had a seat, tucked into one corner of the carriage.

One or two of the passengers were studying copies of the *Racing Post*, and I feared that the front-page headline was shouting out to those around me.

I could almost feel a large red arrow above my head, pointing straight down at me, with *Guilty Party* written on it in large letters.

When we arrived at Ascot railway station, there was a mad rush to get off the train, but I was so crammed in that I had to wait for everyone else to leave before I could even move. In fact, I waited almost until the doors began to close again before I finally stepped out onto the platform.

I was in no hurry.

Cherwell Edge, the Victrix horse I had running today, was in the Hampton Court Stakes, a Group 3 event for three-year-olds, over a mile and a quarter. It was the second-to-last race of the day, not due off until 5.35, and I hadn't arranged to meet up with Toni until after the Gold Cup, because she thought she wouldn't be able to get away any earlier.

She and the Farquhars were lunch guests today of the Ascot Authority, the organisation that runs Ascot Racecourse on behalf of the sovereign, who owns it.

All the train passengers, including me some way behind them, walked up the quarter-mile-long steep pedestrian pathway to the racecourse, to join the throng waiting to gain entry through the turnstiles.

I made a short detour to Car Park 2 first, to check that all was well with my car, that it hadn't been towed away overnight—it hadn't—before gathering up my daily owners/trainers badge, lunch voucher, and parade-ring pass from the collection marquee at the east end of the car park.

The nice lady who gave out the badges looked up and smiled at me. "Hello, Mr Newton. I greatly enjoyed reading that lovely piece about you in today's *Racing Post*."

"Lovely piece?" I said, confused.

"Yes. The piece about you and Potassium. On page five."

I realised I hadn't looked past the horrors of the front.

I unfolded my copy of the paper, which was still tucked under my arm, and opened it to page five.

"Chester Newton and the Ever-Rising Star of Victrix Racing" was written across the top of the page, with a large colour photograph beneath, taken at Owen Reynolds's yard, of me with Potassium.

Meanwhile, a queue of impatient owners was forming behind me.

"Thank you for telling me," I said to the lady, taking my badge and lunch voucher from her hand. "I'll go outside and read it."

She smiled at me again, and then her gaze moved right to the next person in the line.

Overall, Jerry Parker had been true to his word in the feature, and very kind about Victrix Racing and about me. Only at the end did he refer obliquely to his own front-page story of the missing Lingfield weights as being the only blemish on an otherwise spectacular three weeks for the company.

I didn't know whether to be happy or fearful. Maybe a bit of both.

It would be the front-page story that everyone would see. For most people, after that, they would only be interested in the runners for the races ahead and the tipsters' views on each horse's prospects, to help them decide on which to stake their cash.

The feature would pass them by completely.

I closed the newspaper, refolded it carefully with the front-page headline well hidden, and went through the turnstiles into the racecourse.

Once inside, it was very easy to tell that everywhere was much busier than it had been during the first two days. In fact, some twenty-five thousand more people would be here today, compared to yesterday.

The queue to have your photograph taken against a Royal Ascot floral backdrop was noticeably longer, and even though it was not yet one o'clock, the spaces around the parade ring from which to watch the Royal Procession were already full.

My phone rang.

It was James.

"I've spoken to the letting agency. They said they really need to see my actual passport to satisfy the regulations, but they're happy just to have a scanned copy of it for the moment. But they need that by first thing tomorrow, at the latest, or they can't hold the flat for us any longer."

"Okay," I said. "I'll scan it this evening when I get home, and send the scan direct to them by email. Text me their email address. I'll copy the email to you."

"And you'll also send the physical passport to me?"

"I'll do that tomorrow morning by post. Text me your address again to be sure I have the right one."

We disconnected.

Not having had any breakfast other than sex, I realised I was hungry. So I made my way to the Owners and Trainers' Dining Room to get some lunch.

Even that was busy, with a queue for tables.

"Hello, Chester," said the man joining the line behind me.

I turned around.

"Oh, hi, Richie."

Richie Mackenzie, the Newmarket-based trainer of five Victrix horses, including Balham, who had been beaten a nose at Windsor ten days ago, and also of Cherwell Edge, my runner of this afternoon. As usual, we had spoken on the phone earlier, albeit briefly.

"All well?" I asked.

"Fine. Edgie arrived safely, and he's raring to go. He'll be doing his best."

I felt he was being tactful.

"I'm not really expecting too much," I said.

Cherwell Edge had only run twice before, both in Class 4 novice stakes. He had finished second in one and fourth in the other, but today's race was a huge step up to a Class 1, Group 3 contest against some highly rated horses.

Both Richie and I knew that I had entered him under pressure from one of the syndicate members, who had desperately wanted just to have a Royal Ascot runner to impress his friends, even if the horse had little or no chance of winning.

"He's been working really well at home, and he might surprise you yet," Richie said. "As long as the jockey weighs in at the same weight as he weighed out."

I looked at him.

"Are you referring to the front page of today's *Racing Post*?"

"I certainly am," he replied. "How did that happen?"

"What exactly?"

"That someone removed weights from Dream Filler's weight cloth."

"I don't believe anyone did," I said, trying to keep my voice calm, even though my heart was beating fast. "Why would they? I think that either Tim Westlake sweated off two pounds—after all, it was an extremely hot day—or some weights fell out of the weight cloth during the race."

"And you really believe that?" he said, sounding very sceptical.

"I don't know what to believe," I said. "Owen Reynolds reckons they must have made a mistake when weighing Westlake out."

"Well, he would say that, wouldn't he, if he was the one responsible."

"Come on, Richie," I said. "You can't possibly think that a trainer of Owen's standing would do such a thing on purpose."

"I reckon it was the jockey who did it," said the large man in front of me, who had clearly been listening to our conversation. "It's always the jockey who's at fault when they lose. Untrustworthy little people."

I thought he was joking, but he obviously wasn't.

This unwelcome bigoted intervention seemed to put a stop to any further discussion on the matter between Richie and me. And for that, at least, I was grateful.

Finally, a table for two became free, and I was invited to sit down.

"Can I join you?" Richie asked. "As we're both on our own."

"Sure," I said. I wanted to say *Just as long as we don't talk about missing weights*, but that might have sounded a bit suspicious.

But we didn't talk about it anyway, other than to discuss the large man who had intervened into our conversation and who was now sitting far enough away for us to talk about him without him hearing.

"It's people like him that give racing a bad name," Richie said quietly. "Do you know who he is?"

"No idea," I replied. "I don't think he's a trainer."

"I'm sure he isn't. Must be an owner. One of the old school who still believes that the jockey is their servant."

As it had always been back in the bad old days.

But even now, professional jockeys are still considered somewhat inferior by some organisations. The Jockey Club is a hugely influential self-elected group that had regulated British horseracing well into the twenty-first century. However, in spite of its name, there is not one current or former professional jockey amongst its membership.

Richie and I collected our food from the buffet.

"So who do you think will win the Gold Cup?" he asked as we sat down again.

"I think that the Irish hurdler has a really good chance."

"Manor House?"

"That's the one. It won the Mares' Hurdle at Cheltenham in March and the Irish Mares' Champion Hurdle at Punchestown in April. And it will be at a good price too. Might be worth a punt."

It was not unusual for horses that predominantly raced over hurdles to occasionally run on the flat. Many of the long-distance flat handicaps were regularly won by jumpers. The Ascot Gold Cup was not a handicap, but it was raced over two and a half miles, making it one of the longest flat races on the calendar—and the same length as the Mares' Hurdle at Cheltenham.

"I'm not sure she'll have the pace," Richie said, taking another mouthful of excellent poached salmon. "I fancy the Johnson colt. Won the Yorkshire Cup last time out. He'll surely start as a favourite."

We took the opportunity to discuss the future plans for the other four Victrix horses in his yard, sorting out when and where they would run next.

"Right," Richie said, standing up. "I must be off. I have one running in the Ribblesdale, so I must go and sort that out. See you later."

The Ribblesdale was a mile-and-a-half contest for three-year-old fillies, the third race on today's card. It was named after the fourth Baron Ribblesdale, who had served as Master of the Royal Buckhounds towards the end of the nineteenth century.

The Masters of the Royal Buckhounds had run Ascot Racecourse, on behalf of the Crown, from its inception right up to 1901, and several other races at Royal Ascot were also named after former masters, including the Coventry, Jersey, Chesham, and Hardwicke Stakes.

Richie walked away, but I decided to stay sitting at the table for a while longer and to watch the Royal Procession on one of the many televisions hung around the walls of the dining room. The TVs showed the afternoon's racing, not only from here at Ascot but also from the day's other meetings at Ripon and Chelmsford.

In order to keep the betting shops happy, race times at the various meetings were staggered so that races didn't clash, with a new race starting somewhere every ten to fifteen minutes.

Remaining in the Owners and Trainers' Dining Room would also mean I didn't have to meet anyone else who wanted to talk about the *Racing Post* headline, at least for a while. So I lingered in the same spot to watch Ascot's first race of the day, the Norfolk Stakes.

I hoped that now that the afternoon's racing had finally begun, people might have something else to talk about other than the *"Mystery of the Missing Weights."*

24

I HAD AGREED TO meet Toni at 4.40 next to the Moët & Chandon Champagne Bar, where we had shared a bottle of fizz the previous morning, and I arrived there a few minutes early.

The Gold Cup had just finished with a stunning two-length victory for Manor House, the Irish hurdling mare, and at a starting price of ten-to-one. I now sorely wished I'd had the strength of my convictions to invest some cash on her nose.

For the umpteenth time, I looked at my watch.

It was now a quarter to five.

Toni was late.

I wanted to be along at the saddling boxes by five o'clock, to be there in good time for when Richie arrived to saddle Cherwell Edge.

Toni arrived at ten to, coming up and throwing her arms around my neck, and giving me a big kiss on the lips.

"Not here," I said, pushing her away. "Too many eyes."

She pulled a face.

"Come on," I said, turning to go. "We need to get to the saddling boxes."

She didn't move.

"Yes, thank you," she said. "I've had a lovely day."

I turned back to her.

"I'm sorry," I said. "I'm glad you've had a lovely day. Good lunch?"

"Excellent. The Ascot Authority suite is fabulous. It's right next door to the King's, and it has a great view of the racing."

I knew. I'd been in there too.

"Now, can we go, please," I said. "I want to be there in time to watch my horse being saddled."

We walked up the slope, past the fast-food outlets, to the parade-ring concourse, and then on beyond to the pre-parade ring and the saddling boxes.

The fifth race was in progress as we arrived, and I was relieved to see that Cherwell Edge was still being led around the pre-parade ring, and without a saddle on his back.

We stopped and leaned against the white rail around the ring, waiting for Richie Mackenzie to arrive.

"Are you coming back to the hotel with me tonight?" Toni asked.

I looked at her and longed to do so.

"I can't," I said. "I have to go home."

"To your wife?"

"No. Not that. My wife has gone to stay with her parents. But I still have to go home. I need to do something for my son."

"Is he also at home?"

"No, he's not," I said. "He's away at university in Bristol, but I have to find his passport for him and then send him a copy. It's urgent."

"Can't someone else do it?" she asked.

"There's no one else there to do it."

"So I can go home with you?"

Suddenly, it felt like this was going too far—although how much farther could one go than full-on sexual intercourse? But taking her back to my house seemed to be elevating things to a different level, one I wasn't sure I wanted to reach. Not yet, anyway.

"How about your clothes and hat for tomorrow?" I asked, fishing for an excuse for her not to be able to come back with me.

"I would just have to wear the same as I am today."

"Won't the Farquhars think that strange?"

"I don't think they'd even notice. It's all about them, not me. I've already told them that they should go back to London tonight without me. I said I wanted to stay for the singing around the bandstand after the races. Everyone on my table was talking about it over lunch."

"So how do they think you'll get back?"

"I said I'd take the train. I'm a big girl." She smiled at me. "And I could also tell them that I will take the train back here in the morning. I'm sure they would be delighted not to have to make the detour to pick me up."

"Where are you having lunch tomorrow?" I asked.

"With you, I hope. The Farquhars have been invited by some friends to something called the Royal Ascot Racing Club. They said this morning that they were very sorry, but the invitation doesn't include me. Seems there are only two guest places available. I told them not to worry. I'd be fine." She smiled at me again. "Maybe we won't even bother to come here at all. We could spend the morning in bed and then watch the racing on the TV in the afternoon."

I had to admit that it sounded like a very attractive proposition.

"But I've made some appointments tomorrow," I said. "I need to be here."

"So we shall be," she said. "No problem."

At this point, Richie arrived with the saddle for Cherwell Edge, and he called the stable lad to bring the horse over to one of the saddling boxes.

"You stay here," I told Toni. "I'll be back."

I went over to the saddling box, but I didn't go in. Richie had brought his assistant to help him, and they soon had Cherwell Edge saddled and ready for the main parade ring.

"All in order?" I asked Richie as the horse was walked away.

"Absolutely," he said. "Weight cloth and all." He smiled at me.

"Good," I said, doing my best to ignore his little jibe. "I'll join you in the parade ring in a few minutes."

He walked on, following the horse, while I went back to Toni, who was still standing by the rail where I'd left her.

"I need to go into the parade ring now to meet up with the owning syndicate," I said to her.

"Can't I come with you?"

"I'm afraid I don't have a badge for you," I said. "And you know how strict they are. Why don't you go and wait at the spot where we watched the Royal Procession on Tuesday, and I'll join you to watch the race."

She didn't like it, but there was nothing I could do. And if I were being honest, I was really quite glad that she couldn't come in with me. There would be many people in the parade ring who knew me very well and who also knew Georgina. And there was nothing that moved so fast in horseracing circles as a nice, juicy piece of matrimonial gossip—even the quickest of the specialist five-furlong sprinters had nothing on that.

* * *

Just as his trainer, Richie Mackenzie, had predicted earlier, Cherwell Edge did surprise me.

Not that he won, or even came close to winning, but he kept on well over the last couple of furlongs to finish a very creditable fourth of the sixteen runners, collecting over eight thousand pounds in prize money.

Toni and I watched the race from the seats on level four.

"So," she said as the horses crossed the finish line, "can I come home with you tonight?"

Of course, I should say "no."

There were so many reasons why it was not a good idea.

What if someone saw us leaving the racecourse together?

Or our neighbours, Victoria or Brian Perry, popped around this evening—as they often did just for a chat or to borrow some sugar or milk?

Or Amanda decided to come home again?

Or the hundred other things I could think of that would give me away?

I turned in my seat to look at Toni.

"All right," I said.

But I could never have imagined what actually did happen.

* * *

Toni and I left while the last race was being run, in the hope that there would be fewer people I knew in Car Park 2 at that time.

When I climbed into the Jaguar, I noticed that there was a piece of paper tucked under the windscreen wiper.

Oh God, I thought. *Not another note from Squeaky Voice.*

But it wasn't that.

It was a letter from the Ascot Authority stating that vehicles were not to be left in the car parks overnight. However, as I had a valid car-park pass for both days, no action would be taken on this occasion, but if it happened again, there would be every likelihood that my car would be towed away.

I drove it out of the car park, wondering what on earth I was doing.

In less than three weeks, since Potassium had gone down to the start for the Derby, my whole mundane life seemed to have been turned upside down.

My business had racked up its greatest ever success in that Epsom race, but it had then been placed in serious peril, both by my own actions and by those of others, jeopardy that was ongoing, with Squeaky Voice still out there somewhere, and today's headline in the *Racing Post* likely to produce more awkward questions for me to answer.

On top of all that, my marriage had begun to disintegrate, and my children had deserted me. And that was not even mentioning the fact that Amanda had been kidnapped from our party by an unknown assailant, and she was, even now, being threatened with death—not that she knew anything about it.

On the plus side, Potassium had again proven himself to be the real deal by winning the St James's Palace Stakes, and my other Victrix horses were performing either at or above expectations. And perhaps best of all, my long-term sexual slumbers had been reawakened by a beauty from Lexington, Kentucky.

* * *

It took me just over an hour to drive from Ascot to home, arriving back at half past seven.

Surprisingly, Toni and I didn't talk much on the journey, although she did occasionally say how "cute" she thought the English villages were that we passed through.

Maybe there was too much going on in our heads for conversation.

I know there was in mine.

I turned in through the white-painted gates onto my driveway.

"How lovely," Toni said as I pulled up close to the front door.

"It's mock Georgian," I said, looking at the house. "It was built in the 1970s but was made to look much older."

I got out of the Jaguar.

"Just wait there a minute," I said to her. "I need to check something."

I went in through the front door.

"Anyone home?" I shouted loudly in the hallway, just in case Georgina had returned without telling me, or Amanda was back at home—even though there was no sign of her car in the driveway.

There was no reply, but I climbed halfway up the stairs and shouted it again, to make sure that I could be heard in the bedrooms and the bathrooms. But there was still no reply, and I could hear no running water, such as in a shower.

All was silent.

The house was deserted.

I went back out to the car, and having looked all around to ensure there was no one walking up the drive and no nosey neighbours peering over the fence, I opened the car door and ushered Toni quickly into the house, firmly closing the front door behind her.

She wandered around the ground floor, looking into every room.

"It's really nice," she said.

"Do you want a drink?" I asked. I was quite sure I did.

"What have you got?"

"Everything."

"Wine?"

"Red or white? I'm going to have some red."

"That'll do just fine," she said. "I've had so much champagne over the last few days that it's given me acid."

We went into the kitchen, and I opened the larder, where I stored the good wines—those saved for special occasions—and selected a 2017 Châteauneuf-du-Pape, which Georgina and I had been given the previous Christmas.

I removed the cork and poured two generous glassfuls.

I gave Toni one, and she drank from it.

"How long have you lived here?" she asked.

"Seventeen years."

What am I doing, putting all of this at risk?

"Food?" I asked, going across the kitchen to look in the fridge.

"Sex first," she said. "Food second."

I hesitated, but not about *if*, more about *where*.

I baulked at the idea of having sex with someone else in the bed I normally shared with Georgina, and Toni seemed to read my mind.

"Living room," she said decisively.

She turned on her heel and walked briskly out of the kitchen.

I picked up my glass of wine and followed her.

25

WE DID IT on the sheepskin rug in front of the fire, not that the fire was lit.

It was us that generated all the heat.

She started by making me sit on the sofa while she stood in front of me and undressed, slowly and seductively removing every piece of her clothing, not that she had been wearing very much in the first place.

Then she made me stand up, and she undressed me.

"I still can't get over all these goddam buttons," she said, struggling to undo the fly of my trousers. But she managed it.

Our lovemaking was more measured this time, more sensual, and to my mind, far more satisfying.

We lay together naked for some time afterwards, side by side on the rug.

"That was lovely," she said.

I snuggled into her. "It certainly was."

My phone started ringing in the kitchen.

"I'd better get that," I said, thinking it might be Georgina.

I jumped up and ran to the phone, catching it just before it went to voicemail. *Amanda* was the name of the caller, as shown on the home page.

"Hello, darling," I said, answering it. But it wasn't Amanda.

"Mr Newton," said a male voice. "This is Darren."

"What's wrong?" I asked.

"Amanda has gone missing again."

My heart missed a beat, or even more.

"When?" I asked.

"She popped out to get me some beers from the local shop just after seven o'clock, and she hasn't come back."

I looked at the digital clock on the electric cooker. It read 21.05. She'd been gone for two hours.

"Have you been out to look for her?"

"I went down to the shop, but they said she never came in."

And she obviously didn't have her phone with her because Darren was calling me on it.

"Had she taken anything?" I asked.

"Like what?"

"Drugs."

"Just a bit of weed."

Me getting angry with him about that wouldn't help the situation.

"Did she say anything to you before leaving?" I asked.

"She said that she'd only be a few minutes."

"Did she take any money?"

"Only the fiver I gave her for the beer."

"How about her car?" I asked.

"It's still parked across the road. I'm looking at it now. And she's not in that either. I looked. And the keys are still on the side."

"Did she take anything else?"

"I don't think so."

"What was she wearing?" I asked.

"Jeans and a black T-shirt."

"Shoes?"

"Flip-flops, I think."

It was hardly a dress code of choice if she was running away from him.

But how could anyone simply vanish in broad daylight? And it was broad daylight until almost ten o'clock at this point in June.

"Do not defy me. You were warned what would happen."

Toni came into the kitchen, still naked.

"What's wrong?" she asked in a whisper.

"Get dressed," I said equally quietly, and she went back towards the sitting room.

"What should I do?" Darren asked.

"Stay right where you are, in case she returns. I will call you on this number later, but call me first if she comes back in the meantime."

We hung up.

I stood there in the kitchen, stark naked, shaking uncontrollably, but not from cold. It was from fear.

Toni came back into the kitchen, now again wearing her yellow dress.

"What's wrong?" she asked with a concerned look on her face.

"My daughter, Amanda, has gone missing." I could hardly speak.

"Missing? How?"

I explained how she had gone out to a local shop to buy beers for her boyfriend, but had not returned to his flat.

"Where's the shop?" Toni asked.

"In Didcot," I replied. "It's a local town about three miles away."

"Do you think she might be coming here?"

I hadn't thought of that.

"You'd better get dressed, just in case."

My phone rang again, and I grabbed it.

"Hello."

"Hi, Dad. Have you scanned my passport yet?"

It was James.

"I'm just going to look for it now," I said, doing my best to keep my voice calm. "I haven't been back long from Ascot."

"I texted you the agency email," he said. "And also my postal address, to send it to me tomorrow. Don't forget,"

"I won't. I promise."

"Good. Must dash. Me and Gary are off to a party."

He disconnected.

"What was all that about?" Toni asked.

"That was my son, James. He wants me to scan his passport and email it to a letting agency. He's trying to rent a flat and they need to see his passport to prove he is who he says he is."

"Why didn't you tell him about his sister?"

"I don't want to worry him. Not until we know what's happened to her."

Oh God. What *had* happened to her?

And was it my fault for allowing Potassium to win?

But how could I have stopped the horse from winning anyway?

I'd never had the chance to remove any weights from the jockey's weight cloth, even if I'd wanted to—which I hadn't.

*   *   *

I collected my clothes from the sofa and went upstairs. Toni came up with me, and while I dressed in jeans and a polo shirt, she had a wander around the bedrooms.

The house was basically rectangular, with a bedroom in each corner. There were also two bathrooms, built between the bedrooms on each long side. One was en suite to the master, and the other opened onto the landing, and was shared between the other three bedrooms.

"So what are you going to do?" Toni asked.

"About what?"

"Your daughter, of course. You need to call the cops."

Did I?

"She's not been missing for long enough," I said. "They won't do anything."

"You need to call them anyway."

"Let's see if she turns up here first."

Although I couldn't think how she could get here. I knew that five pounds wasn't enough to pay for a taxi all the way from Didcot. There were no buses in the evenings, and she surely wouldn't walk three and a half miles in flip-flops.

I didn't want to let my mind settle on the most obvious conclusion—that she'd been abducted again by Squeaky Voice.

"I think I ought to go out and look for her," I said.

"But where?"

"I don't know." I could feel the panic rising in my throat, just as it had on Tuesday after I'd received the *Do not defy me* text message. "I just don't feel I can sit here doing nothing."

"How about finding your son's passport?" Toni said.

"That will have to wait."

"No. Do it now. Then it'll be done, and it will also occupy your mind for a while to stop you panicking about your daughter. In the meantime, she might show up, either here or back with her boyfriend. What's his name?"

"Darren," I said. "And I don't like him."

She laughed. "No father ever likes his daughter's boyfriend. It's a given."

"But Darren is very controlling, and he also gives her drugs. If Amanda has gone missing because she's run away from him, I'd be delighted."

"There you are, then," Toni said. "Maybe it's a good thing."

But deep down, I knew it wasn't.

* * *

James's passport was more elusive than he had claimed.

I went through the top drawer of his desk, where he'd said it could be found, but it was nowhere to be seen. The drawer was absolutely crammed full of stuff. In the end I turned everything out onto his bed. But still I couldn't see any passport.

I put everything back into the drawer, one item at a time, but there was definitely no passport present.

The desk had three drawers, and I opened the second one down. It was equally crammed full of stuff, all of it in a complete jumble. I tipped it all out onto the bed and went through it piece by piece. But there was still no sign of any passport.

The third drawer was deeper than the top two, and tidy by comparison. There were four large, black, hardback notebooks in a stack, and under them, a couple of printed leaflets.

I lifted the notebooks out and separated each one, flicking through the pages just in case the passport was hiding amongst them. It wasn't.

As a last resort, I removed all the drawers completely, and there was James's passport, at the back, at the bottom, leaning up against the rear panel.

"There you are," I said, relieved.

I reached in and picked it up.

"Found it?" Toni asked, coming into the room.

"Finally," I said, holding the passport up triumphantly. "It must have fallen down the back from the overfull top drawer."

"What's all this?" she asked, waving a hand at the stuff still lying on the bed.

"I emptied the drawers out."

Toni lifted one of the printed leaflets off the bed, one of those that had been under the black notebooks.

"BUGS," she said.

"What's that?"

"BUGS. That what it says on this flyer." She held up one of the leaflets. "The Bristol University Gambling Society."

"What about it?" I asked.

"This flyer. It's advertising material: *Join the Bristol University Gambling Society and get a guaranteed return on your stake money.*'"

"Guaranteed return?" I said. "They must be joking. Have you ever met a poor bookmaker?"

"I've never met any bookmakers," she replied.

"I just hope that James isn't wasting his money." I held up the passport. "Come on. Let's go and scan this in my office."

"How about this mess?" Toni said, pointing at the stuff still lying on the bed.

"I'll deal with it later."

We went downstairs, through the kitchen and utility room, to my office.

"This house just keeps on giving," Toni said in her broad Southern accent. "I have two beds and a bath upstairs, and a kitchen and living room downstairs. That's it. No frills. No extras."

I put the picture page of the passport face down on the scanner and made the copy, which I then emailed to the letting agency, using the address James had texted to me, with a cc to him. I left the passport lying on my desk.

"Remind me to post that to him in the morning."

Toni put the BUGS leaflet down on my desk next to it.

"Now what?" she said.

She had been right. Scanning the passport had taken my mind off the most pressing issue of the moment, if only for a while. Now it all came flooding back with a vengeance.

"Hadn't you better call your wife?" Toni said.

"I'll call the boyfriend first."

I pressed Amanda's number on my phone.

"Hello," Darren said, answering at the first ring.

"Is she back?" I asked.

"No."

I looked up at the clock on my office wall. It was ten minutes to ten. She'd now been missing for almost three hours.

"Did you and Amanda have another argument?" I asked him.

"No," he replied, but there was something in the tone of his voice that slightly worried me. But it might just have been because he didn't like me.

"I think I should call the police," I said.

"The police?" He didn't sound at all happy about that.

"Yes," I said. "The police. No doubt, they will want to interview you. Are you sure there is nothing more you want to tell me? Like, are you responsible for Amanda's disappearance?"

"What do you mean?" he said.

"Have you done something to her?" I asked him outright.

"No. Of course not."

Did I believe him?

Maybe I did. Or maybe I didn't.

CHAPTER

26

AMAZINGLY, DETECTIVE SERGEANT Christine Royle answered her phone at the first ring.

"I didn't think you'd be working at this late hour," I said.

"I'm not. I redirect my office line to my mobile. Who is this?"

"Chester Newton," I said. "My daughter, Amanda, was abducted three weeks ago. You came to my house."

"Yes, Mr Newton," she said. "I remember. How can I help you?"

"She's gone missing again."

"Where from?" the DS asked.

"From Darren Williamson's flat in Didcot. It seems she popped out to go to the local shop at seven o'clock and has not come back. Darren says he went to the shop, looking for her, but the shopkeeper told him she never went in."

"Where is this flat?"

"Above the Raj Tandoori takeaway, near Didcot station."

"What was she wearing?"

"Jeans and a black T-shirt. And flip-flops."

"Did she take anything with her?"

"Nothing," I said. "Not even her phone. Just a five-pound note."

Not even some honey and plenty of money, I thought, my mind wandering for some reason to Edward Lear.

"No other clothes or shoes?"

"No," I said. "Darren Williamson told me she took nothing. She told him that she'd only be a few minutes."

"Lots of people say that who want to go missing."

"But why would she?" I said, getting somewhat agitated by the detective's lack of urgency. "If you remember, she didn't *want* to go missing last time. Someone injected her with ketamine and abducted her."

"Are you implying that the two events are linked?"

"Bit too much of a coincidence otherwise."

"But why would the same person take her again?" she asked.

What could I say?

Because I didn't stop Potassium from winning the St James's Palace Stakes.

I don't think so.

I now so wished I'd told the police at the very beginning, after I'd received that first telephone call in the middle of the night at the Royal Berkshire Hospital.

But I hadn't.

And now I was complicit in race fixing.

My whole future life flashed before my eyes: financially ruined; warned off by all the worldwide racing authorities, with my reputation totally destroyed; divorced, and quite likely homeless—that's if my home wasn't a prison cell by then. And, worst of all, maybe with a dead daughter on my conscience as well.

"But you must think it's odd for someone to go missing twice in such quick succession."

"Mr Newton," she said slowly, "there are several members of the public in the Thames Valley Police region who go missing regularly, some of them almost on a weekly basis."

"I can assure you," I said firmly, "that my daughter is not one of those. She wouldn't be missing without good reason. I believe she must have been abducted again."

"Do you have any evidence for that?" she asked.

Yes, of course I do.

"No," I said.

"I will file a missing person report, which will mean that all police officers will be looking out for her. At this stage there is nothing more I can do."

"You could organise a search."

"Not at night," she said. "And not until we have some further information."

"So will you go now and interview Darren Williamson to get that further information?" I asked.

"We will speak to him in the morning—that's if your daughter is still missing. In the meantime, please inform me if she contacts you."

"Is that all?" I asked in frustration.

"All for now," said the detective. "Call me again in the morning."

She hung up.

"Why do you believe that someone would abduct your daughter?" Toni asked intently, having listened to my conversation with DS Royle, or at least my side of it.

"I don't know," I lied. "But someone did it before."

I told her about Amanda going missing from the party and turning up several hours later in Pangbourne, agitated and with ketamine in her system.

"But that's crazy," she said. "Who goes to all the bother of kidnapping someone and then lets them go without demanding a ransom?"

"You sound like an expert," I said.

"But it stands to reason," she said. "Kidnapping is a major crime. In the States, after the Lindbergh baby kidnap in the 1930s, right up until the 1960s, you could get the electric chair for kidnapping. That's before our stupid lawmakers worked out that no one would ever be released alive, even if a ransom was paid for them, because the kidnapper had nothing more to lose by then killing their hostage."

I rather wished she wouldn't talk about killing hostages.

But she was right.

Why would anyone go to all the bother of kidnapping Amanda, only to then let her go again?

The answer, of course, was to intimidate me into fixing races.

So what would be the value in killing her this time?

None at all.

If whoever was responsible wanted me to fix another race, then killing my only daughter would not be the sensible thing to do. Taking her for a second time must be just further intimidation to make me comply with his demands.

Either he must let her go again or keep her alive as his hostage while demanding that I fix more races. He would surely work out that to kill her would be totally counterproductive to his cause, not only because then I certainly wouldn't agree to any of his future demands, but also because it would bring the full force of the police down on his head.

But would he work it out in time? Before he carried through with his threat?

"Are you going to call your wife now?" Toni asked. "To tell her?"

"No," I said decisively. "I'm not. Not tonight. It would send her into a blind panic, and there is nothing she could do anyway, not from Harrogate."

"Harrogate?"

"Where her parents live. It's in Yorkshire."

She looked blank.

"About two hundred miles north."

"So she's not about to turn up here tonight?"

"Very unlikely," I said. "But Amanda might."

"Do you really think so?"

Did I?

Keeping a hostage safe, well, and unfound for days on end was not an easy task, especially if the kidnapper was intent on keeping his identity a secret from his victim. The necessary interactions between the two, to provide food, water, and sanitation, were fraught with difficulty and danger.

From a kidnapper's point of view, the ideal scenario was to receive a large ransom payment quickly, preferably before any such interactions were needed. But in this case, the ransom would likely be a demand for me to fix a horse race, and that would require considerable time to set up, maybe as long as five or six days, if I had to enter a horse for a specific contest for the fix.

In the meantime, I would demand proof that Amanda was still alive— perhaps a WhatsApp video of her holding up the front page of that day's *Times* newspaper—something that would likely place the kidnapper in even greater danger of her discovering his identity.

The obvious scenario, at least to me, was that Squeaky Voice would do what he had done before—release her and give me another opportunity to acquiesce to his demands, and threaten that the next time I didn't . . . it would be body bag time.

He would probably say that there would be no third chance. Except that the same arguments would still apply. If I didn't do what he wanted, would he actually kill Amanda, simply out of revenge? Or would he give up on me and find someone more compliant to terrorise?

So was it time for me to tell him to get stuffed and finally call his bluff?

That's if it was a bluff.

Could I afford to take that risk?

There was nothing more I could do now anyway, short of driving aimlessly around South Oxfordshire searching for Amanda. I had called the police to tell them she was missing, but I had no means of making contact with Squeaky Voice.

I simply had to wait for him to call me.

* * *

Toni found some spaghetti in a kitchen cupboard, plus some pasta sauce in the fridge, and set about making us a late supper while I went upstairs to put the things back into James's desk.

I put his middle drawer on the bed and put back into it all the stuff I had tipped out of it. Next I did the bottom drawer.

I put everything back just as I'd found it. I briefly flicked through the notebooks, but they were just full of equations and calculations, and a few lists, presumably something to do with his university maths course.

"It's ready," Toni called from downstairs.

"Coming," I shouted back.

I went down and we both sat at the kitchen table, eating spaghetti and drinking the rest of the red wine.

"So what now?" Toni asked as she laid down her fork.

"We wait. There's nothing else we can do. I've told the police, but they said they won't do anything until the morning at the earliest. If she *has* been kidnapped, I expect that there will be some sort of ransom demand."

"Why aren't your cops taking it more seriously?" she asked. "Back home, this would be a big deal."

"I suspect it's because she was taken before and released unharmed. And they also seem to think that she might have gone missing on purpose."

"Did they also think that last time?"

"I fear they did," I said. "But I don't know why. She was injected with ketamine and went missing from her own birthday party, when all her friends were here. She turned up three hours later, nine miles away, in a highly agitated state, and she couldn't have walked that far in the high heels she was wearing. She could hardly stand up in them."

"So how come the cops thought she disappeared on purpose?"

"Because she wasn't raped, and there was no ransom demand."

At least, I hadn't told them of one.

"But even so," Toni said, clearly quite angry on my behalf, "they should get a search party out now, looking for her."

"They don't have the manpower to search for everyone. I was told by a policeman that a person goes missing in this country every ninety seconds."

"And he's getting pretty fed up with it," she said, laughing at her own joke.

I smiled, just. It might have been funny under different circumstances.

"Sorry," Toni said.

My phone rang loudly into the silence.

I looked down at it lying on the table. *Georgina* was the name on the screen.

I picked up the phone and walked out of the kitchen into the sitting room, leaving Toni alone at the kitchen table. I closed the doors so she couldn't hear my conversation.

"Hello," I said, answering.

"I've been waiting for you to call me," Georgina said with a hint of irritation. "I'm going to bed now."

"Sorry. I fell asleep in front of the television. It was such a hot day at Ascot today. I'm totally exhausted."

"How are things at home?" she asked.

What could I say? "Fine, except your daughter has been kidnapped again, and I've just been screwing an American blonde on the rug in the sitting room?"

"All good," I said. "How's your father?"

"Remarkable, considering what he was like when I arrived. The new carers started today, and amazingly, he seemed to like them. He was even flirting with the girl."

"When are you coming home?" I asked.

"Are you missing me?"

"Of course."

"I think I should be here for the carers tomorrow, and maybe on Saturday as well. Mum seems a little better and slightly more positive, but it's hard for her, and I hate them being so far away. We've discussed about Dad going into a home, but Mum's not very happy. I think it's mostly because she doesn't want to be left alone in this house. She says she'll look after him for as long as she can. And the carers coming in every day will make a big difference."

"You stay there for as long as you need to," I said.

"I'll look up the trains for Sunday," Georgina said. "I'll have to come home soon because I'm running out of my medication."

"Sunday will be fine. I'll pick you up from the station."

My phone beeped and showed that I had another incoming call, but there was no indication of who was trying to reach me.

"I've got a call waiting," I said. "I'll speak to you in the morning."

"Okay," Georgina replied. "Night, night."

She hung up and, with a degree of trepidation, I touched the "Accept" button on my phone's screen.

"I told you it was easy to take your daughter," said the squeaky voice.

CHAPTER

27

"WHERE IS SHE?" I demanded.

"Safe and well," replied Squeaky Voice.

"Where is she?" I repeated.

"I'm giving you one last chance," he said, ignoring my question. "You will do as I tell you."

"No, I will not," I said adamantly. "You will release Amanda immediately, or I will go to the police and tell them all about these calls and give them your texts. I am sure they will be able to use them to trace you. They just do a tri-angulation from the mobile phone masts to your handset, and there you are."

I wasn't sure if that was true, but it sounded good—at least to me.

"How much do you value your daughter's life?" asked the voice.

"How much do you value your freedom?" I asked him in reply. "The maximum sentence for kidnapping is life imprisonment. You'd probably get a whole life term if you also kill your hostage."

I was still guessing, but he wasn't to know.

"You would die in prison. And kidnappers never get an easy time inside. You'd have to continually watch out in the showers, the cold showers, or you might get your balls slashed off. Or they'd keep you in solitary, year after year after every bloody year, for the rest of your rotten life. You'd go barking mad. Are you ready for all that?"

There was a slight pause.

"You will not get another chance," he said.

"Nor will you," I said straight back at him. "Release her right now or I'll call the police and tell them everything."

Well, almost everything.

"She's already released," said Squeaky Voice.

Did I detect a touch of contrition? Or was I imagining it?

"So where is she?" I asked.

He didn't answer. He just hung up.

I ruefully smiled at myself in the mirror above the fireplace. I thought that had gone rather well. But had I really removed that particular monkey from my back, or would he still come back for more?

Now I had to make sure that Amanda had indeed been released and that she was unharmed.

As if on cue, my phone rang again, and *Amanda* appeared on the screen. I grabbed it, but it wasn't her calling me.

"She's back," Darren said.

Thank God, I thought.

"Let me speak to her," I said.

"She doesn't want to speak to you."

"I don't care. Give her the bloody phone."

There was a slight pause.

"Dad?" said Amanda, coming on the line.

"Darling, are you all right?" I asked in my most compassionate tone.

"I'm fine," she said.

"Where have you been?" I asked.

"I was on my way to the shop when someone came up behind me and put a sack over my head and shoulders. I was bundled into the back of a van. Then I've been driven around for ages."

"How did you get away?"

"The van stopped and the back door was opened. I was told to get out, and then just left on the side of the road. The van drove away."

"Where were you dropped?"

"In Didcot. Not far away. I walked back here."

"Did you see the man?" I asked. "Or the van?"

"I had the sack over me all the time. I was told not to remove it or he would hit me. I was so scared."

"It's all right, darling. You're safe now."

Or moderately so, considering she was still with Darren.

"Do you still have the sack?" I asked.

"No. After I heard the van drive off. I took it off. I left it there."

"What sort of sack was it?"

"It was just a sack."

"But was it made of plastic, like a rubbish sack? Or was it hessian?"

"Dad, I don't know. Okay?"

But there were so many other questions I also wanted to ask her.

"Can I come over and see you?" I asked. "I could bring you home."

But what will I do with Toni? I thought.

I looked at the clock on the mantelpiece. It was quarter past eleven. I knew that the last train from Didcot to Paddington wasn't until after midnight. Toni would have to catch that and take a taxi back to her hotel.

"No, Dad," Amanda said firmly. "I'm fine here. I want to go to bed now."

"Are you sure?"

"Quite sure."

"Then call me in the morning," I said.

"Okay," she said, but I wasn't that confident that she would.

We disconnected and I went back to the kitchen.

"Amanda is back," I said.

Toni looked up at me sharply. "Back where?"

"At her boyfriend's flat."

"For a moment, I thought you meant she was here."

"No, but she *was* abducted. Someone put a sack over her head and shoulders and then bundled her into a van. Whoever it was drove her around for four hours, then let her go."

"Is she all right?" Toni asked.

"Seems to be. Obviously a bit shaken. And she said she was scared."

"But why?

"Why what?"

"Why kidnap someone and then not ask for a ransom? It doesn't make sense."

She was right, there.

None of this made any sense.

*   *   *

Toni and I spent the night together in the double bed in the guest room, but somewhat embarrassingly, my enthusiasm for more sex had evaporated. Even if my mind had been willing, my body wasn't.

Maybe it was because I had so much else going on in my head.

Having intercourse with Toni in the sitting room of this house, and also lying to my wife about having fallen asleep in front of the television, suddenly made me feel incredibly guilty.

"I'm sorry," I said.

"That's all right," Toni said. "We'll have another try in the morning."

She seemed to go straight to sleep while I lay awake in the dark for ages, trying to sort other things out.

Had I finally rid myself of Squeaky Voice?

I liked to think so, but I wasn't so sure.

Maybe he would try a different tactic.

So far, he hadn't actually harmed anybody—not physically anyway—apart from a single injection into Amanda's neck. I had called his bluff about killing her, but that didn't mean he couldn't now threaten to hurt her, maybe cut her face or throw something corrosive over her, or over Georgina, or even over James or me.

How ruthless was he? And would he react badly to my determination not to do as he asked?

Was it now time for me to try harder to find out who he was?

But how?

I had to start by talking to Amanda, to find out if there was some clue she had found out, even if she didn't realise it, and use it to build a trap.

*　*　*

Toni tried her best to get me interested in more sex on Friday morning, waking me by cuddling up to my back, and allowing her hands to wander down between my legs.

It was successful to a degree, insofar that my body was now willing, but my mind was seemingly elsewhere, and I don't think she found the experience hugely satisfying. Neither did I.

With a slight sigh, she climbed out of bed, and I heard her in the shower.

I also stood up and went downstairs to my office in my dressing gown.

My first call of the day was to DS Royle's number.

She answered almost immediately.

"My daughter is safe," I said. "She returned home to her boyfriend's flat late last night."

"Good," said the detective. "Did she say where she'd been?"

"Someone put a sack over her head and bundled her into a van. She was driven around for several hours and then left at the side of the road in Didcot."

"Did she see the person who did this?"

"It seems not. She had the sack over her head all the time until after the van had driven away."

"Was she harmed? Or abused?"

"No, other than she said she was very frightened."

"Did you pay a ransom?" the DS asked.

"No," I said. "I never received a demand for one."

"How strange."

"What are you going to do now?" I asked. "Will you interview her?"

"I may send my detective constable to see her in due course."

That sounded very much like a "no" to me.

"Surely an abduction of a young woman in broad daylight demands the attention of at least a detective sergeant."

"That's if an abduction did take place."

"Are you calling my daughter a liar?"

"I just think it's odd that no ransom was demanded and she was released totally untouched."

What the detective didn't know was that a ransom had been demanded. Maybe not a monetary one, but a ransom, nevertheless.

I wondered if I should tell her about it, but there would then be too many difficult questions to answer, not least why I hadn't mentioned it to her before.

If I had finally managed to rid myself of Squeaky Voice, it would surely not be a good time, or a good idea, to unnecessarily open myself to allegations of race fixing.

After the police detective, I called my list of trainers, the first of whom was Malcolm Galbraith, the jump trainer who'd been at the party, and who lived in the village over the hill. The one Victrix horse in his yard, Casillero, had been declared to run that afternoon in the Summer Plate Trial Handicap Steeplechase at Market Rasen in Lincolnshire, about a hundred and sixty miles north.

"Morning, Malcolm," I said. "All good for today?"

"Fine," he said. "Cassy went up yesterday. She's not a very good traveller, so I've given her overnight to recover. She'll be fine by this afternoon."

"Are you going?" I asked.

"No. My travelling head lad will do the necessary. He went up in the horsebox with her. I'm off to Ascot for the day."

"So am I. I might see you there. I'll watch Cassy's race in the Owners and Trainers' Bar. What time is it?"

"Five to four. I'll meet you there to watch it with you."

We disconnected and I quickly rang the rest of the trainers on my list.

At about half past eight, as I was finishing the last of my calls, Toni came into the office, wearing her yellow dress and holding her hat.

"I've decided not to go to the races today after all," she said. "It seems a shame to come all this way and not see something else of England other than the Ascot racetrack. I was too tired Monday, and this is my last day, so I'm going to go see some of the sights instead. Can you put me on a train to London?"

"Of course," I said. "But it's a shame when you've already paid for your badge."

"The Farquhars bought it for me."

That was all right, then.

"How about tonight?" I asked.

"I'm going to have an early night," she said. "My flight to Cincinnati departs at half past eight in the morning, so I need to be at Heathrow soon after six. I have a car booked for five-thirty. Sorry."

To be honest, I was relieved.

I felt this adventure had run its course, and I think she did too.

* * *

I dropped her at Didcot station at a quarter to ten.

She reached up and kissed me goodbye.

"It's been great," she said. "Thank you."

"Thank you too," I replied.

"If you're ever in Lexington, give me a call. We could do it again—just for old times' sake."

I watched her walk away from me, and she turned once to wave before disappearing into the station entrance.

I sighed. It had indeed been great. A reawakening.

In fact, I wondered if my life could ever be the same again.

I climbed back into the Jaguar, feeling slightly forlorn that she had gone.

"Come on," I said to myself. "Pull yourself together."

I started the car and drove out of the station forecourt without so much as a backward glance, putting that chapter literally and symbolically behind me.

Next I went to the post office on the Broadway, to send James's passport to his current flat address, paying extra for Special Delivery by one PM on a Saturday.

When I'd sat at my desk earlier, packing the passport into an envelope, I'd enclosed with it the Bristol University Gambling Society leaflet, but only after I'd written across it in bold black marker pen: *Don't get involved with this. There's no such thing as a guaranteed return on your stake.*

As I was already in Didcot, I decided to drive to the Raj Tandoori.

I parked on the road opposite and called Amanda.

"I told you never to call this number," she said, answering at the second ring.

"But I need to talk to you," I said.

"Is Grandpa all right?" she asked.

"He's fine," I said.

"So why are you calling?"

"I need to talk to you about last night."

"What about it?" she asked. "I told you what happened."

"Have you remembered anything else, something that might help catch the person who did this to you?"

"No."

"How about the sack? Where did you leave it?"

"On the road?"

"Which road?"

"Dad, I don't know. I was panicking. I ran until I found something I recognised. Then I came home."

She was getting quite agitated.

"It's all right, darling," I said. "I'm sorry. I didn't mean to upset you. But if you do remember anything else, please call me."

"There is one thing," she said. "Either the sack or the van smelled of dogs."

"Dogs?"

"Yes, you know, that musty smell you get from wet dogs."

Or maybe from wet hessian, I thought.

"Where are you now?" I asked her.

"At work. I'm on earlies at the supermarket this week. It's my break time."

So I was wasting my time being here outside Darren's flat.

"What time do you finish?"

"Four."

I'd be at Ascot watching Casillero's race from Market Rasen in the Owners and Trainers' Bar. There was no way I could be here to collect her.

"I have to be at Ascot today at four o'clock. So can Darren come and collect you from work, to take you back to his flat?"

"Stop being silly, Dad."

"I'm not being silly. I'm worried about you."

"Don't be. I'm fine."

"Please be careful," I said. "Don't go out on your own at night, and keep away from dark alleys."

"I promise I'll be careful," she replied in a sort of "please don't treat me like a little girl" tone. "I have to go now as I'm due back at work."

She hung up.

Who did I know who owned dogs?

28

THE OFFICIAL ATTENDANCE numbers showed that there were slightly fewer people at Royal Ascot on Friday than there had been for the Gold Cup the previous day, not that you would have noticed it.

Not having an invitation to lunch or a complimentary meal on offer as one of the day's owners, I didn't arrive at the racecourse until after the Royal Procession, to avoid the worst of the traffic.

I had spent the rest of the morning, after my trip to Didcot, ensuring that all was as it should be in the house. I had stripped the guest-room bed and put the linen in the washing machine, and placed all our dinner and breakfast things in the dishwasher.

Georgina was a stickler for having everything in the kitchen just as *she* wanted it, and she was not happy if anyone put something back in the wrong place. So, I'd been through all the drawers checking that Toni hadn't inadvertently put a wooden spoon back in with the metal ones, because Georgina would have noticed.

I'd had a good look at the sheepskin rug in front of the fire to search for any stray blonde hairs, and I checked for the same in the plugholes of the family bathroom where Toni had showered.

Satisfied that everything was in order, and there were no traces of Toni's perfume lingering in the air, I changed into my morning dress and set off for the races.

The highlights for Friday were two Group 1 races: a six-furlong dash for three-year-olds of either sex, and a mile trip for three-year-old fillies only, the girls' equivalent of the St James's Palace Stakes for the boys, which Potassium had won on Tuesday.

There are currently eight Group 1 races over the five days of Royal Ascot, but age and sex restrictions, and differing distances, mean that for any given top horse there is really only one Group 1 race on offer, even though a few horses have raced in the five-furlong sprint on Tuesday and then again just four days later in the six-furlong Jubilee Stakes on Saturday. Some have even won both, a five-year-old bay stallion called Blue Point being the most recent, in 2019.

All the races are part of the British Champion Series of thirty-five Group 1 races, which culminates in the championship finals on British Champions Day, back here at Ascot in October.

I wandered into the enclosures as the first race of the day was being run.

I had two appointments with potential future syndicate members in addition to the one with Malcolm Galbraith to watch Casillero's race from Market Rasen.

Even though I had not been invited to lunch, a long-standing multi-syndicate member of mine, Jim Green, had rented a private box for the day, and he wanted me to pop along for a drink, to have a quiet word with a friend of his. The friend was considering dipping his toes into horse ownership, and Jim thought that his joining one of my syndicates was a sensible first step.

"Come up after the first race," Jim had said when he'd called me earlier. "Box 359. We'll have finished lunch by then."

So I now made my way up to the third level, to Box 359 at the far eastern end of the grandstand, knocked on the door, and went in.

Eight people were sitting around a table down the centre of the box and, of course, they hadn't finished their lunch, but at least they were on dessert. There were four men and four women, with Jim Green at the end closest to the door.

"Come in, Chester. Come in," Jim said effusively, standing up. "May I introduce Patrick and Lucinda Hogg, Geoff and Virginia Sterling, Martin and Elizabeth Atherton—and you know Gemma. This is Chester Newton, who runs the syndicates I was telling you about."

I waved at them. "Good to meet you."

"What would you like to drink?" Jim said.

"A small red wine would be great," I replied.

One of the two catering staff in the box handed me a glass of red, which no one could ever claim was small. It must have contained about a third of a bottle.

"Sit here," Jim said, pointing at his chair. "I've finished anyway."

He stood to the side.

"Now," he said loudly, "Chester is going to talk you all into becoming racehorse owners by joining one of his syndicates. Isn't that right, Chester?"

"If you say so, Jim," I responded with a laugh.

It was hardly the "quiet word" I'd been promised.

I gave them my usual spiel about how, by signing up with Victrix Racing, they could have all the excitement of horse ownership but without the huge outlay or the worry of ever-expanding bills to pay.

For between eight and thirty thousand pounds initially, and about half of that in the second year, depending on the cost of the horse, they could enjoy all the benefits and fun of being an "owner." And they would get to share not only in the prize money but also in any resale proceeds.

I explained how each of the twelve shareholders of Potassium had received fifty thousand pounds in prize money as a result of him winning the Derby, with another twenty-one thousand for his victory here on Tuesday, all of it completely free of tax, and all for an initial outlay of only nineteen thousand, to say nothing of the millions that the horse was now worth.

"So what's the catch?" the man at the far end of the table asked bluntly.

"The catch is that you might very well lose the lot," I said, looking straight back at him. "Horses as good as Potassium are extremely rare. Don't go into horse ownership if you are looking for a sound investment, one that gives you a safe return on your capital. It may, but that will be only if you are very, very lucky. Far more owners lose money than make any. Look upon it as buying into a way of life—an indulgence—and then you might enjoy losing your cash."

I could see some of the women shaking their heads, as if they had other plans for between eight and thirty thousand pounds of surplus family funds.

I wondered if Gemma had the slightest idea how much Jim had invested in horseflesh through me over the years. Perhaps I wouldn't ask her.

"I like you, Chester Newton," said the man at the far end. "You talk straight, which is more than I can say for most of the bloodstock agents I've met."

I didn't think of myself as a bloodstock agent, but I wasn't going to argue.

The second race, the Group 1 six-furlong dash, The Commonwealth Cup, was about to start, so we all went out onto the balcony to watch it.

Such is the length of the huge grandstand at Ascot that Jim Green's box was almost nearer to the start than it was to the winning post.

I found myself standing next to the man who had asked me about the catch.

"Patrick Hogg," he said, holding out a hand.

"Good to meet you," I said, shaking it.

"I think Jim asked you here because of me," Patrick said. "I've been interested in becoming an owner for some time."

"They're off," shouted the commentator over the PA system.

The thirteen runners jumped out of the starting stalls in a jagged line.

Patrick and I watched the race unfolding in front of us.

"Have you had a bet?" I asked him.

"Just a small one," he replied. "To make it interesting."

"It would be more interesting if you owned one of them," I said, turning to him.

He laughed. "Okay, okay. Enough. You have me already. Where do I sign?"

Now it was me who was laughing. "Nowhere yet. But I'll send you an invitation to our yearling parade in October, when I'll be showing off the horses that Victrix will buy at this autumn's sales. We also have a good lunch. You can sign up then if you still want to."

We watched the end of the race together.

"Hopeless," he said, screwing up his betting slip.

"What do you do for a living?" I asked.

"I'm a lawyer," he said. "A barrister."

"Like in court?"

He nodded. "Wigs, gowns, and wing collars. But, thankfully, no longer white lace cuffs, black britches, and silver buckled shoes—except on very special occasions." He smiled.

"Do you do criminal work?" I asked.

"Most of the time these days," he said. "I did do civil stuff in the past— mostly highly contested divorces—but I got fed up with dealing with people who were consumed with hate for someone they once loved enough to marry. So I switched to criminal work. Not that the hate disappeared completely. But in recent years, I seem to have found my niche in fraud, where the hate is minimal."

I wondered if race fixing was fraud, and decided it probably was.

"Prosecuting or defending?" I asked.

"Both," he said. "But obviously not in the same case. It depends on which side's solicitors instruct me first. But I also do quite a lot of prosecution work for the government—tax evasion cases mostly."

"Do you always win?" I asked.

"What sort of question is that from someone involved in horseracing?"

"I'll take that to be a "no" then."

"Some juries just don't seem to understand what I'm telling them."

He laughed again, and I laughed with him.

I liked him, and I felt that the feeling was mutual.

"Here," he said, smiling. "Take this."

He handed me one of his business cards—Patrick J Hogg, KC, Middle Temple. I took it and put it in my pocket.

"Thanks, Patrick," I said. "I'll be in touch about the yearling parade."

* * *

Malcolm Galbraith was at the Owners and Trainers' Bar ahead of me.

"What are you having?" he asked as I arrived. "A pint?"

He held up his own.

"No, thanks. Just some fizzy water. I have to drive later."

And I hadn't got out of Jim Green's box without having a second large glass of red wine thrust into my hand, even though I'd hardly touched it.

The two-mile five-furlong Summer Plate Trial Handicap Chase was the feature race of the day at Market Rasen.

As its name suggested, this race was a trial for the Summer Plate Handicap Chase, the premier steeplechase of the summer months, which would be run at the same course in four weeks' time. A good showing in today's trial might encourage Malcolm and me to enter Casillero for the main one.

In the past, jump racing had always been a winter sport while flat racing took place in the summer, but both now occur pretty much throughout the year.

When I was a child, the thought of there being a jumps fixture on the same day as Royal Ascot would have been laughable, yet this year, three of the five days were now shared with a jump meeting somewhere in the country.

"How do you think Cassy will go?" I asked Malcolm.

"Fair to middling," he replied.

Malcolm was never one to be overly confident about any of his horses' chances. "Fair to middling" was about as good as I could have expected, and was certainly a step up from his other favourite prediction: "Should get round."

Market Rasen is a slightly undulating, right-handed, ten-furlong oval track, with sharp bends at either end. There are four fences in the back stretch, two of which are open ditches, and three more plain fences in the home straight.

The two-mile five-furlong start is in front of the grandstands, and the ten runners in this race therefore had to negotiate two complete circuits of the course, jumping each of the seven fences twice, making fourteen in total.

Malcolm and I watched on one of the television screens as the horses circled before being called into line by the starter.

Unlike in flat racing, where starting stalls are used, jump races are started behind a tape, and there is no draw for starting position. When the starter was satisfied that all were ready, he lowered his flag and released the tape, and "They're off!"

The early pace was rather pedestrian, and the group of ten were bunched closely together around the first bend, with Casillero running in fifth or sixth. They all negotiated the first plain fence in the back straight with no problem. Next up was an open ditch, but the fences at Market Rasen are considered fairly easy, and it also caused no concerns.

Only when the group turned into the home straight for the first time, did the tempo really pick up, and that was because Casillero's jockey took the initiative and pushed her to the front.

"About bloody time," Malcolm said under his breath. "I told him not to let it go too slow for too long. Cassy is well placed in the handicap, and we need to make sure that lower weight has its full effect."

The injection of pace quickly spread out the field such that there were twenty lengths or more from first to last as they made their way along the back straight for the second and last time.

Casillero was still in front as they turned for home, but she hadn't shaken off two of the others, and one of those came past her going into the last fence, in spite of it carrying six pounds more on its back.

"Second," Malcolm said as they crossed the finish line. "Not too bad, I suppose."

But I could tell he was disappointed.

"They went too slow on that first circuit," he said. "I should have been there."

"Don't beat yourself up," I said. "Second is good. I think we should enter her for the Summer Plate next month."

"It's quite a step up," Malcolm said, always being cautious. "Today's trial was only rated as a Class 3 contest. The Plate itself is a Class 1."

"I think we should still give it a go. Especially if she remains favourably handicapped."

I had to be careful, though. Consistently aiming a fairly average horse too high could easily produce a string of mediocre results. No syndicate member would prefer their horse to be fourth or fifth out of twelve runners in a Class 1 contest, when they could have won at Class 4.

In horseracing, winning was everything, even if the prize money was small. And my number-one priority was keeping my syndicate members happy, to keep them coming back to me, year on year.

"Are you here tomorrow?" I asked Malcolm. "Victrix has a four-year-old called Wayleave running in the Wokingham."

He laughed. "Well, good luck with that," he said. "I'm taking a rare day off from the gee-gees tomorrow. I'm going to a wedding. Mind you, I'll still be dressed up like this." He waved up and down at his morning dress. "Barbara's nephew is getting married in Bath."

"Aren't you wearing a kilt?"

He looked at me. "You'd do well to mind your language." He laughed again. "Actually, I do have a kilt somewhere, but the waistband is a good eight inches too short for me these days. Can't imagine why. It must have shrunk in the wash."

He took another large swig of beer, and I reckoned I knew the real culprit.

My phone rang.

I looked at it: *No Caller ID.*

Oh God, I thought. *Not again.*

"I'd better take this," I said to Malcolm, turning and walking away from him.

"What the bloody hell do you want?" I said, answering the call.

"I just wanted to know if you liked my piece about you in the *Post* yesterday," said a normal voice.

"Oh, Jerry," I replied. "I'm so sorry—I thought you were someone else."

"I should hope so."

"The piece was lovely, thank you. Although I wasn't so happy with your front-page article."

"I'm sure. And I have more news on that. I've managed to acquire a copy of the CCTV footage from the Lingfield weighing room from that day, and it clearly shows that Tim Westlake weighed out correctly at nine stone seven pounds. So Owen Reynolds assertion that they must have made a mistake weighing him out is definitely not correct."

"So what are you going to do about it?" I asked, trying hard to keep the worry out of my voice.

"Not much I can do," he said. "I've asked the online gambling companies, in particular the exchanges, to tell me if there was any unusual betting recorded on that race, especially any evidence of anyone taking large number of lays on Dream Filler or offering better lay odds than everyone else. I'm still waiting to hear. The lawyers won't let me accuse anyone without cast-iron proof, and short of searching people's houses, I won't get that."

"You can search my house, if you like."

He laughed. "You had nothing to gain by fixing the race."

"But why do you clearly think that Owen did?"

"Owen is a gambler," he said. "Everyone knows that. But you're not."

That's what he thought.

29

I FOUND THE HOUSE quite lonely again on Friday evening.

I arrived home from Ascot about seven, having spent an hour with another prospective syndicate member discussing the minute details of the syndicate contract. By the time I managed to prise myself away, I wasn't at all sure I wanted him as one of my future syndicate members anyway. I could see that he was going to be far too demanding, and it was trouble I could probably do without.

I took the guest-bedroom linen out of the washing machine and placed it in the tumble dryer rather than hanging it outside on the washing line. I didn't want Brian or Victoria Perry, our nosey neighbours, telling Georgina how domesticated I had been, washing the bed sheets, while she'd been away at her parents.

But the linen made me think of Toni, in particular her naked body curled up next to mine.

I cooked myself some scrambled eggs on toast, all the time wondering what Toni was doing at that very moment.

She had given me her phone number, but she'd also specifically told me not to call it while she was in the U.K., because of the exorbitant price her cell company charged her for overseas calls.

Should I call her at the hotel instead?

I got as far as looking up the hotel phone number on the internet before good sense took over.

"It's over," I told myself. "It was just a two-day dalliance. Leave it."

But I still couldn't stop thinking about her, especially when I took my food into the sitting room to eat while I watched the television, my feet resting on the sheepskin rug.

Georgina called me at nine o'clock.

"I'm missing you," she said. "And to be honest, I'm getting fed up with both of them."

"Your parents?"

"Yes. I've told Mum that I'll stay until Sunday, but I'd much rather come home tomorrow."

"I'll be at Ascot all afternoon," I said. "I have a runner in the fifth race."

"I can always get a taxi home from Didcot station. I'll let you know."

"Is everything else okay?" I asked.

"Yes. I think so."

"What do you mean, you think so?"

"I've had a few strange calls today on my mobile."

"What sort of calls?" I asked slowly.

"Calls with no one there, or at least no one who talked. Whoever it was just waited a few moments and then hung up."

"How many calls?"

"Five or six. I didn't answer them after the first three."

"Did the caller's number show up on your phone?" I asked.

"No. It just said *No Caller ID.*"

"Don't worry about it," I said. "They were probably auto-dial marketing calls."

"It's just a bit unnerving, that's all," she replied.

It certainly was.

*   *   *

Saturday morning dawned to grey skies and heavy rain. The hot, dry spell had definitely ended, with a weather front moving in from the Atlantic, and rain was forecast for the rest of the afternoon.

I thought about not bothering to go to the races, but Victrix had a runner, and I'd told both the trainer and the syndicate members that I'd be there.

I made my usual morning calls to all the trainers, discussing entries for the following week and making plans for the upcoming racing festivals at Newmarket, Goodwood, and York, for which some entries closed early.

Just after I finished the last of the calls, my phone rang.

No Caller ID.

I wondered if it was Jerry Parker again.

It wasn't.

"Chester Newton?" said the squeaky voice.

"Leave my wife alone," I shouted at him down the phone.

"Then do as you're told. Wayleave will lose today."

"Get lost."

I hung up.

Wayleave would probably lose anyway, whatever I did. There were twenty-nine declared runners for the Wokingham Stakes, a six-furlong handicap dash, and this particular race had a reputation for being a bit of a lottery.

But how did Squeaky Voice get Georgina's mobile number?

My number, yes—it was available on the Victrix website—but hers?

*   *   *

If anything, the rain was falling even heavier as I turned into Car Park 2 just before two o'clock. It was clearly going to be a very damp Royal Procession.

I had spent quite a lot of time, before I left home, remaking the guest-room bed and checking that everything was in order in the house, with no tell-tale signs of Toni's presence, such as a discarded wineglass with lipstick on the rim, just in case Georgina did decide to come home today rather than tomorrow.

I had also looked up on the internet that Toni's flight from Heathrow to Cincinnati had departed on time at half past eight—it had—and I felt somewhat bereft that she was, even now, hurtling through the atmosphere, away from me, at five hundred miles an hour.

Royal Ascot in the sunshine is delightful—gorgeous even. But in the rain, it can be a nightmare, especially on the Saturday with nearly seventy thousand people having bought tickets. There is simply insufficient cover for everyone.

Ladies splash through puddles in their open-toed Jimmy Choos while their male companions do their best to hold up large, plain golf umbrellas—no commercial logos or club crests allowed—to prevent the rain from making complete disasters of their wives' expansive—and expensive—headgear.

I made my way, under my own plain umbrella, to the Owners and Trainers' Dining Room for some lunch.

It was even busier than on Thursday, but some people were already finishing their meal and leaving, so I didn't have to wait too long for a table.

The Wokingham Stakes was the fifth race of the day, not due off until five o'clock, and I'd arranged to meet Wayleave's trainer outside the weighing room after the third, so I was in no hurry.

I was eventually shown to a table by the window, and thankfully this time I was on my own, so I didn't have to answer any awkward questions about missing weights.

I also wanted time alone, to think.

* * *

Wayleave didn't win the Wokingham Stakes, but it wasn't from his lack of effort.

He'd been drawn right in the middle, in starting stall fifteen, and as was often the case in these large-field handicaps, the horses split into two groups, one on either side of the racetrack.

Wayleave's jockey had the option of going either way, or even of staying alone down the centre. Having burst out of the stalls quickly to make the early running, he chose to join the group closest to the crowd, drifting to the left, towards the near running rail.

Indeed, most of the main action was taking place on the near side, with that group making the most of the better ground after the heavy rain earlier.

Wayleave held the lead until well inside the final furlong, before he was swallowed up close to the line by three from the group behind him. He finished a highly respectable fourth, collecting more than eight thousand pounds in prize money for his syndicate, all of whom seemed delighted with their horse's performance when I met them in the unsaddling enclosure.

Overall, I was also very happy with Wayleave's showing, but there was a bit of me that had really hoped that he would have hung on to win, just to poke Squeaky Voice firmly in the eye, and maybe also in his pocket.

Although it had probably made my life a little easier that he hadn't.

* * *

I arrived home just after seven-thirty.

During the journey, I had called Georgina on my hands-free.

"Are you home?" I'd asked.

"No. I'm still in Harrogate. Mum was so disappointed when I tried to tell her at breakfast that I was leaving today that I didn't have the heart to go. But I have booked my ticket for tomorrow. The train is due to get in to Didcot just after six, but I'll call you from Paddington to confirm I'm on it."

"All right. I'll be there."

I walked into the house feeling quite low. Not only would Toni have recently landed at Cincinnati, but it was also the end of the five days of Royal Ascot.

The excitement was over for another year.

I often had similar emotions at the conclusion of the other great four-and five-day annual racing festivals—Cheltenham in March, Goodwood in July, and then York in August—even though I always found them totally exhausting at the time.

I was like the schoolboy who couldn't wait for the term to end and the holidays to begin, only then to find that he was missing all his classmates.

I went upstairs to change, putting my morning-dress back in its protective sleeve in the wardrobe, and my top hat in its box, ready for next year.

In its place, I put on jeans and a polo shirt and went back downstairs, feeling much more comfortable. But I was hungry, so I went in search of something to eat. However, it was all a bit Old Mother Hubbard in the kitchen, insofar as not only was the cupboard bare, but also the fridge and the freezer.

Six days without Georgina being here, and without her usual weekly Waitrose delivery, had clearly taken its toll on the Newton family food stocks. There was not even enough milk left for me to have a bowl of cereal.

I reached for my phone and dialled.

"The Red Lion."

"Hi, Jack," I said. "It's Chester Newton here. Are you serving food this evening?"

"We sure are. Last orders at nine o'clock."

The cooker clock showed me it was ten to eight.

"Do you have room for one more?"

"No problem," he said. "The restaurant is full, but I'll find you a place in the bar."

"That'll be fine. Thanks. I'll be along shortly."

I poured myself a glass of red wine, the regular cheap stuff this time, rather than the Châteauneuf-du-Pape I had shared with Toni.

I'd just have one glass now, I thought, before going to the pub, where a glass of Merlot cost almost as much as a whole bottle at home. Then I'd buy a second glass to have with my dinner.

I stood by the kitchen sink, looking out the window at the lawn, with the stables and paddock beyond. At least the earlier rain would have done the grass some good, as it had begun to turn brown in the heat of the past week.

I finished my wine and put the glass down in the sink.

That's odd, I thought. There was another glass already in the sink, a tumbler, and I was sure it hadn't been there when I'd left that morning.

Was I going mad?

I shook my head. I must have just missed it during my cleanup.

*   *   *

The rain had stopped, and there was even a hint of watery evening sunshine as I walked around to the Red Lion, which was packed, with many of the customers having spilled out into the garden with their drinks.

"I've saved you a space," Jack said breathlessly as he saw me come in. "It's crazy here tonight. Everyone's celebrating England's win at the Euros."

"Who did we beat?" I asked.

He looked at me as if I were from another planet.

"Germany," he said. "On penalties. Didn't you watch it?"

"I was at Ascot," I said. "I had a runner."

He shook his head in disbelief.

Jack showed me to my table, a small one in the corner of the bar.

"Here do?" he asked.

"Lovely."

He handed me the menu. "I've run out of the fishcakes. Everything else is good. Specials on the board." He pointed at a blackboard hanging on the wall. "Drink?"

"Large Merlot, please."

He went off to fetch it while I studied what was on offer.

"Here you are," he said, returning and putting the glass of red on the table. "Have you decided?"

"I'll have the Red Lion Burger."

"Good choice. Fries and onion rings, or a salad?"

I now looked at him as if he were from another planet.

He laughed. "Fries and onion rings, then. Starter?"

"No thanks," I said. "Just the burger."

"Coming up."

Jack hurried off towards the kitchen with my order while I had some of the wine and did some more thinking.

"Is this chair free?" asked a female voice from somewhere above my head.

I looked up to see a young woman staring down at me.

"Oh, hello, Mr Newton. I was wondering if this chair is free."

She pointed at the chair opposite mine at the table.

"Of course," I said. "Sorry, I don't know your name."

"Louise Bannister," she said. "I was in Amanda's class at primary school."

She pulled the chair out and sat down on it.

"That's better." She smiled. "I'm sorry. I can't stand for very long at the moment." She clasped her hands around her expansive front. "I'm eight months gone. Can't wait to get the little bleeder out now."

"It must be a very happy time for you," I said.

"You've got to be joking," she said with a forced laugh. "It's a bloody disaster. It's totally screwed my plans to go to college this year, and the father pissed off as soon as he saw the positive test. My mum is furious with me, but she can't really talk. I was a mistake too." She laughed again.

Perhaps I should be more grateful that our family doctor, Duncan Matthews, had been prescribing the contraceptive pill for Amanda these past three years. I had another sip of wine.

"How is Amanda?" Louise asked.

"She's fine," I said. "She's living in Didcot at the moment, with her boyfriend." I didn't mention that her boyfriend's flat was immediately above an Indian takeaway, with its all-invasive aroma of curry.

Jack arrived with my burger.

"More wine?" he asked, looking at my almost empty glass.

How did that happen?

"Yes, please." I said. "How about you Louise? Glass of wine?"

She smiled but shook her head. "I'm afraid I'm off alcohol at the moment." She tapped her bump. Then she stood up. "I'll let you eat your dinner in peace."

"You're welcome to stay."

"Thanks, but I'm all right now. I just needed to give my back a rest for a minute. Give my best to Amanda."

"I will."

Louise went back to the group she was with while I tucked in to my food, which was excellent.

I went back to thinking—trying to make a mental list of people who could be Squeaky Voice. That was assuming I knew him in the first place. If he were a complete stranger, I'd have no chance of finding him.

I finished my burger and debated with myself whether to have yet another glass of wine. In the end, I passed the motion in my head to have another one at home, so I stood up and went to the bar.

"All good?" Jack asked as I presented my contactless card for payment.

"Great," I said. "Thanks for fitting me in."

"No problem," he said. "Always room for a member of the Newton family. It was good to see James in here earlier."

"Earlier?" I said. "What? Earlier today?"

"Yes. About five o'clock. He came in to watch the last part of the match."

How odd, I thought for the second time this evening.

30

"You might have told me," I said to James. I'd called his mobile when I got back to the house, where there was some decent phone signal. "It cost me a small fortune to send your passport with guaranteed delivery on a Saturday."

"Yes, sorry, Dad. But it was great that you did send it. It arrived here about eleven, and I took it straight round to the letting agency before they closed. We now have our next year's flat confirmed."

"Good," I said. "But why did you come here in the first place?"

"Gary needed something from his parents' house. He said he was driving home to get it, so I decided to go with him. That's all."

"Did you come into this house?" I asked.

"No need. We went to the Red Lion for a bit, just to watch extra time in the match, and then the penalties. It was a great win."

"So I believe."

"But we had to get back to Bristol. A group of us had a booking at Roxy Lanes to go bowling at seven-thirty. We've just finished. We're on our way now to have a quick pizza, then we're off to a party."

The busy social life of the modern student.

"Okay," I said. "Mum's back here tomorrow evening. Grandpa is doing better, at least for the moment."

"That's great news. But I must dash now, Dad, because we've arrived at the pizza place. Bye."

He disconnected.

I went into the kitchen to get some more wine.

I lifted my glass out of the sink and poured a good measure into it.

I stood there wondering what Toni would be doing right now.

I had looked up the Cincinnati Airport on Google Maps.

While the city of Cincinnati itself is in the State of Ohio, the international airport is just south of the Ohio River, in northern Kentucky, just eighty miles north of Lexington, along Interstate 75.

She'd probably be home by now, I thought, in her "two beds and a bath upstairs, and a kitchen and living room downstairs."

I told myself to stop thinking about her.

She's gone. It's over. If you're not careful, you'll be calling Georgina 'Toni' when she gets back tomorrow, and then you'll be in trouble.

I took another glass of wine into the sitting room, but that just seemed to make things worse. Would I ever be able to come into this room again, to look down at the sheepskin rug, without thinking about what had occurred on its surface?

Probably not—but I suddenly realised that it was not totally a bad thing.

Overall, the memory made me happy, not sad. It was something to cherish.

I tried watching some television, but there were Saturday-night reality-TV programmes on all channels, and I didn't give two hoots which one of the so-called celebrities—none of whom I'd ever heard of—was about to be voted out of the jungle, or even which young operatic prodigy would receive the huge cash prize as the nation's future possible answer to Luciano Pavarotti or Maria Callas.

I flicked off the set and went upstairs, but I didn't go straight to bed. Not yet.

I had other things to do first.

*   *   *

I had a restless night, tossing and turning and only sleeping in short snatches.

My mind was too active to allow me to rest, in spite of the wine.

At half past four, after a particularly long session awake, I finally got up, put on my dressing gown, and went downstairs.

With the summer solstice being this week, the sky was light even at this early hour, and the sun would be up within the next fifteen minutes.

I made myself a coffee in the kitchen and took it through to my office.

It was too early to call the trainers, even those whose first lots went out soon after five o'clock during the mid-summer months. But I hadn't come down to use the phone anyway, but to use my computer.

I spent the next hour or so searching through various social media sites and other web pages.

Then I looked up betting systems.

I thought I knew everything there was to know about gambling on horseracing, but I was wrong, very wrong.

Sure, I knew the basics.

I knew you could simply bet on a horse to win, or to place—usually meaning to finish in the first three—and that you could group those two bets together to make an each-way wager.

You can place those bets either with a bookmaker or on the Tote, and the term *bookmaker* here includes all the high-street betting shops and their websites as well as the men and women standing shouting the odds at the racecourses.

Bookmakers, as the name suggests, make a "book" on each race. In the past, the book was what the bets were recorded in, by hand, but nowadays they are typed into a computer. But the bookmaker still has to decide the fixed-price odds he is offering on each horse in the race.

If a horse is thought to have a high probability of winning, the bookmaker will choose to offer only short odds, say at two-to-one, whereas if the horse is considered to have little chance, the offered odds will be longer, maybe at twenty-to-one or even higher.

The longer odds are to tempt people to back the outsider.

As the time of the race nears, the bookmaker may vary his offered odds either up or down. In this way he regulates how much is bet with him on each horse, and that allows him to calculate his liability for every possible outcome.

The Tote, however, is not a bookmaker. It is a "parimutuel" or "pool" betting system. All the money that is bet "to win" on all the horses in a race is added together into the pool. The Tote then deducts a percentage to cover its costs and profit. The remainder is then divided by the number of winning tickets to determine the payout. So no one "decides" the Tote odds, they depend solely on how many people have backed each horse.

Racetracks in the United States operate parimutuel systems as their only form of gambling. Bookmakers are not allowed.

But there are all sorts of other bets you can make too. Exactas (or trifectas) are where you have to select two (or three) horses to finish first and second (or first, second, and third), and in the correct order.

Then there are also coupled bets for multiple horses in different races.

Doubles, trebles, and other multi-race accumulators require that all the chosen horses must win for the bet to succeed. If any one of them doesn't win, you lose your stake.

Whereas the chances of that happening may seem small, the returns can be huge. And much stranger things than that do happen in racing.

Who could have imagined that Frankie Dettori would ride all seven winners in one afternoon at Ascot? But he did—Frankie's Magnificent Seven—and the cumulative starting price of all seven was more than twenty-five-thousand-to-one.

And then there are "special" accumulators like the Tote *Jackpot* or the *Scoop6*. They are both six-fold accumulators—you have to pick the winners of six races in one day to win—but with a major difference. If no one wins it on any given day, the prize pot rolls over until the next day, and so on, building and building until somebody does win it.

The largest ever Tote *Jackpot* payout was almost one and a half million pounds to a single one-pound ticket, and in 2014, after an unprecedented twelve weeks of *Scoop6* rollovers, eight lucky punters shared nearly eleven million.

All those bets were fairly straightforward. I understood all of them.

But I found there were so many other ways to lose your shirt, or make your fortune, which I was only vaguely aware of.

I'd heard of people placing a *Yankee* or a *Lucky 15*, but I didn't really know what they were. So I looked them up on the internet. They were both multiple-bet combinations on various horses in separate races. And there were many other multi-bet variations too, all of them with exotic names such as *Trixie, Heinz,* or *Goliath.*

But the development of internet gambling has opened a whole raft of new and unconventional ways to stake your cash.

The creation of the "betting exchange" is the most obvious new addition, where anyone and everyone can now act as the bookmaker, taking bets from other people by "laying" a horse, which is essentially betting that the horse will lose.

In recent years, this has allowed the emergence of something called "matched betting," where you place two bets on opposing outcomes.

For example, you bet on a horse to win with a bookmaker and then lay it to lose on an exchange. Clearly, the horse will either win the race or lose it—there is no other possible outcome—so one of your bets will definitely win, and the other one will surely lose.

Now, at first glance this might seem rather pointless, especially if the odds are the same for both. You would end up with no loss, but also no profit.

However, if there is a slight difference in the odds, such that the bookmaker is offering a fractionally higher price than you lay on the exchange, you can turn this variation to your benefit. Provided you calculate the relative stakes correctly, if the horse wins, you end up with a profit, and if it loses, you're even.

It's a "no loss" bet with only an upside.

It is as close to a guaranteed return as you can get while betting on horses, as long as you do your sums right and also remember to factor in the small commission charged by the exchanges.

In financial circles it is known as *arbitrage* and involves buying and selling the same shares simultaneously at slightly differing prices on separate stock markets, in order to make a profit.

But such opportunities are normally few and far between.

However, the gambling business is very competitive, and almost all bookmakers, and even some of the exchanges, are always making offers of free bets to encourage new customers to open an account—*"Bet £10 and get £30 in free bets"*—or to make existing customers bet more.

These "free" bets make matched betting much more attractive.

But bookmakers aren't stupid—far from it. If they believe you are matched betting, and winning, they stop offering you any sort of promotion, and if you then go on winning, they will close your accounts.

In effect, all bookmakers, and all casinos for that matter, will only go on taking bets from people who lose. For all their seeming joy at the occasional big winner, they don't like those who do it all the time, and they won't continue to do business with them.

I leaned back in my chair and stretched.

My brain hurt from concentrating so much.

But things were beginning to crystallize in there too.

By now, it was too late to go back to bed, so I made myself another coffee, swallowed a couple of ibuprofen tablets, and toasted the last remaining slice of bread, which I found hiding in a dark corner at the back of the fridge.

I decided I must go to the supermarket and stock up on some essential items before Georgina returned. I didn't want to give her the pleasure of thinking that I was totally useless at looking after myself when she was away.

After a while, I went back to my office and called the Victrix trainers.

Royal Ascot may be over for another year, but racing across Great Britain went on regardless.

There were three race meetings today, four tomorrow and Tuesday, and five or six each day for the rest of the week—thirty-three meetings in total over the seven days, with over two hundred separate races involving nearly two thousand different horses.

My target was that at least six of those horses should be owned by Victrix syndicates, and preferably more, because I had learned over the past
twenty-four years that, more than anything, my syndicate members wanted
their horses to race, and to race often, rather than be standing idle in their
stables at home.

By the time I had finished my calls to the trainers, and I'd emailed all
the syndicate members of those horses we planned to enter and run this coming week, it was nine o'clock.

I sighed. It felt more like midday.

I went upstairs to shower and dress.

* * *

Tesco in Didcot at eleven on a Sunday morning was as busy as I had ever
known it, with cars waiting in line to get into the car park.

I'd made a list but I was still in a bit of a trance as I pushed my trolley
up and down the aisles, collecting items off the shelves in a random order.

I'd worked out that Georgina wouldn't be wanting to cook when she
arrived home after several hours on the train, so I bought a tasty, simply-
heat-up ready-meal for two, of chicken jalfrezi and rice, packaged together in
two wooden ovenproof trays.

I also remembered to add a bottle of Châteauneuf-du-Pape to the trolley,
to replace the one I'd drunk with Toni, just in case Georgina had been saving
it for a special occasion. And I put two of the cheaper bottles of Merlot in
there too, along with a bottle of Sauvignon Blanc.

I queued to go through a regular, old-fashioned, staffed till rather than
using one of the bank of self-service checkouts. I looked around but couldn't
spot Amanda. She was probably off shift.

A young man scanned everything through as I packed it into bags.

"Two hundred and sixteen fifty," said the young man.

"How much?" I asked in surprise.

"Two hundred and sixteen fifty," he repeated.

I looked down at the three bags of groceries now back in the trolley.

Granted, the bags were fairly large and almost full, but I had clearly lost
touch with the current price of food. And the four bottles of wine didn't
help.

I inserted my payment card into the slot on the reader and entered my
PIN.

"Thank you," said the young man, giving me my long receipt before
turning to the next customer.

I pushed the trolley out to the Jaguar and placed the bags in the boot, but I didn't go straight home. Instead, I went to a pub for Sunday lunch.

In fact, somewhat strangely, I went to three pubs for Sunday lunch.

I had a starter in one, a main in the next, plus a pudding in the third. I had a list of all the pubs in Didcot, and was prepared to visit them all, but it was in the third one that I went to, the Railway Tavern, close to Didcot station, that I found the information I was looking for.

31

G EORGINA CALLED ME at five o'clock from Paddington to tell me that she
would be on the expected train, getting in to Didcot at ten past six.

"Shall I buy something for supper from Marks and Spencer?" she asked.

"If you like," I said. "But I have already bought us a ready meal for
tonight. But it will keep until tomorrow if you want something else."

"What did you get?"

"Chicken jalfrezi and rice."

"That's great. I could really do with a curry. All the food Mum cooks is
so desperately bland. Neither of their systems can cope with anything spicy.
She doesn't even put salt in anything because she thinks it's bad for Dad's
blood pressure. I tell you, I can't wait to get home."

She sounded so excited at the prospect.

But how did I feel about it?

Georgina and I had now been apart for a whole week—far longer than
ever before during the twenty-five years of our marriage.

I had to admit that, in spite of a few lonely moments, I had quite enjoyed
the separation, and not just because I had been brazenly seduced by a blonde
beauty from across the Atlantic.

Part of me was actually looking forward to having Georgina back, to
returning to normality. But another part of me ached for someone thousands
of miles away in Kentucky.

I again resisted the temptation to call Toni, partly because I was afraid
she would tell me to go away and stop being so silly. Didn't I realise that it
had simply been an away-day fling—at least for her—and we had to now get
on with our lives as they had been before?

So did that mean I had to return to tiptoeing around on the eggshells? To always do what Georgina wanted, to go back to having a quiet but boring domestic life?

Or should I become more uncompromising in my approach to our marriage, more resolute, and more determined to lead my life in the way I really wanted?

Or would that result in the marriage being over?

Was it, in fact, now time for Georgina and me to go our separate ways physically, as we had done emotionally for quite some time?

With all these thoughts swirling around inside my head, I set off for the station to collect her.

* * *

I was standing by the car when she came out of the station.

Once upon a time, at the start of our relationship, we would have run towards each other, embracing and kissing passionately, even if we'd only been away from each other for a few hours, never mind a whole week.

But now there was hardly a flicker of emotion between us.

We simply pecked each other on the cheek.

"Good journey?" I asked.

"Yes, very good," she replied. "I paid an extra ten pounds to upgrade to a first-class seat between Leeds and Kings Cross. It was a weekend offer."

"That was good."

I put her suitcase in the car boot, and we both climbed in.

In spite of us having been apart for a whole week, I drove home in silence.

"Have you spoken to either James or Amanda?" Georgina asked as we turned into the driveway.

"Both of them," I said. "They're fine."

I'm not sure why I didn't mention Amanda's second disappearance to my wife, either previously or now. I suppose it was mainly not to worry her, but it also may have had something to do with me not having to explain to her why I hadn't immediately gone out searching. And Thursday evening seemed like a very long time ago now, and in more ways than one.

We went in and I took Georgina's small suitcase upstairs. She followed.

"It's so good to be home," she said. "I only really took enough clothes for three days, so I'm looking forward to putting on something different."

"You unpack and change," I said. "I'll go down and put the oven on. Do you fancy a glass of wine?"

"Is there any white?"

"I bought you some Sauvignon Blanc. It's in the fridge."

"Lovely."

I went downstairs and opened two bottles, white for her and red for me. Whereas we had once always shared a bottle, even our taste in wine had now gone its separate ways.

I switched on the oven to heat up and then took her wine up to her. She was in the shower, so I left it on her dressing table and went back down again.

Why did I suddenly feel that my life straitjacket, which I had so spectacularly discarded during this past week, was suddenly being refitted tightly around my body?

I took my wine into the sitting room, but that only seemed to intensify my discomfort. It also made me think about Toni and what she would be doing.

There was a five-hour time difference between the U.K. and Lexington, so it would be about two o'clock in the afternoon there. Would she also be thinking of me, or would she be just getting herself ready to go back to work at Keeneland Racetrack the following morning?

I shook my head. *Stop it*, I told myself silently.

I went back into the kitchen for some more wine.

Georgina came downstairs in pyjamas and a dressing gown.

"Everything looks fine," she said, walking around and running her finger across the worktop as if she was looking for dirt.

"Don't sound so surprised," I replied sharply. "I'm quite able to look after the place on my own."

"I didn't it mean as a criticism," she mumbled. "Quite the reverse."

Why was I being so tetchy with her?

"Sorry," I said. "It's good to have you home. More wine?"

*   *   *

We went to bed early, but not for any excitement in the sexual department. More because we were both tired.

Georgina was asleep before I'd even finished in the bathroom.

At least the chicken jalfrezi had been a success, even if Georgina had reprimanded me for finishing the rest of the bottle of red wine with it.

"That's far too many units," she'd said, tut-tutting as I'd poured the last bit into my glass.

It was a good job she wasn't here last night, I thought. I'd drunk a whole bottle of red wine at home, plus two more large glasses of it at the Red Lion.

I lay awake for a short while, sorting out some plans in my head, but I must have drifted off fairly quickly, because the next thing I knew the alarm on my phone was sounding at seven o'clock.

I left Georgina in bed and went downstairs in a pair of shorts and a T-shirt to make some coffee. I took a cup up to her.

"Sleep well?" I asked, putting the coffee down on her bedside table.

"Like a log," she replied. "There's nothing like sleeping in your own bed."

Except, maybe, sleeping in Toni's, I thought.

"I need to go down to make my calls," I said.

"Are you going racing today?" Georgina asked.

I nodded. "At Bath, this evening. Victrix has a runner in the 7.10."

The runner was Dream Filler, and it was his first outing since his infamous disqualification at Lingfield sixteen days ago.

"I should be back home by nine o'clock, nine-thirty at the latest."

"Will you have eaten?"

"Probably. I'll find out for sure when I know how many of the syndicate will be there and how many dinner tickets we have available. Would you like to come with me?"

"No," she said firmly.

"But you always liked going racing at Bath, especially since they've spruced up the whole place with that new grandstand."

Bath Racecourse is not in the city itself, but three and a half miles away to the northeast, up on top of Lansdown Hill. At seven hundred and eighty feet above sea level, it is the highest racecourse in the country for flat racing, and there are some spectacular views of the city and the surrounding Somerset countryside.

"I still don't want to come," Georgina said. "I'd rather spend the evening here at home, catching up on some correspondence."

"Okay," I said, somewhat relieved. It was always easier, and safer, for me to go to the races alone.

I went downstairs to my office and logged on to my computer.

I skimmed through the daily emails from my remote assistants, one of which said that there would only be four of Dream Filler's syndicate at Bath this evening, two of them accompanied by their wives, which meant that there would be a complimentary dinner for me, that's if I wanted it.

I emailed back, thanking her, and saying that yes, I did want.

Next I made my regular morning calls to the trainers.

Owen Reynolds was the last one.

"All set for this evening at Bath?" I asked.

"Are you coming?"

"I certainly am," I said. "I want to watch Dream Filler put everything to rights after last time."

"But this race is two steps up in class from the one at Lingfield. And the bloody handicapper has raised his rating by four points despite him being disqualified."

"Are you saying that he won't win this evening?" I asked.

"Let's just say that I'm not as confident as I was last time. But he should still run well. I've decided to put Tim Westlake up on him again, to make up for Lingfield. He deserves it. But this time, I'll be in the weighing room when he weighs out, to check for myself that he's at the correct weight."

"Good idea," I said, trying to keep my voice calm.

We arranged to meet outside the Owners and Trainers' Restaurant before the first race, and then we disconnected.

As I put my phone down on my desk, it started ringing.

I looked at it.

No Caller ID.

I didn't answer, and after about six rings it stopped.

It started again, but I still didn't answer.

It rang for a third time. I switched the phone to silent, but it went on vibrating. I ignored it.

Then a message notification popped up on the screen

Dream Filler will lose again today.

He might well lose again today, I thought—but it certainly wouldn't be due to anything that I did.

* * *

Bath races on a warm summer's evening is truly delightful, although the same cannot always be said of their early April or late October meetings, when an icy wind off the Atlantic can cut through you like a knife on the exposed hilltop.

The course itself is kidney shaped, which gives those in the stands a great view of the action, as the horses are never too far away. As you might expect for a track built on the top of a hill, there are numerous undulations, including a steady climb over the last three furlongs, all the way to the finish line, which can prove a severe test for even the most experienced horse and jockey.

It also has one of the prettiest approaches to any racecourse in the country, as you drive between Cotswold dry-stone walls and through the centre of Lansdown Golf Course on arrival.

I parked my Jaguar in one of the spaces reserved for owners and walked into the enclosures, collecting my owner's badge and meal voucher on the way.

I was very early.

The first race was not for another hour, at 5.40.

But I'd had something to do in the centre of Bath beforehand, to meet someone, and it hadn't taken as long as I'd allowed for.

I sat at a table, under a sun umbrella, on the lawn outside the owners and trainers area and made a call to Patrick Hogg, KC, the barrister from Middle Temple, whom I'd met in Jim Green's box at Ascot.

"Do you have time to talk?" I asked.

"Court adjourned early at half three today," he said. "So fire away."

"Can I speak to you in confidence?"

There was a pause.

"Strictly speaking," he said finally, "the confidentiality rules exist only between a lawyer and his or her client. I am not your lawyer, and you are not my client."

"Can I be?" I asked.

Another pause.

"I am not what is known as a "public access barrister," so I can only be instructed by a solicitor or the Crown Prosecution Service, not by members of the public."

"Could you give me some advice then, just as a friend?"

Yet another pause.

"Not that you could rely on in court. And if you tell me you have been money laundering or avoiding your taxes, then I would be honour-bound to report you straight to the authorities."

"I haven't been doing either of those," I assured him with a laugh, hoping that he didn't ask me about race fixing.

"So what sort of advice?" he asked with a huge degree of wariness in his voice.

Maybe it hadn't been a good idea to contact him, after all.

"It's about a family matter," I said.

I spoke with him for the next twenty minutes or so.

"Look, Chester," Patrick said, interrupting my flow. "I'm sorry, but I have to go now. I have to get to Paddington to catch the train home. We have a family event this evening. Perhaps we can speak again tomorrow morning. Call me any time after eight and before a quarter to ten."

At least he hadn't said, "Don't ever call me again."

Did he say train home from Paddington? That was our direction.

"Where do you live?" I asked quickly.

"Near Reading," he said. "A village called Upper Basildon."

"But that's only nine miles away from my house."

"Sorry," he said. "I must dash now."

He hung up.

I sat there for quite a while, thinking and staring into space.

"Penny for your thoughts," said a voice above my head.

I looked up. The voice belonged to Bill Parkinson, one of the Potassium syndicate.

"Oh, hi, Bill. What are you doing here?"

"Enjoying myself at the races," he said. "I'm a member here."

"Beautiful evening for it," I said.

"Does Victrix have any runners?" he asked.

"Dream Filler in the fourth."

"Isn't that the one that was disqualified at Lingfield a couple of weeks ago for weighing in light?"

"Sure is," I said. "We're hoping he'll make up for that this evening."

"Then you'd better keep your eyes firmly fixed on his weight cloth," he said with a chuckle. "That was a rum business."

"It certainly was," I agreed.

"Are you any closer to finding out what happened?"

I shook my head. "It's all water under the bridge now, anyway."

Thames river water, I thought, *under Goring Bridge.*

Owen Reynolds arrived to join us.

"Evening, Owen," said Bill. "How's that horse of mine?"

"If you mean Potassium," Owen said, clearly not amused, "he's fine."

"Have you two decided where he's running next?" Bill asked us. "How about the King George and Queen Elizabeth back at Ascot?"

"He is entered for that," Owen said. "But he's also entered for the Sussex Stakes at the Goodwood Festival, and he won't run in both, that's for sure, as they're only a few days apart. He's also still in the Eclipse, but I think that might be too soon after last week. And entries close tomorrow for the International at York in August, so I've already put him in that."

"You and I have much to talk about," I said to him. "When do we have to decide?"

"Confirmation for the Eclipse would have to be made by noon next Monday. We have another week to decide on the others. Let's have a proper chat about it on Sunday, when I've seen how he performs on the gallops this week."

For a racehorse trainer, choosing the correct races in which to run their horses is as important as ensuring that the animals are fit and healthy. Without both of these things being just right, they will have no chance of fulfilling their potential and winning the big races.

"Right," I said. "Owen, you and I now have to talk about this evening."

Bill took the hint.

"Good luck later," he said, and wandered off.

"He's a real pain, that one," Owen said to me under his breath when Bill was far enough away not to be able to hear. "He's always ringing me up at home to ask about Potassium and tell me where he should run next, or even what feed supplements I should give him. And he always refers to him as 'his' horse."

"But I specifically instruct all my syndicates to contact only me with their concerns, and never to call the trainers direct."

"Well, he takes no notice of that."

"Sorry," I said. "I'll send a reminder to all the members."

Yet another thing to add to my 'to-do' list.

"So how about Dream Filler?" I asked.

"He should do all right," Owen replied. "But he won't start as favourite this time. It's that Gosden filly that's the main danger. And I'm a bit worried that the ground may be too firm for our boy. They don't water up here, and it's still as hard as iron after all the hot weather we've been having. If it hadn't rained early on Saturday morning, I'd have probably not declared him. But I don't think the rain has made any difference. I just hope he comes home sound."

"Apart from that, is everything else okay?"

He smiled. "Yes."

"Good," I replied. "Are you going to eat?" I pointed behind me at the Owners and Trainers' Restaurant.

"No time. I have another runner in the second. I had a cheese sandwich before I came out."

"All right, then. I'll see you later."

I went inside the restaurant and used the meal voucher to collect from the buffet my free supper of cod in a white wine sauce.

As I was sitting down, I was approached by two members of Dream Filler's syndicate, plus their wives.

"Hello, Chester," one said. "May we join you?"

"Of course," I said with a forced smile.

They pulled across some chairs and another table to abut the one where I was sitting.

In truth, I would rather have been left alone to think, especially when I found out that the sole topic of discussion between them was the disqualification of Dream Filler last time out.

"Let's hope it doesn't happen again today," one of the wives said.

"I don't think it will," I replied.

In fact, I was quite certain it wouldn't.

32

I WENT TO THE saddling boxes before the fourth race, but I didn't go in.
Owen had help from his assistant and from the stable lad, so I wasn't
needed. Instead, I walked over to the parade ring to meet up with the syndicate, and presently we were joined, first by Owen, and then by Tim Westlake
wearing the Victrix silks.

"All set?" I asked.

Tim nodded at me, but Owen still wanted to give his final
instructions.

"Remember," he said earnestly to Tim, "the track falls away slightly after
the start, and then there's a very sharp turn back towards home. Try and get
to the inside rail before the turn, and then stick to it all the way round. Some
of the others farther out may have difficulty negotiating the bend, so you can
gain an advantage on them. But leave something in reserve. It's quite a stiff
climb up to the line. Got it?"

Tim nodded again.

The bell was rung, and Owen went over to Dream Filler with Tim and
gave him a leg up into the saddle, while the owning syndicate and I went
along to the viewing areas on the grandstand to watch the race.

Tim Westlake followed Owen's instructions to the letter, sticking like
glue to the inside rail around the turn, but it wasn't quite enough. The four
extra pounds that Dream Filler had been forced to carry because of the
increase in his rating by the handicapper was the deciding factor.

The Gosden filly beat him into second place by half a length, it only
drawing ahead within the last fifty yards.

I wasn't quite sure how I felt about it.

Was I disappointed? Or relieved?

Perhaps a bit of both.

I'd certainly done nothing to adversely affect the result, and for that alone I was happy. And the syndicate members seemed relatively content too, in spite of some obvious disappointment. They'd all been able to cheer for their horse in a close finish—which is what it was all about. And it gave them hope for future successes.

On this occasion, there was no objection by the Clerk of the Scales.

Tim Westlake had weighed in at the correct poundage.

*   *   *

I arrived home at quarter past nine to find Georgina in her dressing gown, lying flat out on her back on the sheepskin rug in the sitting room, with her eyes shut.

"What are you doing?" I asked, slightly perturbed at finding my wife in such a state, and particularly on that specific spot.

"Mindfulness," she replied without opening her eyes. "There's a post on Instagram that says it should be good for my anxiety. It said that meditating should help me to always remain calm."

"And does it?"

"I'm not sure. I don't think I'm doing it right. I mostly just seem to nod off."

We both laughed together. A first for ages.

"Did you win?" she asked.

"Second. But he ran well."

"Good. Have you eaten?"

"I had some fish around five. But I'm quite hungry. I think I'll make myself a slice of toast, maybe with some of that pâté I bought."

She stood up. "I'll get it. Do you want a glass of wine as well?"

"That would be lovely."

Maybe her mindfulness meditating was working after all, but was it too little too late?

Georgina went up to bed at ten o'clock while I stayed downstairs to watch the television news and enjoy a second glass of red wine. However, after listening to the headlines, I flicked the TV off. The news was all bad, and I was quite distressed enough without adding to it any further.

But I had one more thing to do before I went to bed, so I took my wine through to my office and sat at my desk to do it.

I composed a text to my children concerning the state of my marriage to their mother and demanding that they come to a meeting to discuss matters.

It took me a long while, but in the end I was happy with it, or as happy as I could be under the circumstances, and I pushed "Send."

Now, only time would tell if it had been a good idea or not.

* * *

I phoned the barrister Patrick Hogg at five past eight, in between my calls to the Victrix trainers.

"I've been thinking quite a lot about what you told me yesterday," he said. "I'm not sure you need my advice. You're doing fine on your own."

I could hear an announcement being made in the background: "The next station is Reading."

He was on a train, and it reminded me of where he lived.

"Could you do me a huge favour?" I asked.

"Depends on what it is."

"What are you doing this evening at seven o'clock?"

I explained what I was planning to do and asked him to be there.

"I will try," he said. "It all depends on whether the judge finishes in good time today."

"What sort of case are you on?" I asked.

He hesitated, as if deciding whether that information was confidential, and obviously decided it wasn't.

"Insurance fraud," he said. "Six years ago, the defendant reported to police that his classic Ferrari had been stolen, and he claimed on his car insurance policy for half a million pounds. But the man subsequently found in possession of the vehicle insists he paid the defendant for it, and in cash."

"Half a million in cash?"

"He says that he paid the defendant three hundred thousand."

"That's still a huge amount of cash. Where did he get it from?"

"Drug dealing. He used to control much of the London cocaine market, mostly by using extreme violence against his opposition."

"Used to?" I said.

"Let's just say that when he came to the Old Bailey to give evidence, it was in a prison van from Belmarsh Prison. That's how the police found the car. It was part of a proceeds of crime seizure at the man's house."

"Is the defendant guilty?" I asked.

"Quite possibly. But the Crown's case relies solely on the testimony of a violent drug dealer. Someone who is serving a twenty-year stretch behind bars. And the jury know it.

"Are you prosecuting or defending?" I asked.

"Defending. The judge starts his summing up this morning. That will take a couple of days, and then it'll be up to the jury. My job is basically finished now. Unless he gets convicted. Then I'd make representations to the judge on his behalf prior to sentencing."

"How long would he get if he's guilty?" I asked.

"Something between two and four years."

"Is that normal for fraud?"

"The maximum sentence under the Fraud Act is ten years, but that would only be for a highly sophisticated fraud or repeated offences. But don't forget, the money obtained by the fraud also has to be repaid. If my client is found guilty, the insurance company will demand back the half a million, and with six years of compound interest added."

"And if he's not guilty?"

"Then he'd be a free man. But the insurance company might still sue him through the civil courts for the return of their money. In criminal trials the standard of proof is 'beyond a reasonable doubt,' whereas in civil cases it is only 'on the balance of probabilities.' All they would have to do is prove that it is more likely than not that he sold the car for cash and defrauded the company."

"That doesn't seem very fair."

He laughed. "No one ever claims that the law is fair. It just is what it is."

"So will you come tonight?" I asked.

"I will if I can."

* * *

I spent the rest of the morning working out in my head what I was going to say to my children and to my wife. I made some notes to act as an aide memoire.

Meanwhile, Georgina went for a day's shopping at the Bicester Village designer shopping outlet, which suited me just fine.

"I'm meeting Yvonne there," she said, coming into my office as I was finishing my calls.

Yvonne was a long-standing friend of hers from the years they had worked together in a recruitment office in Manchester, from the time before Georgina and I had even met. Yvonne now lived in Birmingham, so Bicester was about halfway between them.

"When will you be back?" I asked, slightly concerned that she wouldn't be home until late.

"About six. We'll have had more than enough by then."

"That'll be fine," I replied. "See you then."

Should I tell her that I had instructed her children to be here by seven? Just to make sure she was back in time?

I decided not to. It would almost certainly involve telling her why they were coming, and I didn't want to ruin her shopping day with Yvonne, even if I might then ruin the rest of her life.

As the day wore on, and seven o'clock came ever nearer, I became increasingly nervous.

What if I were wrong?

Would it be better to do nothing and carry on as before?

But things were no longer as they had been before.

Trust had been eroded.

It was time to grasp the nettle and sort things out, once and for all.

But I was about to open a can of worms that I hadn't bargained for.

33

GEORGINA ARRIVED BACK at ten past six. I had been watching out for her through the hall window.

She came into the hall carrying a couple of designer-branded carrier bags.

"Only two?" I said.

She laughed. "Yvonne and I spent most of the time chatting or having lunch. The place was so full, mostly with Chinese. Even the menu was in Chinese. The waiter told us that Bicester Village is the number-two destination for Chinese tourists, only behind Buckingham Palace. And I can believe it."

"James and Amanda are coming," I said.

"Coming where?" Georgina asked, seemingly confused.

"Here. This evening. Soon. To welcome you back from Yorkshire."

"Oh. That's great." But she didn't seem totally excited or pleased. "But I haven't got any food for them."

"I'm sure that won't matter."

"What time are they coming?"

"Seven."

At least, I hoped they were both coming. Neither of them had texted back to confirm. But that might have been because my text to them had given them strict instructions not to contact me or their mother—just to make sure they were at the house by seven o'clock.

"So I've got less than an hour," Georgina said. "I'll have to see what I can rustle up." She was not happy, and she was also getting quite agitated. "Why didn't you call me? I could have stopped to buy something on the way home."

She started to go towards the kitchen.

"I thought it would be a nice surprise," I said. "And there might be more of them than just James and Amanda."

She stopped and turned around. "More of them?"

"I said they could each bring a friend."

In fact, I had told both James and Amanda in my text that they should bring someone with them, to provide them with some support.

"Why don't we just order a takeaway?" I said. "Then we can ask them all what they'd like when they get here."

Georgina relaxed a little. "Sure. But I'm still going up to have a shower and to change into something smarter."

"There's no need," I said. "You look fine as you are."

She gave me a stare, which implied that I obviously didn't know what I was talking about. She went upstairs.

James arrived at ten to seven and, as expected, brought Gary Shipman with him—or rather Gary Shipman brought James, as they arrived in Gary's car.

I opened the door to them before they could ring the bell, James in shorts and tee shirt, while Gary sported jeans and a leather jacket.

"What's all this about, Dad?" James asked immediately. "Are you and Mum getting divorced?"

"You'll find out everything soon enough," I said. "Go into the sitting room with Gary."

He looked worried but did as I told him. I went back to staring out the window.

At five to seven, Amanda's battered blue Ford Fiesta turned in through the gates, and I could see that she had brought Darren with her.

I went out to meet them.

"What's going on, Dad?" Amanda asked, clearly quite distressed.

"Come on in," I said in reply, standing aside to let them through the front door. "Hello, Darren."

He grunted something at me in reply, which I didn't comprehend, and I wondered if he was high.

I ushered them into the sitting room to join James and Gary, and into this rather glum-faced gathering walked Georgina, all smiles and happiness, with fresh makeup and wearing one of her smartest dresses.

"How lovely," she said, walking over to give each of her children a kiss.

"Lovely?" James said in obvious surprise. "What's lovely about it?"

"Having you here, of course," Georgina replied.

"Hasn't Dad told you the real reason why we're all here?"

"No." She suddenly sounded concerned. "Why are you all here?"

There was a long pause as my wife looked in turn at the four young faces staring back at her.

"Because Dad wants a divorce," Amanda said finally.

At that point, the front doorbell rang.

I went out into the hall to answer it while the others remained in the sitting room in a stunned silence.

When I went back in, with Patrick Hogg, KC, all five of the others were staring at me. I closed the sitting-room door, as if to close us all in privately together, both literally and symbolically.

"This is Patrick," I said. "He's a lawyer."

"So it is true," Georgina said almost in a whimper.

Patrick went and leaned against the wall at one side of the room, between the windows, taking his mobile phone out of his pocket. Meanwhile, I stood on the sheepskin rug in front of the fire place, facing all of them.

"As a matter of fact," I said slowly, "it's not true that I want a divorce. But I did give James and Amanda that impression strongly in the text I sent to them late last night."

I looked down at Georgina who was now slumped on the sofa, with tears running down her cheeks, which were making an awful mess of her newly applied mascara.

"I'm so sorry, my darling," I said to her with a smile. "I didn't want to distress you like this, but I couldn't think of anything else I could have said to the children that would have guaranteed that they would both be here this evening and also that they would bring Gary Shipman and Darren Williamson with them."

She looked up at me, trying to smile back.

"Hold on a minute," James said. "So if you don't want a divorce, why are we all here? What's the real reason?"

Now it was my turn to look in turn at the four young faces in front of me.

"Because I know that one of you is Squeaky Voice."

*　　*　　*

They all stared at me again.

"What?" Georgina asked.

"For the past three weeks, someone has been calling me, and in a squeaky voice he or she has been demanding that I make Victrix horses lose races. And it's one of these four youngsters here. And I want to know which one."

"Don't be ridiculous," James said.

"Being ridiculous, am I? So speaks someone who blatantly lied to me, his own father, about whether he came into this house last Saturday afternoon."

I stared at him, but he said nothing.

"I know you did, so why didn't you say so when I specifically asked you? You came here to collect something from your room, even though you told me that it was Gary who had to collect something from his house. You also left a dirty glass in the kitchen sink. Had a drink of water, did you? But forgot to put the glass back in the cupboard?"

I paused but still James said nothing. Neither did Gary. So I went on.

"And what was it in your room that was so important that you came all the way from Bristol to fetch it, and at such short notice?"

James just sat there, looking up at me.

"No answer?" I said, looking down at him. "Okay, I'll tell you. You came to collect some black notebooks, four of them, from the bottom drawer of your desk."

"You shouldn't be going through my things," James mumbled.

"I went through your desk because you asked me to. I was looking for your passport, remember. It had slipped down the back, from the top drawer to behind the bottom one. Hence I found the notebooks, and the printed BUGS flyers, one of which I sent to you, along with your passport. It must have given you a huge fright, because you knew where the flyers had been. Under the notebooks. Which meant I must have seen those too."

"So what was so important about these notebooks?" Georgina asked.

James didn't answer, so I answered for him.

"The books contained lists of names, amounts, and calculations for the Bristol University Gamblers Society, something that James and Gary, here, have been running together for the past two years."

You could have heard a pin drop.

"I suspect you wrote everything down in the notebooks by hand so that it couldn't be found on your computers. And I imagine you kept them here in case your flat in Bristol was broken into or raided by the police. Because operating a gambling club without a proper licence is illegal.

"But you hadn't reckoned on me finding them. So you decided to come and fetch them before I realised what they were. And I probably would never have realised except that James lied to me about coming here, and I was determined to find out why. So I searched his room again, and the notebooks were gone. I had briefly flicked through them all when I'd been looking for James's passport, so I sat down and worked hard at remembering what I had seen."

"But what has this got to do with someone phoning you about horses losing?" Georgina asked.

"The Bristol University Gambling Society has not been having a good time in recent months, especially as they guaranteed a return on stake money to all the students who joined—hundreds and hundreds of them, maybe even thousands, each of whom handed over their cash in good faith."

I looked at both James and Gary, but they went on sitting, stony-faced, saying nothing.

"Matched betting was it?" I asked. "Using James's mathematical skill to work out the stakes. For risk-free returns."

Still no response.

"And all was going fine as long as you kept getting the bookmakers free bets. But when they dried up, it was more difficult, especially after some of the Bristol betting shops stopped taking your bets altogether. So you tried to force me into stopping the Victrix horses, so you could lay them big on the exchanges without having to also bet on them to win with a bookmaker."

"But how could they force you?" Georgina asked.

"By kidnapping Amanda and then threatening to kill her if I didn't obey their instructions."

Even Georgina was now silent, with her mouth hanging open in shock.

"Now you *are* being ridiculous," James said, finally finding his voice. "How could Gary or I have possibly kidnapped Amanda when we were both at the same party as you and Mum. And we were there all the time."

"Because no one did actually kidnap Amanda, did they?"

I looked straight at Amanda who was sitting next to her mother on the sofa in front of me. She went bright pink.

"Amanda simply walked out of the garden when no one was looking and then drove herself away. Gary's car, was it? You drove to Pangbourne, parked the car somewhere in a back street from where Gary could collect it later, and then you waited for a while before banging on someone's front door with a cock-and-bull story that you couldn't remember anything."

"But she'd been drugged," said Georgina. "How could she drive?"

"Ah, yes," I said. "The ketamine. Are you aware that you can inhale it as a white powder? Or even take it by mouth as a liquid?"

"But there was an injection puncture on her neck."

"Indeed, there was," I said. "But that wasn't how the ketamine got into her system. That puncture mark had been made earlier, probably by our medical student here." I pointed at Gary. "It was conveniently covered up at the party by a white scarf tied tightly around her neck. The same scarf that was dramatically left behind on the ground, to further make it look like she had been taken away by force."

James stood up. "This is all fucking nonsense. I'm going."

"Sit down!" I said sharply. "I'm not finished."

"You might not be, but I am. Come on, Gary—let's go."

"If you step out of this room, James, I will have no option but to call the police and hand them all the evidence I have."

"You don't have any evidence," Gary said, also standing up. "It's all just a fanciful story you've made up, and I've heard enough of it."

"Do you know someone called Mike Mercer?" I asked.

"Never heard of him," Gary said, but his body language shouted otherwise.

"Well, he knows of you, all right. He told me all about you when I went to see him in Bath yesterday afternoon. He left Bristol University last summer, and he claims that your gambling society is a huge con trick. And he's been saying so on social media for months. He says that you tried threatening him, to make him stop. But he wouldn't stop, would he? Instead, he went to the local papers. That's how I found him."

"He doesn't know what he's talking about," Gary said. "And what he says is not evidence."

"Are you willing to take that risk? Now sit down, both of you."

Slowly and reluctantly, James and Gary returned to their seats.

I turned towards Amanda.

"And it seems, young lady, that you are making a habit of being abducted by mysterious men. But it never actually happened, did it?"

She said nothing. She just looked at me.

"First at the party," I said, "and then again last week. That's what you claimed. Darren called me at nine o'clock on Thursday evening to say you had gone missing again. He said you'd left the flat at seven to get him some beers from the local shop, but you hadn't come back. He even said he'd been out to look for you. So I called the police again to report you missing. But you weren't really missing, were you, Amanda?"

She said nothing.

"Because you spent the evening sitting in a corner of the saloon bar of the Railway Tavern, in Didcot, waiting for a telephone call to tell you when you could walk home. The landlord remembers you very well because you only bought one soft drink the whole evening and didn't talk to anyone. He told me that he'd felt sorry for you and thought you might have been there to get away from an abusive partner, so he didn't ask you to leave.

"And then, just before closing time, he answered an incoming call for you on his landline. That was because you had left your own mobile phone behind at the flat, so that it couldn't be used to trace where you were, just as you had done on the night of the party. The pub landlord said you called yourself Elizabeth, but he recognised you all right from this picture."

I held up my mobile phone with Amanda's smiling face showing on the screen—a photo I'd taken the previous Christmas Day.

"You even told me that the van smelled of dogs, just to try and confuse the issue. I bet you and Darren had a good laugh about that."

"I knew nothing about it," Darren said.

I didn't believe him.

Amanda was now openly crying and hanging her head in shame, as well she might, considering the terror and distress she had caused her mother and me.

"I'm sorry," she said between sobs.

"So who rang you at the Railway Tavern?" I asked. "Was it Darren?"

She shook her head without looking up. "It was Gary. The whole thing was his idea."

"Shut up!" Gary shouted at her. "You stupid little bitch!"

He leapt up from his seat and tried to hit her, but I took a step forward to stop him, grabbing his raised wrist before he could bring his hand down on her.

"Don't you dare touch my daughter, you little shit."

He wrenched himself free from my grasp and then reached into his jacket pocket. When he pulled his hand out again, there was a flash of reflected light—the hand now held a knife.

"Don't be stupid, Gary," I said, shocked at this sudden escalation. "Put the knife away."

But from his angry demeanour, it was quite clear that he had no intention of putting the knife away.

Anger plus a knife.

Together they made for a very dangerous combination.

CHAPTER

34

MY CAREFULLY CONSTRUCTED plan was unravelling, and doing so very quickly.

I had fully expected the four youngsters to admit to their collective foolishness, to be full of remorse, and then for Patrick Hogg, KC, to explain how they could try and prevent themselves being sent to prison for fraud.

But I had not accounted for Gary's explosive temper, or his knife, and we had suddenly gone way beyond that.

Holding the knife in his right hand, he went behind Amanda, wrapped his left arm around her from behind, and lifted her over the back of the sofa into a standing position. And he had the blade of his knife against her throat.

James stood up.

"Sit down," Gary screamed at him.

"Come on, Gary," James said, still standing. "Stop it. Let Amanda go."

But Gary took no notice of his friend. And he was now looking somewhat manic, with the whites of his eyes showing large. I was worried that he had lost all reason and was about to do something really reckless.

Amanda whimpered, her eyes also wide, but in her case from terror.

"It's all right, darling," I said, looking straight at her in the hope that she might even believe me. "Just stay calm and do what he says. Make no sudden moves."

She stared back at me, but with a mixture of understanding and sorrow.

I wondered why she had become mixed up in all of this.

Georgina, meanwhile, was moaning and hyperventilating, by now almost lying horizontally across the sofa.

Patrick Hogg, who had so far said nothing, seemed the calmest of us all.

"The maximum sentence for wounding with intent is life imprisonment," he said slowly. "And under English law, wounding means simply to break the skin, even with the slightest of cuts."

The prospect of a long prison sentence didn't seem to have any deterrent effect on Gary, who went on holding Amanda, and his knife remained precariously close to her neck.

"I'm leaving now," he said, backing towards the door. "And I'm taking Amanda with me. So don't try and stop me."

"The maximum sentence for false imprisonment is also life," Patrick said, almost matter-of-factly.

"Shut up!" Gary shouted at him.

"I'm only telling you what will happen to you if you leave this room. Where would you go? Do you think your parents might help you? I doubt it. If my son had kidnapped someone at knifepoint, I'd immediately turn him into the police. What do you think that would do to your parents? And to any future relationship for you with them?"

"Shut up!" Gary yelled at him again.

But Patrick went on talking to him, slowly and distinctly and without emotion, as I imagine he often did to a jury.

"The law is very unforgiving," he said. "Trust me—I know. I've been working in the courts for almost thirty years. If you walk out of here now, the police will find you, and because you are armed, they will come hunting for you with guns. And they won't stop looking until they either arrest you or kill you. So put the knife down, Gary, and let Amanda go."

It sounded like very reasonable advice to me, but Gary was having none of it. He was clearly no longer in a fit state to process any logical thoughts. Instead, he continued to back up towards the door to the hall, pulling Amanda along with him.

"Leave my girl alone," Darren said suddenly, standing up and moving purposefully towards them.

"Get back!" Gary shouted at him. "Or I'll kill her." He moved the knife over her throat.

Darren took another step forward.

"I mean it," Gary shouted, his manic eyes now wider than ever.

At that precise moment, none of us doubted him.

Darren stopped moving and stood still, about three feet away.

Gary inched backwards towards the closed door. He glanced down behind him, as if looking for the door handle.

As he moved his hand holding the knife down and backwards, away from Amanda's neck, in order to open the door, Amanda abruptly sat down onto the floor, slipping out of Gary's grasp.

As Gary bent down to grab her again, Darren leapt at him.

"I told you to leave my girl alone," he shouted as he aimed a punch at Gary's jaw.

But even as the blow landed, Gary's right arm was already swinging round in an arc, and he stabbed Darren in the upper left abdomen, angling the knife up under his ribcage.

* * *

The whole thing had seemed to occur almost in slow motion, but there was nothing slow about the way blood started pouring out of the wound in Darren's body.

Within seconds, the front of his white T-shirt was saturated bright red, and a steady stream was already cascading from it, down onto the wooden sitting-room floor.

Amanda screamed.

For a couple of seconds, Gary seemed transfixed by what he had done, staring down at the ever-increasing pool of scarlet liquid on the floor, but then he turned and ran, first out into the hall, then on out through the front door, leaving it wide open.

I rushed forward to where Darren had now sunk to his knees, with Amanda supporting him.

"Lie him down," I ordered. "We need to apply pressure."

I pulled off my own polo shirt, made it into a ball, and then held it very tightly against the wound. Darren moaned as I did so, from the pain.

"Sorry," I said to him, pushing hard against him. "It needs to be done to stop the bleeding. Otherwise you'll bleed to death."

Amanda and I laid him down, and I used my weight to push down even harder. He stared up at me with wide, frightened eyes, and with good reason.

The initial rate of bleeding suggested that the knife had punctured something critical, perhaps his liver or one of the blood vessels connected to it. Without the pressure, he would bleed out in a matter of minutes, maybe even seconds. But what he also needed now, and urgently, was proper medical help.

"James," I shouted, turning my head towards him. "Call an ambulance. And the police."

He hesitated, instead looking out the sitting room window towards the gateway onto the road through which his friend was driving away at high speed.

"James, do it now!"

"I've already called them," Patrick said. "They're on their way."

He still held his phone, and I suddenly realised that he had been filming everything that had been going on. He saw me looking at him and shrugged.

"Evidence," he said. "Sorry. Force of habit."

Amanda kneeled down beside Darren and stroked his forehead.

"You're my hero," she said to him.

He tried to smile at her, but he was clearly in great pain and in shock. His face was very pale.

"But he will be all right, won't he?" Amanda asked, looking across at me, searching for some reassurance.

I didn't like to tell her that it depended on how long the ambulance took to arrive, but she could probably read that in my face.

I knew that, in spite of the external pressure, Darren would still be bleeding internally, and much would depend on how much blood he was losing into his abdominal cavity. If it was too much and it couldn't be replaced in time, it might result in not enough oxygen getting to his organs, and his body would begin to shut down.

I looked down at him.

"How are you doing?" I asked.

"I'm cold," he said. "Yet I'm sweating."

I thought sweating was not a good sign.

Keeping the pressure on Darren's abdomen with one hand, I reached for his wrist with the other. His pulse seemed strong enough, but it was very rapid, and I didn't know whether that was good or bad. I was just thankful that there was a pulse at all.

"Where's the bloody ambulance?" I asked of no one in particular.

It had probably only been two or three minutes since Darren had been stabbed, but it felt more like half an hour.

Indeed, time in that room seemed to have almost stopped altogether.

James went on staring out the window, perhaps contemplating the disastrous mess that he was now part of, while Amanda remained kneeling on the floor next to Darren, stroking his forehead and constantly telling him how sorry she was.

And Georgina had recovered her composure.

"I think I'll put the kettle on," she said, standing up from the sofa as if nothing had happened and there wasn't a young man quite likely bleeding to death on her sitting-room floor. It was as if she had blocked out everything.

She didn't quite have to step over Darren's prostrate body to reach the door on her way to the kitchen, but it was a close-run thing.

Meanwhile, Patrick continued filming.

*   *   *

We all heard the ambulance's siren long before it arrived.

"James," I said, "go out and meet them. To make sure they get the right house."

He didn't move but went on looking out the window.

"James!"

He slowly turned his head to face me, but there was a rather disturbing blankness in his eyes, as if he didn't care about anything anymore.

"Go outside and meet the ambulance," I said. "Show them where to come."

With clear reluctance, he dragged himself off the back of the armchair on which he'd been perching, and walked out of the house, hardly giving Darren a second glance.

I looked down.

If anything, Darren had gone even paler, and I felt we were getting close to losing him.

"Stay with us, Darren," I said urgently. "Keep awake. Don't go to sleep."

Amanda looked up at me with increasing dread, and perhaps for the first time, I realised how much she cared for him.

The siren came much closer, filling the house with noise. Then it stopped.

Two ambulance men in green uniforms came running in, each carrying a large red backpack. They went down on their knees, one on each side of the patient, while Amanda stood up. I remained where I was, still pushing down on Darren with my ball of polo shirt.

"He's been stabbed in the abdomen," I said. "Initially there was a lot of blood, but I've been applying pressure now for about ten minutes."

"Is the knife still in him?" one of them asked as he started removing equipment from his backpack.

"No," I replied.

"Do you know if he has any other injuries? Was he hit with something, or was there anything else done to him that could have broken any bones? Or did he hit his head on the floor when going down."

I shook my own head. "No. Nothing like that. Just the single stab wound."

"Right. You keep up the pressure on that while we assess him."

He slipped a blood-pressure cuff over Darren's right arm and placed a large clip on his index finger while his colleague put a cannula into the back of his other hand.

"How much blood did he lose?" asked the other one.

"What you can see."

But Darren was lying in most of it.

"More or less than if you'd broken a bottle of red wine on the floor?"

"About the same, maybe a bit more. But that's only externally. There's probably quite a lot more inside him."

"Eighty over forty-seven," one of them said, reading it off the blood-pressure monitor. "Too low. And oxygen saturation is less than ninety per cent. He urgently needs some intravenous fluid."

I watched as he reached into his bag and pulled out a large transparent bag of liquid, with a plastic tube attached.

"Saline," he said, connecting the tube to the cannula in Darren's hand. "Not as good as whole blood, but it's all we've got."

He held the bag up and squeezed it to speed up the transfer of the liquid into Darren.

"Now it's time to blue-light this chap to hospital. He'll need immediate surgery to stop the internal bleeding."

His colleague went out and returned with a stretcher, a high-tech black and yellow contraption on wheels, which he positioned alongside Darren. The two ambulance men then moved so that one was at his head, the other at his feet.

"All right, ease the pressure slightly as we lift him. One, two, three—*lift*."

Grabbing his shoulders and his ankles, they lifted Darren easily onto the stretcher.

"Thank you," said one paramedic to me. "I'll take over the pressure now."

I lifted my saturated polo shirt off Darren. Blood immediately started to leak out of the wound, but not as fast as before. The paramedic replaced my shirt with a large sterile pad, to which he applied pressure with a blue-gloved hand.

Far more hygienic.

The other one hung the saline drip on a pole attached to the stretcher, before placing a bright red cellular blanket across Darren's legs and feet. I wondered if ambulance blankets were coloured red so that you couldn't see the blood.

Together the two men wheeled the stretcher quickly out of the house, and then up the ramp into the ambulance, while Amanda and I followed with the rest of their equipment.

"Where are you taking him?" I asked the one who slammed shut the back doors of the ambulance and ran forward to drive.

"The nearest emergency department is at the Royal Berkshire Hospital in Reading."

I knew it well.

"Will he live?" I asked him quietly so Amanda wouldn't hear.

"I don't know," he said, shooting me a forlorn glance. "But we'll do our best."

He gunned the engine and they were away, the siren again blaring loudly.

And at that point, to further complicate matters, the police finally arrived.

35

I THINK IT WAS fair to say that the police were less than impressed concerning the contamination of a crime scene, not least because, even as Darren was being wheeled out to the ambulance and driven away, Georgina was already starting to clean his blood off the sitting-room floor with a mop and bucket.

"Before it seeps through the cracks between the floorboards, and into the underfloor insulation," she insisted.

My wife was nothing if not practical.

Needless to say, she was immediately stopped from cleaning up any more, and we were all ushered out of the sitting room by the two uniformed policemen who had arrived first. Indeed, we were required to leave the house altogether—until the detectives arrived—although not before I was able to collect another polo shirt from my wardrobe.

As we waited outside the front door, our neighbours, Victoria and Brian Perry, walked up the drive.

Alerted by the ambulance siren, they had come to see if everyone was all right. At least, that's what they claimed, although I believed it was more because they wanted to know what had happened so that they could be the first to inform the rest of the village, but that might have been slightly unfair on my part.

Fortunately, the two police officers politely told them to go back home and stay there, leaving just my family of four, plus Patrick Hogg, standing on the gravel of the driveway.

* * *

It was Detective Sergeant Christine Royle who arrived next, in an unmarked car, along with her sidekick, DC Abbot.

"We meet again, Mr Newton," she said without any warmth. "What's been going on here then?"

Patrick stepped forward.

"Officer," he said. "My name is Patrick Hogg. I'm a barrister. A King's Counsel. I am here at the invitation of Mr Newton, as an observer. And I have a video on my phone of everything that happened, up to and including the stabbing of the young man."

"Do you, indeed?" said the DS. "Then I had better see it. Please come and sit in my car."

Patrick and the two detectives walked to the car and climbed in.

I would have much preferred it if Patrick did not show the detectives the first part of the meeting but, as he'd said, I had asked him to come as an observer, and it was a bit late now not to want his observations, including his video.

"What's going to happen now?" Amanda asked. "I'm really worried."

"We'll just have to wait to see how Darren recovers," I said.

"It's not just Darren. What about me?"

There was not much I could say, so I said nothing.

James, meanwhile, still seemed somewhat distant.

"Where would Gary go?" I asked him.

"What do you mean?" He stared blankly at me.

"I mean, where would he be going right now?"

He shook his head. "No idea."

"How about Bristol?" I said.

"Why would he go there?"

"How about for his passport? And for clothes? To get away."

"And some money," James said. "We have a bit stashed away."

"How much?"

"A few grand. It's in our flat, under my bed."

I didn't feel it was appropriate at that particular moment to ask how an impoverished university student had several thousand pounds of cash hidden under his bed. That would be a question for later.

I had the flat address on my phone. It was where I had sent James's passport only the previous Friday.

I walked down to the police car and tapped on the window.

DC Abbot climbed out.

"My son and I think it's possible that Gary Shipman may have gone back to Bristol, to a student flat they share. He might be trying to collect his passport and some cash they have there."

I gave him the address of the flat.

"Thank you, sir," said DC Abbot. "I'll get on to Avon and Somerset to send someone to check."

"Tell them he's armed. He took the knife with him."

"I will, sir."

The constable got back into the car.

What a mess, I thought. *How on earth are we going to survive this as a family?*

* * *

Finally, their film show being over, the two detectives, plus Patrick Hogg, emerged from the car and walked up towards us.

"I should arrest you for wasting police time," said DS Royle sharply, pointing straight at Amanda.

"I'm so sorry," Amanda said quietly, unsuccessfully trying to hold back the tears.

"And your boyfriend too—that's if he recovers. Reporting someone missing when you know they're not is also a crime."

"But Darren didn't know. He's not involved in any of this. It was all planned by Gary and James. They made me do it."

"How did they *make* you do it?" asked the DS with obvious cynicism.

"Gary has a film of Darren selling some crack. He must have been set up. Gary threatened to give it to the police unless I went along with their plan. They said that all I had to do was quietly walk out of the party, drive myself to Pangbourne in Gary's car, wait a bit, snort some ket powder, and then knock on someone's door, claiming I couldn't remember anything, just as Dad said earlier."

"How did you get the ketamine?" asked the detective.

"Gary gave it to me. In the Red Lion during the afternoon. That's when he also made the needle mark on my neck. Out the back. I had to hide it from Darren. And it bloody hurt."

No one expressed any sympathy towards her, not even her mother.

"Gary promised it was all I had to do. But then James called me last week and said I had to go missing again, and to tell the van story, or Gary would send the film to the police."

"That sounds suspiciously like blackmail to me," said the DS. She turned her gaze towards James. "So what have you to say for yourself?"

James just stared at the ground. It was clear he had nothing to say for himself, or for anyone else.

"And as for you, Mr Newton, you should have come to us rather than conducting your own Hercule Poirot impression. Then this stabbing could have been avoided."

I couldn't argue with that.

"And don't think you're getting off scot-free either," she said, pointing at Georgina. "What possessed you to degrade a crime scene with a mop? Tampering with evidence can constitute perverting the course of justice. In fact, I have half a mind to arrest all of you."

"I'm not sure that would be sensible," Patrick Hogg stated calmly.

And mostly, good sense prevailed.

* * *

DS Royle and DC Abbot finally left our house at about half past ten, by which time everyone was exhausted.

Each of my family was asked in turn to give their own account of the events leading up to and including the stabbing.

"Do I need legal representation?" I asked.

"That depends on whether you've done anything wrong," answered the detective.

How deep would she delve? I thought. *As deep as the Thames under Goring Bridge?*

I decided against the need for a solicitor, at least for myself for now. But I wondered if James should have one, and maybe Amanda as well.

In the end, both of my children refused the detective's request to give any further voluntary statements anyway, exercising their right to remain silent.

I suppose you couldn't blame them.

While all the talking was going on—or not—a forensic team measured, photographed, and swabbed everything in the sitting room, as well as the drops of Darren's blood that had dripped from the knife as Gary had run across the hall as he'd made his escape.

"Why do you bother?" I asked DS Royle, "when you've got everything that happened recorded on video?"

"Protocol," she answered. "And also because the defence might claim that the footage is inadmissible as evidence because it was made without Gary Shipman's express permission. So it's best to get everything else done properly at the beginning."

"Does it require his permission? You surely don't need a person's consent to capture their image on a security camera. And it's my house, so I should decide."

"You or I might think that was a reasonable argument, but you never know what his lawyers are going to say in court. They can be slimy bastards."

"Oh, thanks," said Patrick, who had been listening to the exchange.

"Present company excluded." She almost smiled.

There were two significant pieces of news that were reported to us during the evening.

The first was that Darren Williamson had managed to cling to life during the seventeen-mile journey to the Royal Berkshire Hospital, and also that he'd survived emergency surgery to stop the internal bleeding from a ruptured spleen.

Although he was still in a serious condition, the doctors were now expecting him to make a full recovery.

And the second piece of news was that a team of firearms officers from the Avon and Somerset Police had detained Gary Shipman as he tried to leave the flat in Bristol with a bag containing his passport, some clothes, and the hidden cash, together with two burner phones.

Patrick Hogg, KC, went home to Upper Basildon.

I went out with him to his car.

"Thank you for coming," I said. "I'm sorry you got more than you bargained for."

"Wouldn't have missed it for the world," he said with a smile. "Not often a criminal barrister gets to witness such a serious crime firsthand. Most of the time, in court, we have to rely on what other people say to try and work out what really happened. And I don't suppose we get it right even half the time."

"Well, thanks to your video, everyone will know the true facts of this one."

"Yes, and I'm glad Darren is going to be all right and that the police have caught Gary. But I would advise your son to get a good fraud solicitor, and quickly. He could be in a lot of trouble."

"Can you recommend one?"

"I'll send you an email."

We shook hands, and then he climbed into his car and drove away.

Amanda wanted to go to Reading to see Darren, but she was told by the hospital that, after his surgery, he would be spending the night in the intensive care unit, and visitors were not allowed.

Consequently, we all went upstairs to our own home beds, and I wondered if it might be for the last time that we were together only as our nuclear family of four.

I lay awake for a while, going over and over in my mind everything that had occurred earlier that evening.

"Are you still awake?" Georgina asked quietly into the darkness.

"Yes," I replied.

"Do you really want a divorce?"

Four Months Later

O N WEDNESDAY, I checked in early at Heathrow Terminal 5 for my British Airways flight, and made my way through airport security.

I was so excited that I could hardly stop myself from skipping along the terminal concourse towards the business-class lounge.

Much had happened over the preceding four months.

* * *

Gary Shipman had pleaded guilty at his first opportunity in the Magistrates Court, to unlawful wounding with an offensive weapon, occasioning grievous bodily harm, and also to threatening an individual with a knife such that the said individual was in fear for their life.

He was full of remorse and regret, and the Crown Prosecution Service accepted his plea that he had not intended to injure anyone. He claimed the stabbing had simply been a defensive reflex action when Darren had leapt towards him.

Three weeks later he was sent to the Crown Court, where a judge handed down a sentence of two years in custody for each offence, but to run concurrently rather than consecutively, for which Patrick Hogg thought he was a very lucky boy.

But that was only the start of his problems.

Following the seizure of Patrick's video by the police, both Gary and James had been arrested on suspicion of fraud, and over the following month the whole sorry business of the Bristol University Gambling Society had been fully exposed, and it was a much bigger mess than I had expected.

Basically, it had developed into a Ponzi scheme.

Initially, with only the cash from a small handful of their closest friends, Gary and James had used the free bets and other promotions provided by the bookmakers to make a healthy return using the matched-betting technique.

They had distributed the winnings to their "investors," which in turn had encouraged them to invest more, and by word of mouth, more and more students had then joined, such that Gary and James suddenly found they had thousands of pounds each week to bet with.

And that number soon became even bigger as the apparent returns kept coming and word spread throughout the university student population. But in reality, the boys had resorted to paying out "winnings" that didn't actually exist, in order to further increase the number of members joining.

By now, most of the local Bristol and online bookmakers had *gubbed* their accounts, which meant they had excluded the society from receiving any more free bets and other promotions, and some had limited the amount they could stake. A few bookmakers had even closed their accounts altogether.

So the "payouts" were in fact now being made straight from the money new society members were bringing in, rather than from any actual winnings.

At one point, they'd had more than two thousand members, some "investing" a hundred pounds or more at a time, and all was fine for a while, as long as the flow of new members kept bringing in more cash to fund everything.

However, it all started to go wrong when the ex–University of Bristol student Mike Mercer had gone to the local newspaper, claiming it was all a con. Suddenly, the supply of new members joining began to slow, and even to dry up, and those already in wanted to cash out from their accounts.

But the society didn't have enough money to pay them what they'd been promised.

So, in a last-ditch effort to turn around their fortunes, Gary hatched the plan to kidnap Amanda in order to force me to make Victrix horses lose races so he and James could lay them for huge amounts on the exchanges.

Although James claimed he was reluctant to do it, he had gone along with the plan because they were desperate, and he had set up the filming of Darren selling cocaine to force Amanda into agreeing.

When Dream Filler has been disqualified at Lingfield, and Hameed had then been beaten at Newbury, they had managed to recoup some of their losses. But Potassium's win at Ascot had cost them dearly, so they had decided to give me a "reminder" that they could kidnap Amanda anytime they liked, and I'd better do what they told me.

It had also been James who had suggested calling his mother's phone several times before hanging up without speaking. He reckoned, correctly, that she would tell me about the calls, and that would add further pressure for me to do what they wanted.

In all, it was estimated that in excess of a hundred and fifty thousand pounds had "disappeared," although a substantial proportion of that had been erroneously paid out to society members as "winnings" to which they weren't legally entitled. Much of the rest had been lost to bookmakers or to other gamblers on the betting exchanges.

Certainly Gary and James hadn't pocketed very much from the scheme, maybe less than ten thousand pounds between them.

Bad as it was, at least it wasn't even close to being in the Bernie Madoff league. His asset-management Ponzi scheme in the United States had involved the embezzlement of an estimated sixty-five billion—yes, *billion*—U.S. dollars.

However, it was still bad enough for the University of Bristol to abruptly boot both Gary and James out of their courses and to ban them for life from ever again setting foot on the University premises.

All that effort to secure the tenancy of a new Bristol flat had been in vain, and it had been my searching for James's passport, needed by the letting agency, that had been the catalyst for me to start working everything out.

In court, at Patrick Hogg's urging, they both pleaded guilty to profiting illegally by knowingly making false representations, contrary to the 2006 Fraud Act, and they were both jailed for eighteen months. This time, Gary's term was to run consecutively to his other sentences.

Now, the only accommodation the two of them would have for the coming year and beyond, rather than being their much hoped-for flat, would have no door handles on the inside, and bars across the windows.

As to the other business, the "kidnap Amanda" plan and the threats made to harm her if I didn't do as I was told to fix races, no action was taken by the police, mostly because I did not wish to make any complaints against my own children.

That may have been seen by some as just generous parenting, but I also didn't want to be asked any difficult questions about any missing lead weights.

However, one of the burner phones in Gary Shipman's bag had contained details of calls and texts made to my mobile number. There had also been an electronic voice changer found in the bag, confirming him as Squeaky Voice.

While Amanda had not been arrested or charged with anything, she had been issued with a ninety-pound Fixed Penalty Notice for wasting police time, which, of course, I had paid.

* * *

Darren spent four nights in the Royal Berkshire Hospital, recovering from the stabbing and his abdominal surgery.

Amanda collected him on Saturday afternoon in her battered Fiesta, and the first stop they made was to the scene of the attack.

They were in the sitting room when I arrived back from watching a Victrix horse run at Newmarket.

"I've come to thank you," Darren said, standing up nervously in front of me. "I've been told that without your prompt application of pressure to the wound, I would have surely died. Even with it, it was a close-run thing."

He held out his hand to me, and I shook it.

"I also want to apologise for being such a bloody idiot. Amanda and I have been talking a lot over these past few days, and I'd like me and you to make a fresh start."

I shook his hand again.

"Then no more drug dealing," I said, holding firmly onto his hand.

"No more drug dealing," he agreed, although I had my severe doubts that he'd stick to that.

Thanks and apologies over, he and Amanda had departed in the Fiesta, back to their love nest above the Raj Tandoori.

* * *

Georgina's father died at the end of July, his heart having finally given up the futile struggle to pump a limited oxygen supply around his failing body. There had been no fuss. He had simply slipped away in his sleep, only discovered the following morning when his wife brought him in a cup of tea.

On hearing the news, Georgina and I had immediately driven north to Harrogate, but there was not much we could do other than to help with undertakers and funeral arrangements.

After two days I returned south, leaving Georgina behind to continue supporting her mother. It wasn't planned as such, but looking back, I think it was at that precise moment that our marriage finally ended.

I kissed Georgina goodbye, standing in her mother's driveway, with the now-customary peck on the cheek.

"I'll call you," I said.

"Fine," she replied.

And that was that. I had driven away, and Georgina had not.

Ten days later, I returned to Harrogate for my father-in-law's funeral but came back home again the same night, and here we were, eleven weeks later, still living apart and speaking only occasionally on the telephone, mostly about the plight of our errant children.

While we hadn't yet discussed a formal separation, or a divorce, the state of our independent lives seemed to be more than satisfactory for both of us. Maybe there would be legal proceedings in the future, but neither of us seemed in any hurry to precipitate them—not yet, anyway.

* * *

Meanwhile, while everything else going on, Potassium had continued to excel, proving himself to be the champion British racehorse of the year.

Owen and I had decided to give the King George VI and Queen Elizabeth Stakes at Ascot a miss, as had always been our intention, but in early July, Potassium had won the Eclipse at Sandown over a mile and a quarter.

A month later he captured the mile-long Sussex Stakes at Goodwood, by two lengths, from the winner of the Prix du Jockey Club, the French Derby, in what was headlined in the following day's *Racing Post* as the *"Battle of Agincourt of the Derby Winners"*—another overwhelming victory for the English, with a cartoon of Potassium holding up a two-finger salute towards the French—even though horses don't actually have any fingers.

Two and a half weeks after that, I had gone north again, this time on the train to York, and I was in confident mood.

Horse races were first held at York some eighteen hundred years ago, to mark the visit to the city of the then Roman emperor Septimius Severus, but the modern racecourse opened for its first meeting in 1731, on open marshy land just a mile south of the city centre, known as the Knavesmire.

The current one-mile six-furlong start is close to the place that had been used for public executions since the fourteenth century, the most notable being that of the highwayman Dick Turpin, who was hanged at that very spot some eight years after the racecourse was established.

Nowadays, the four-day Ebor Festival—from *Eboracum*, the Roman name for York—is the highlight of the northern racing calendar, with three Group 1 races plus the Ebor Handicap, the most valuable flat-racing handicap in Europe.

Yorkshire folk certainly know how to have a good time, and they flock to York races in huge numbers to do just that, especially during the Ebor meeting.

It had always been one of my favourite events. But this year was extra special, with Potassium being the main attraction on the first day, as a runner in the million-pound International Stakes over a mile and a quarter.

Such was Potassium's reputation that he had frightened off most of the other good horses, so there were only four others in the race, and he lived up to his star billing, winning easily by three lengths.

He had now won five of his six runs this year, all of them at Group 1, and so it was an easy decision for Owen and me to accept the invitation from America to run in the US$7 million Breeders' Cup Classic at Keeneland, rather than the £1.3 million Champion Stakes at Ascot.

Potassium had nothing more to prove at home, and now was his chance to take on the best of the international horses, to try to emulate Raven's Pass, the only other English-trained winner of the Breeders' Cup Classic, way back in 2008.

So, here I was at Heathrow, waiting for my flight to Cincinnati.

*   *   *

The autumn was always the busiest time of my year anyway. Not just because of the ongoing racing, but mostly on account of the bloodstock sales.

It was when the annual fresh crop of yearlings go under the hammer in either the U.K. or Ireland, and it's only then that I find out if my many months of talking and visiting the breeders has paid off.

By the time the sales started, I had compiled a long list of possible targets, so I spent many days inspecting and vetting each one, and then either I sat on my hands, or I raised them to bid in the auctions, hoping that I could secure the purchase within my budget.

All too often, the bidding went beyond what I was prepared to pay, leaving me rueing the outcome, but there were other times when I believed I had bought a future winner, and at reasonable cost.

At the end of the sales, I had fulfilled my aim of buying sixteen quality yearlings at a fair price, all of which I believed were excellent prospects, and now all I had to do was find the syndicate members to share their ownership.

They were the new blood—next year's Victrix two-year-old racers.

At the other end of the line, most of the company's current three-year-olds would shortly be going to the horses-in-training sales, to be moved on to new owners for further racing or to become broodmares or whatever.

It was like a constant conveyor belt of new blood in, old blood out, and it was the part of my job that I found most exciting, Derby winning excepted.

The previous week, I had held my annual yearling parade, and it had gone as well as I could have possibly wished. There was nothing like having had the Derby winner to bring in the clientele, and my books were filled to overflowing such that, for the first time ever, I had a waiting list of prospective members who all wanted to buy into the lifestyle and to chase the ultimate dream.

And I was delighted that Patrick Hogg, KC, was now a Victrix syndicate member, securing a share in one of my favourite purchases. I just hoped that I could repay his kindness by providing him with a future winner or two.

* * *

My flight was called over the airline-lounge public address system, so I started to make my way to the gate.

The previous day I had finally plucked up the courage to phone Toni Beckett, to tell her that I would be coming to Keeneland for the Breeders' Cup races and that I hoped to be able see her there.

Far from receiving the brushoff that I had feared, she had been hugely excited.

"Is your wife coming with you?" she had asked warily.

"No," I'd said. "In fact, she and I are now living apart."

"Yee-haw! So you'll be staying at my place?"

I'd been booked into a suite at the Hilton Hotel, in downtown Lexington, all courtesy of the Breeders' Cup organisation.

Bugger that.

"I'd absolutely love to stay at your place."

* * *

My flight touched down at Cincinnati airport at a seven o'clock, local time, on Wednesday evening, after an eight-and-a-half-hour hop over from London.

The long journey across the Atlantic gave me the time to relax, to unwind my mind from the stresses of the past months. There were no phone calls to worry about, no emails or texts demanding an answer, just a few glasses of an excellent Bordeaux to consume, along with some decent food and a chance to catch up on some sleep in my business-class flat bed.

Toni had offered to pick me up from the airport, but I already had a car arranged for me by Breeders' Cup, so I told her not to bother.

The car took me to the Hilton, where I checked in to my suite and dropped off some of my luggage before exiting through a side door and climbing into Toni's white Jeep Cherokee SUV.

Her *two beds and a bath upstairs, and a kitchen and living room downstairs* was part of a modern development on the western side of the city, just off Versailles Road, convenient for Keeneland Racetrack.

And we only needed the one bed, not two.

* * *

The Breeders' Cup races are widely advertised as the annual end-of-year world championship of horseracing, and consists of fourteen different top-rated races over two days in early November, crowning fourteen different "world champions."

Race distances range from just over five furlongs to a mile and a half. Five are for female horses only, two for males only, whereas the rest are for both sexes competing together.

There are five races scheduled for Friday, all for two-year-old "juveniles," three on the grassy turf track and two on "dirt," which at Keeneland is a blend of sand, silt, and Kentucky clay. And then nine more races on Saturday, all for horses aged three and older, five on dirt and four on turf.

All are designed to be truly "international," but in truth, most of the American horses run on the dirt, while the Europeans all prefer the turf. Potassium, however, was bucking that trend as a starter on the dirt in the Breeders' Cup Classic, the most prestigious and the most valuable of all the fourteen.

He had made his own trip across the Atlantic almost three weeks ago, to give him time to recover from the journey and the time change, but more importantly, to get used to running on the dirt surface, something he appeared to enjoy according to the reports I had received.

Owen Reynolds had sent two of his stable staff over with the horse, and all three seemed to have settled in well in Keeneland's own training centre, which was adjacent to the racetrack. Owen and our Derby-winning jockey, Jimmy Ketch, were also making the trip over, to maximize our chances of success.

* * *

Thursday was mostly taken up with media interviews and press photo shoots, culminating in a reception and gala dinner at the Kentucky Horse Park for all the international and out-of-town guests. All of them, that is, except the main stars of the show, the horses, who remained in their stables at the race-track, totally unaware of all the fuss that was going on around them.

But Owen Reynolds was there, along with his wife, Eleanor.

"Hi, Owen," I said, going over to him at the reception. "Good journey?"

"Yes, thank you," he said. "We arrived this morning from New York. Eleanor wanted to go there for a couple of nights on the way. To go shopping."

He rolled his eyes and I laughed.

"Is Georgina with you?" Eleanor asked, ignoring her husband.

"No. Her father died, and she's in Harrogate looking after her mother."

"Oh, I'm so sorry."

"Thank you," I said.

A waiter came and refilled our glasses.

"Have you been to see Potassium?" I asked Owen.

"Sure have. I went straight to the stables, even before checking in to the hotel. He looks in great form. Raring to go."

"Good."

As so often in the United States, dinner was served early at six, so the whole event was over before nine, which was just as well as I was having difficulty keeping my eyes open during the final speeches because of the jet lag.

Toni picked me up, and I was asleep before we arrived at her place.

But she woke me up again.

*   *   *

Potassium's race was the very last one on the Saturday afternoon, the climax, with all the other races acting as appetizers for the main event.

The organizers had invited everyone connected to runners on Saturday to attend Friday's racing if they wanted to, but Toni had somehow wangled some time off—she said that all the ticketing was now complete—so we spent a while seeing some of the local sights and then went back to bed at her place, which was much more fun.

On Saturday morning, she had to go in to work early to make up the hours she had taken off on Friday, so she dropped me at the Hilton, and I arranged for one of the official cars to get me to the track by noon.

Arriving at Keeneland Racecourse was an experience to savour.

The long avenues of maple trees leading in from the main road were in full red and orange autumn colour, and they were truly spectacular in the sunshine.

Add valet parking and a grand entrance hall, complete with high-backed armchairs and a roaring open fire in the grate, made it feel like I was entering a very fancy private members' club rather than a major international sporting venue.

Toni was waiting for me in the entrance hall, and she led me through to the open area between the impressive ivy-clad clubhouse and the new paddock building, both with their grand arched windows.

"I've found you a place in a private suite," she said, obviously rather pleased with herself. "You're having lunch with Herb and Harriet Farquhar."

Now I was worried that I wasn't sufficiently smartly dressed.

Before I'd left home, I had packed a warm suit plus a thick overcoat, expecting that it would be cold at the races, as it would be at Newbury in November. But I had not bargained with Keeneland being so much further south than Newbury. Indeed, Lexington is on the same line of latitude as Athens, and on top of that, central Kentucky was currently experiencing an unseasonably warm spell.

Hence, today I had left my heavy woollen suit and overcoat in the Hilton and had opted instead for my lightweight, blue-checked sports coat plus some navy chinos, both of which I had thankfully thrown into my suitcase at the very last moment. Together with a tie, of course. But was it smart enough for the Farquhars' private suite?

Toni assured me that I looked "just fine and dandy," and she took me up in a lift to the fourth level and along the corridor to the suite, where I was relieved to find our host wearing a seersucker jacket not dissimilar to my own.

"Well, look who it is," said a loud familiar British voice.

Nick Spencer, Potassium syndicate member, was also a lunch guest, together with his wife, Claire. I had known they were coming over, even though I hadn't seen them at the gala dinner on Thursday evening.

"When did you get in?" I asked Nick.

"Late last night. And we're only here until tomorrow. We have to fly home overnight because I have to be back in my office first thing Monday morning. I'm in the middle of a huge deal on a residential block near Tower Bridge. It's worth millions. But I wouldn't miss this for anything." He smiled. "Do you think we'll win?"

"Only if Potassium is fast enough," I said. "But I have absolutely no idea how good the opposition really are."

The eleven other runners in the Classic were all American bred, owned, and trained—the best of their best. And most were older horses—four, five, or six. Only two were three-year-olds, like Potassium.

I had tried to look up their relative form, but many of them raced in different states, and some had never competed against one another before.

We were venturing into the unknown, and in their own backyard.

We would just have to wait and see whether our horse was good enough to beat them all. But it wouldn't be from any lack of trying on our part.

I think I enjoyed my lunch, but if you'd asked me afterwards what I'd eaten, I wouldn't have been able to tell you. I was that nervous.

Our race wasn't due off until twenty minutes to five, and the afternoon seemed to drag by, but eventually it was time for me to go down to the saddling area.

Potassium was already there, as was Owen Reynolds plus his two stable staff, who'd been looking after the horse.

With the three of them, I wasn't really needed, so I stood to one side and watched as Owen went about saddling the horse. At one point, I saw Owen looking across at me, and I smiled and waved at him.

When all was complete, Potassium was led across into the paddock where Jimmy Ketch, wearing the Victrix silks, was given a leg up onto the horse's back.

As the runners made their way out to the track, I went back up to the Farquhars' suite to watch the race.

"Beautiful, isn't it?" said Harriet as we stood side by side looking out across the immaculately manicured infield with its neat hedging, some of it even topiaried into the word "KEENELAND."

The racecourse was a mile and one furlong round, so the ten-furlong start was right in front of the stand, the horses in this race having to negotiate just over one complete circuit.

The twelve runners were expertly loaded into the starting stalls, and then, accompanied by a ringing bell, the gates flew open, and they were off.

As usual, Jimmy Ketch took Potassium straight to the front, and they hugged the inside rail around the first turn. Down the back stretch, he opened up a lead of five lengths, which soon became eight.

Around the final turn, he didn't show any signs of slowing, and if anything, he extended his lead as they straightened up for the final run home.

Potassium totally annihilated the best the Americans had to offer, reaching the wire first, and with a winning margin of almost ten lengths in a new track record time.

Herb Farquhar grabbed my shoulders from behind in excitement.

"Absolutely unbelievable," he shouted with tears in his eyes. "I've never seen anything like it. I simply *must* have that horse as a stallion at my farm. Name your price. Any price."

The most expensive stallion ever sold was Fusaichi Pegasus, winner of the Kentucky Derby. He was bought by the Irish breeding powerhouse, Coolmore, for seventy million U.S. dollars.

Should I ask Herb for the same? Or for more?

But now was not the time for that.

I rushed down to the winner's circle. Like at Epsom, it was in front of the grandstand, and it was already pretty full of people by the time I got there.

Owen had beaten me to it.

I joined him and we leaned against the rail, side by side, waiting for the horse to finish its victory parades up and down the track in front of the adoring crowd.

"By the way," he said casually, without turning his head towards me, "I know it was you who removed the weights from Dream Filler's weight cloth at Lingfield. I've worked it out."

In spite of the warmth of the day, I went cold.

I realised that I shouldn't have worn my blue-checked sports coat here today. That is what Owen had obviously been looking at earlier, in the saddling area. It must have sparked a memory.

I turned and stared at him, but he didn't look back at me. Instead, he continued facing forward.

"You did it while I fetched the parade-ring vet," he said. "All that fuss you made about Dream Filler being lame was only to give you the opportunity." He paused, and finally turned to face me. "I don't know why you did it. And I don't want to know. But I reckon you must have had a good reason."

"So what are you going to do about it?" I asked, realising that it was far too late to start denying anything.

"Nothing," he said. "This year has been the greatest of my life, and that is largely down to you for choosing me to train Potassium. So I'm not going to ruin it now."

I smiled at him.

"But," he added, "you do owe me seven hundred and fifty pounds to cover the fine."

"Will you take cash?"

THE END